RIGHT AS RAIN

A C.T. FERGUSON CRIME NOVEL (#10)

TOM FOWLER

WideningGyreMedia

Editing by Chase Nottingham

Cover Design by 100Covers

Published by Widening Gyre Media

For Lisa and Isabel.

CHAPTER 1

I sat in my car on Fell Street a couple hundred yards from The Inn at Henderson's Wharf. It was a boutique hotel in the historic section. Shops and salons dotted both sides of the cobblestoned streets. My quarry was due to come out any minute. Reaching him at his office would be difficult with all the security he paid for.

It took me a while to track him here, but I found him. Peter Hudson was a wealthy middle-aged executive who flouted his opulence in all the predictable ways. This included keeping a mistress on the side. He eschewed cliché in as much as his lover was someone else's secretary, and I watched her leave for the office ten minutes ago. Hudson's wife filed for divorce a month prior, and he dodged all her attempts to serve him with papers. She turned to me, and I soon discovered his room at the hotel charged to the company card of one of his low-level employees.

Hudson still drove to his office in Baltimore's World Trade Center, and the building's guards could keep me from reaching him. Here, he had no retinue protecting him. The February chill pressed in on me, and I fired up my Audi S4's engine again to get some heat running through the cabin. A couple minutes later, Hudson strolled through the sliding double doors.

I killed the motor, climbed out of the car, and hustled down Fell Street. The apartment building I lived in upon my return to Baltimore sat across the street from the hotel. Between them, a large gated lot offered plenty of parking. Henderson's Wharf guests received a card to open the gate. Hudson slid his into the reader. The gears spun and whirred, and the gate began its slow slide. Hudson walked through, apparently oblivious to me slipping in behind him. I took the envelope holding divorce papers from my coat pocket.

His fancy car awaited about a hundred yards ahead. I pulled even with him. "Good morning, Mister Hudson."

He stopped and turned to me with wide eyes. "Who the hell are you?"

I held the envelope out, then pushed it into his chest when he showed no intention to take it. "Someone who enjoys serving papers to assholes."

He snatched the envelope away and glanced at his expensive gray wool coat. It remained unmarred. "You touched me. I could have you charged with assault."

"You could," I said. "If you do, though, I'm going to knock you on your ass." He frowned. "I believe in earning my charges."

"The bitch paid you, huh?" I didn't dignify his question with a response. "How'd you find me?"

"I'm smarter than you."

"You think so?" he said.

"I know better than to pair a silver tie with a black shirt and black suit," I said. "You look like you work for the Raiders."

"This suit cost three thousand dollars." He sneered and glared at my clothes. The coat hid my sweater, but my jeans and tennis shoes were on full display. "Why don't you take the money my bitch of a wife is paying you and go to a real clothing store?"

This marked the second time he insulted his wife, a lady who didn't deserve his adultery or scorn. I wouldn't tolerate a third. "Why don't you quit while you're only slightly behind and get out of here? I'm sure your paramour will soon be wondering why you're not in the office."

Hudson drew his fist back. I flinched and raised my left arm. He stopped. "Jesus, you're jumpy."

"Yeah," I said, "too much coffee waiting for you." I felt my heart beating faster in my chest. Despite my best efforts to stare conflict in the face, it made me recoil ever since I got shot almost four months ago. "Make sure you and your fancy car show up in court. I'd hate to have to drag you and your three-thousand dollar suit in front of a judge."

This time, Hudson took a swing at me. After the initial panic of a moment ago, however, I was ready. I grabbed his wrist, spun him into a hammerlock, and marched him to his new Maserati sedan. Once we reached the expensive car, I shoved him against the side of it. I hoped it would leave a dent. "Three reasons you're an asshole. Your suit, paying full freight for an Italian car, and the way you refer to your wife. Do it again, and I'll put your head through the window. We clear?"

He wriggled but couldn't get free. "Yeah . . . yeah, sure. Let go of me!" I clamped the hold down for a couple seconds before releasing him. Hudson turned back around with anger flashing in his brown eyes. He didn't make a move, though. I flinched only the first time, and I figured he knew he missed his chance.

"Might want to fix your suit," I said, pointing to the wrinkles on his pants from our little tussle. "Hope you have a five-hundred-dollar iron." While he seethed against the door of his overpriced car, I turned and left the parking lot.

* * *

FROM THE BOUTIQUE HOTEL, I drove to my home in the Federal Hill neighborhood of Baltimore. I steered into the alley and pulled onto the parking pad behind my house. I left the S4 next to a red Mercedes AMG coupe shaped and colored like a rocket. My girlfriend Gloria Reading drove the car, and it was one of the few I liked driving more than my own.

"Morning," she said as I walked in through the rear door. Light coming in the windows danced in her chestnut hair. Even in the dark, though, my pulse always hopped a little whenever I saw her. Gloria stood from her breakfast and planted a lingering kiss on me.

She returned to the table while I remained in the kitchen. Every day we spend together—which is most of them—I wake up before Gloria. When I have coffee and breakfast humming along, she wanders downstairs to join me. This morning, I was out the door early to catch Hudson at the hotel, so I left a few bagels on the counter.

Having already enjoyed a toasted whole wheat model, I grabbed a yogurt from the fridge, poured another mug of java, and joined Gloria at my small table. "How'd it go?" she asked.

"Fine. Guys like Hudson fold pretty easily without their security details to make them feel big and powerful."

Gloria eyed me over her mug. "He didn't give you any trouble?"

"Nothing I couldn't handle," I said.

"So he didn't get physical with you?"

I fortified myself with a sip of coffee before answering. "He did."

When I didn't elaborate, Gloria had to follow up. "And?"

"I handled it," I said.

"You didn't shrink back?"

It took me a few seconds—and some more caffeine—to muster a response. "I did at first." I shrugged. "It turned out all right."

"This time," she said. "It's not the first instance, though."

"I know you're worried about me. I appreciate it . . . but I'm fine. I'll figure it out."

Gloria's neutral expression showed me she remained unconvinced. I couldn't blame her. I didn't even manage to persuade myself. Ever since I took two bullets, this remained the most challenging part of my recuperation. My stamina was mostly back, and my physical recovery went well. Mentally, however, I was still sorting some things out. Gloria, who slept beside me most nights, knew better than most. "I think you rushed yourself back to work," she said.

"Maybe." She probably had a point, but I needed to re-establish my PI business once my parents severed the financial backing of their foundation. "I'm pulling jobs, though. They keep me occupied. I'll get it all sorted out."

"I sure hope so," Gloria said. She paused the inquisition long enough to enjoy a few dainty nibbles of her bagel. What I could devour in a dozen bites, Gloria needed three times as many. When we ate together, I always finished first. "Have you talked to your parents recently?"

"For my father's birthday a couple weeks ago. We Skyped."

Gloria grinned. "I remember because I was on the call, too. Not since then?" I shook my head. "Why not?"

"Nothing to talk about," I said.

"Maybe you could explain what's been happening. They might reconsider the split."

"They won't." And I wouldn't beg them to. They'd made their decision, and so had I.

"You're all stubborn," Gloria said.

"Just part of my charm." I added a wink.

Gloria's lips turned up slightly. "You're lucky I love you."

I was, and I knew it.

* * *

AFTER BREAKFAST, I took my other car to the new office. The vehicle would win no awards for its looks. It was a late-'eighties Chevy Caprice in a couple different shades of blue. I snagged it from a chop shop owner who put in a newer engine and added fortifications against common handgun fire. Most importantly, it looked like the kind of car an honest hard-working private investigator would drive.

I still needed to make up some ground on both of those fronts.

Before I got shot, I rented an office in the CareFirst Building, a blandly-named tower in Canton Square. They'd been itching to get rid of me and move a doctor in, and when they did, I found a new space. I occupied the floor above an auto body shop in Fells Point. It was far from ideal, but it worked, and I needed to be able to pay for it myself.

I parked in the lot, leaving the Caprice among its battered automotive cousins, and walked in the front entrance. A door ahead led into the shop. I took the stairs to the right, unlocked my office, and went inside. Manny, the owner, told me it had been a two-room apartment before he decided to rent it commercially. The smaller portion served as a waiting area. To date, very few people used it for its intended purpose.

Shortly after I arrived, a man in a cheap suit came in. It was the kind of suit which looks fine from across a room, but the illusion cracks up close. I never understood why people didn't just wait for sales on the good stuff. Then, I remembered I might need to rummage around in the bargain bin more than I used to.

The joys of being fully self-employed.

He sat in a guest chair on the other side of my desk and set his briefcase beside him. Whatever passed for decorating was still a work in progress. I had my trusty computer, three monitors, the same number of chairs, a coffee maker, fridge, and a movie poster for *The Maltese Falcon*. In case anyone missed my occupation on the door, the large placard would clue them in. This fellow looked around, frowning in silent disapproval, before fixing his gaze on me. He was slender and wore glasses too big for his face. Whoever let him buy the suit must've also accompanied him to the optometrist. "I'm Elliot Allen."

I nodded but didn't answer. My name was on the door. Introductions seemed superfluous.

"I'm with the local branch of Countrywide Insurance," he continued. I bobbed my head again—after all, I knew this from the appointment he created via my online calendar. "Our client in this case is Good Samaritan Hospital." No nod this time. Gotta keep them guessing. Allen's brows knitted. "Have you worked many insurance cases, Mister Ferguson?"

"A couple," I said, which constituted two more than the actual number. "I focused on individual clients until the end of last year."

"Do you have an issue working for a company?"

"It would depend on the company."

Allen picked up his briefcase and popped the locks. He pushed his glasses up on his nose and sniffed. "Why don't I tell you what this is about?"

"Why don't you?" I said. What the hell else were we doing here? I wondered how many times Allen got stuffed into a locker in high school. If I had one handy, I might've tried it, too.

He dropped a manila folder on the desktop. Someone wrote the name *Stanton, Charles* on its tab with a black marker. "This man is a nurse at Good Sam. He's worked there over fifteen years. A couple months ago, he claims he hurt his back lifting an especially heavy patient. He filed for workman's comp, of course."

I put my hand on the file but didn't open it. "Seems pretty standard so far."

"If it ended there," Allen said, "it would be. Mister Stanton hasn't returned to work yet. He claims he's still injured."

"Your client is a hospital," I said. "They should be able to verify an injury."

"It's more difficult with the back. Mister Stanton could have an older injury which doesn't affect his ability to work or quality of life." I noted the order in which Allen listed those. "It could still appear on an MRI."

"You want me to see if he's faking it."

"Precisely. Observe him for a couple days, see what he does, and send me a report."

I leaned back in my chair. "You know I'm not a medical professional, right?"

"Of course," he said, spreading his hands. "Why?"

"If I see this guy do something, it doesn't mean it's out of bounds with his injury."

"Just write it up and send it in. We'll figure it out."

I didn't care for this potential investigation already, but I also couldn't be as choosy now as I'd been in the past. Without my parents' foundation as a benefactor, I needed to work more than a case a week. "All right. When do you need the report?"

"End of the week would be fine," Allen said. "I presume you want half your fee up front."

"Yes," I said as if I'd determined this payment structure before right now. He cut me a check. I still didn't like the case.

The joys of being fully self-employed.

CHAPTER 2

ANOTHER APPOINTMENT APPEARED ON MY CALENDAR later in the day. I would need to go online and block off some time as unavailable, especially if people kept availing themselves of the Internet bookings. Working more than my usual one case at a time was something I'd reluctantly do, but I didn't need a line of people queueing up at the door. Maybe I could work out a discount on oil changes for my clients with Manny.

I put on a jacket and walked into Fells Point proper for lunch. Even with reduced dining capacity, many choices awaited me. I'm a simple man, and I opted for a simple lunch: a pepperoni and mushroom pie from Brick Oven Pizzeria. After carrying it back to my office, it lost a bunch of its heat but none of its taste. Eating pizza at my desk seemed like a very PI thing to do. I only needed a bottle of whiskey in my desk to be welcomed into the club.

When I'd finished half the slices, I realized I didn't have any way to contain the others. Lacking a better method, I folded the box in half and crammed it into the fridge. Aluminum foil vaulted to the top of my shopping list. A short while later, quiet footfalls came up the stairs. My door opened, and a slim woman walked through. She peeked into my office, and I gestured toward my guest chairs. "Thanks for seeing me," she said.

"Sure." My latest potential client looked to be in her late twenties, making her a few years younger than me. Her blonde hair was impossibly straight and hung past her shoulders. Red, puffy eyes told me she'd been crying. If we met under happier circumstances, I would have called her pretty. She lapsed into silence as she glanced around at my very much in-progress setup. "I still have some work to do on the place," I said, hoping to encourage her out of her shell.

"It's fine." Her smile was more polite than anything, but I counted it as a win. "Wow." She took a deep breath to collect herself. "I never thought I'd be talking to a private investigator." She frowned. "Sorry . . . that probably sounded rude."

"I've heard a lot worse." No reaction. Whoever this woman was, she came here because she needed my help, but she'd clammed up since sitting down. "Want some coffee?"

"OK," she said after a few seconds of silence. I repurposed my old Keurig into the office java station, and I used it to brew two cups.

"Milk? Sugar?"

"Just milk. Thanks." I prepared it as she wanted and set the mug in front of her. It earned me another tight smile. I woke my computer from its slumber and checked the calendar. Amy Sloan sat on the other side of my desk.

"What can I do for you today, Miss Sloan?"

After a sip of caffeine, she answered. "I need your help. I haven't had much luck with the police."

"Lot of it going around," I said when she stopped talking.

"My sister died recently. She was murdered."

"I'm sorry." I knew very well how she felt. About a year and a half ago, I finally learned my older sister's death when I was sixteen hadn't been accidental. While her killer now rotted in a prison cell, I understood the lingering feeling of loss.

"Thanks." Amy Sloan grabbed a tissue from my desk—one of the few supplies I possessed the sense to stock—and dabbed at her eyes. "It happened ten days ago. The police have been investigating, but they haven't told us anything new for a while now." Her eyes glistened. "Suzie was my baby sister." The tears came in full now, and I nudged the tissue box closer. It seemed like a hollow gesture, but I couldn't do anything else for her. Yet.

When Amy muttered something sounding like an apology, I said, "No worries. Take your time." She needed a few minutes and an equal amount of Kleenex, but she bucked up and bobbed her head. "Tell me what happened."

"Someone beat Suzie to death with a baseball bat." Her voice cracked at the end, and I didn't blame her. I winced. There are probably no pleasant ways of being murdered, but getting bludgeoned to death repeatedly ranks among the most brutal ways to go.

"The police haven't found a suspect?"

"Nothing official," she said. "They tell us they have a few persons of interest, the case is ongoing . . . yada, yada, yada. They've been at this a week and a half and have nothing to show for it."

This case immediately took priority over some nurse maybe cheating a rich insurance company in my mind even though ten days didn't constitute a long homicide investigation. "I'll need as much about Suzie as you can tell me." I took out a notebook.

"Sure. She worked for a doctor . . . some big-shot plastic surgeon, I think. She really liked the job, but there was an issue with insurance or something. I don't know all the details, but the guy let her go over it. I thought he was a prick, but Suzie said he was great to work for." She paused. "She has a boyfriend. Nothing super serious. He's older. They were in a good place as far as I know. What else . . .? She's . . . was popular. Everyone loved Suzie."

"At the risk of sounding indelicate," I said, "one person obviously didn't."

"I know." Amy fought back tears again. "The police have talked to everyone. I don't know what else to do."

Shootings can be random. Beating someone to death with a bat is personal. Whoever killed Suzie Sloan knew her and hated her. Most murder victims died at the hands of people they knew. "I'll need to run down her boyfriend and other close acquaintances with you," I said. She nodded. "Do you know any more about what happened with the plastic surgeon?"

"Not really," Amy said. "I work for a construction company. I didn't understand a lot of the stuff Suzie tried to tell me. He came to the service, though. Sent a huge bouquet of flowers. He seems nice."

"What about the boyfriend?"

"No red flags." She shrugged. "I think he runs a gym. He was always pleasant to me."

I looked at my notepad. The answer didn't linger anywhere in my scribbles. "Any exes you'd be concerned about?"

"No. Suzie always had the sense to avoid assholes."

I knew of at least one situation where she failed to, but I didn't want to pile on. We spent a few minutes going over the important names in Suzie Sloan's life. Amy told me everything she could. It wasn't a complete picture, but it gave me enough to start. Suzie was young, pretty, and popular, so I felt confident I could uncover more via social media if I needed to.

Since opening this office, I'd done a lot of minor cases. They helped pay the bills, but I didn't relish the thought of serving divorce papers to smug pricks in expensive suits long-term. A murder case represented someone's family member dying, but it felt good to sink my teeth into something important.

I took a deep breath. Finally, I was back in the game.

* * *

"A MURDER CASE? SO SOON?"

Gloria frowned her concern. We stood at the counter making dinner, which is to say I did the bulk of the work. Gloria was not to be trusted in the kitchen. After forgetting the lid for the blender and nearly summoning the fire department when she made toast, she earned a ban from all duties except chopping vegetables, which she performed capably a few minutes ago.

"It was in the afternoon," I said. "Not too early."

"You know what I mean." Gloria crossed her arms. The hoodie she wore diminished the spectacular effect it had on her breasts, reducing it to merely impressive. I still noticed, though. Gloria's stern expression didn't change.

I stopped stirring the spaghetti sauce and set my large wooden spoon down. "Yeah . . . I do. I appreciate your concern."

"I know there's a 'but' coming here," Gloria said.

"There is." I couldn't help grinning even though Gloria continued to look unamused. "I need to do my job. I can't control who walks through the door or what they need."

"You can control what you tell them, though. You don't have to say yes."

"Her sister got beaten to death with a bat." I picked up the spoon again and tended to the sauce. It smelled of tomatoes, olive oil, garlic, and a few veggies but light on oregano. I added a little more. "How do I walk away from someone in this kind of situation?"

Gloria uncrossed her arms. "I know. Doing work like this gets in your blood. I've met a few of the people who've benefited from my fundraisers. It's always a great feeling."

"I'm glad you can relate."

"Sort of," she said. "The difference is I'm not risking my life."

I swirled the sauce some more. A deep inhalation revealed a better aroma. "You'd need to charge a lot more per plate if you did."

Gloria bit her bottom lip, probably to suppress a laugh. "You've been back to work for . . . what, three weeks now?"

Counting the time I spent finding and furnishing my new office, her estimate seemed accurate. "Sounds right."

"You haven't talked much about your cases. Not like you normally do. How are they?"

"Boring, mostly." I checked the water for the pasta. It was still a couple minutes from a vigorous boil. "I've served subpoenas and divorce papers a lot. Spent too much time in the car waiting for people to come or go. Declined a bunch of adultery cases."

Before I knew she'd moved, Gloria placed a hand gently on my shoulder. "You're back to work, and it hasn't really been meaningful yet,"

"Not really, no," I said. "At least I'm getting paid on time." Now, I needed to track things like invoices, expenses, delinquent accounts, and the like. It was almost enough to make me want to hire an assistant.

"Don't push too hard in your search for a meaningful case," Gloria said. "That's all."

"I'm not." I didn't think I was, at least. Three weeks of waiting in cold parking lots to hand some asshole an envelope, however, constituted a long time to suffer. I might have jumped at Amy Sloan's case because I wanted some "real" work again.

"I hope not."

The water boiled. I dropped a bunch of angel hair into the pot. The sauce bubbled, so I turned the heat down. I sampled a bit from my tasting spoon. "*Magnifique!*"

"Speaking French isn't going to get you off the hook," Gloria said. I handed her the spoon, and she took a taste. "Damn. That *is* good."

"Give it nine minutes or so, and we can eat."

"A girl could get used to her handsome boyfriend cooking dinner every night."

"I thought you already had," I said.

Gloria grinned. "I suppose I have."

Implicit in her words was she needed me to be around to keep up the kitchen routine. I understood, though I was still going to work the Sloan case.

* * *

IN MY HOME office after dinner, I logged onto my laptop. Amy Sloan told me the official investigation into her sister's murder had stalled. Even when I enjoyed the financial backing of my parents' foundation, many of my clients came to me because of their dissatisfaction with the pace of police work. I tried to be realistic about it—solving a murder usually didn't happen in a couple days—but also wanted to help people who felt they had no other recourse.

Now, the dynamic of my relationship with my clients changed. I took money from lawyers and let sleazy insurance executives mar my office. Lysol took the spot below aluminum foil on my supply list. Working something like the Sloan case would get justice for a family and serve as a palate cleanser for me. Win-win.

During my first case a few years ago, my cousin Rich, then a uniformed sergeant with the Baltimore police, made the grave error of leaving me alone at his computer. Armed with a couple vital bits of information, I've since been able to get the BPD's network to accept my computer as one of its own. This clever bit of impersonation allows me access to case files—something they'd be loath to give me most of the time.

Suzie Sloan's file showed an active homicide investigation. The two cops assigned to it were a pair I barely knew. Detectives Davis and Adler were middle-of-the-road as far as closed cases and investigative prowess went. They responded to Suzie Sloan's apartment and found her dead inside. She'd been bludgeoned repeatedly with an aluminum bat not recovered from the scene. I looked at the photos and winced. Suzie's face got battered beyond recognition, and her skull yielded to several cruel blows.

This was a vicious beating. Someone hated her.

Davis and Adler ran down the usual leads. They started with Suzie's boyfriend, friends, and boss. The lack of a murder weapon hampered them. Baseball bats are made to size specifications, and there's little to differentiate a Louisville Slugger from a Tennessee Thumper when local stores sell hundreds, and you're down to impressions on skull and bone. No one claimed to own such a weapon, of course.

The homicide lieutenant, a loudmouth named O'Malley, even got involved. As I would expect, his presence brought no help to the investigation. His best attribute was a booming voice, and his worst were everything else about him. Even Rich, who rarely spoke ill of his fellow men and women in blue, disliked O'Malley and thought him a buffoon.

The file saw no updates for the last three days, during which six more murders plagued Baltimore, so the police didn't lack for other cases. Nothing in the notes jumped out at me. Lovers are always the first to come under suspicion, but Davis and Adler questioned Suzie's boyfriend twice without arresting him. None of her friends looked good for the crime, either.

I knew it couldn't be random. The savagery involved meant Suzie's attacker despised her for some reason. The killer's identity was in the file somewhere.

I would find it.

CHAPTER 3

THE NEXT MORNING, I HIT THE MEAN STREETS OF FEDERAL Hill for a run. A chilly fog blanketed the area. My walk to the area's eponymous park took a couple minutes, which was usually enough time to warm up on all but the most frigid of mornings. The cold stayed with me today, however, and I didn't feel like my blood flowed properly until I passed the halfway mark of my first lap.

Before I got shot, I used to run for about a half-hour. It let me do about three and a half miles, sometimes four if I pushed the pace or stayed out for a few extra minutes. Since two bullets tore up my chest and cost me a lobe of my lung, my endurance still hadn't come all the way back. In the same thirty minutes, I'd be lucky to hit three miles, and I'd sound quite a bit like a septuagenarian chain smoker by the end. Still, I knew I'd never improve if I stopped, so I kept at it and hoped the slow incremental gains I'd seen so far continued.

My route around the park afforded me a great view of the Baltimore harbor. The Maryland Science Center, the carousel, and the struggling retail pavilions looked back at me. Every time I ran here, it forced me to see the place where my shooting happened. On some level, it was probably therapeutic. One of these days, maybe I'd feel a little therapy from it.

I sucked wind strolling up Riverside Avenue, went back inside my house, and took a shower. By the time I'd started coffee in the kitchen, Gloria stirred and joined me downstairs. She planted a minty kiss on me, then prepared her first cup of morning caffeine. I chopped an apple, added the pieces to a small pot of oatmeal, and sprinkled in some cinnamon. Ten minutes later, we enjoyed a classic winter breakfast.

An interruption soon followed as my phone buzzed. I ignored it, but then it did it again. I picked it up. My new client the insurance fellow seemed eager for me to get started.

Mr. Ferguson, it's a new morning. Each day Mr. Stanton is out of work, we owe him more money. We'd like to know if this is a frivolous expense. I expect your prompt report.

"I expect your prompt report," I said in a voice mocking Elliott Allen's nasal tone.

"Don't like the case?" Gloria asked.

"Too soon to say. The man who hired me is probably an asshole, though."

"You could just not work for him."

"Maybe I'll get to tell him off when it's over," I said. "I should probably wait for the check to clear first, though."

Gloria frowned at me, but she didn't say anything else. After breakfast, I grabbed a jacket, kissed Gloria goodbye, and walked out back to my car. I wanted to look into Suzie Sloan's murder, but I needed to get Elliott Allen off my back first.

Most of all, I wanted to reach the point where I could work one case at a time again.

* * *

ABOUT A HALF-HOUR LATER, I sat in front of Charles Stanton's house. He lived off Harford Road in the Hamilton area of Baltimore, a stone's throw from the city-county line. My cousin Rich lived a few minutes away. Homes here dated from before to a few years after World War II, and many were built in the Victorian style.

Stanton owned a medium-sized two-story. Its white paint gleamed in the morning sun. He could boast of the best-looking shutters and fence on the street. I wondered if this served as the genesis of Elliott Allen's concerns. If Stanton could build a fence—or make significant repairs to it—he should have been healthy enough to go back to work.

With no activity in the area, I perused the file Allen gave me. Stanton was a tall, thin, light-complected black man. He graduated from Goucher College with a nursing degree and worked in the field ever since. Until his alleged workman's comp incident, he'd been a model employee, including earning a promotion to shift supervisor five years ago.

Stanton's front door opened, and he walked down his four stairs into the yard. The spring in his step, as my father would say, didn't indicate any kind of lingering injury. He carried a power trimmer in his hand and fired it up. Stanton's front yard contained a lot of azaleas and other bushes. They didn't look unruly from where I sat, and it seemed at least a month early to do much landscaping.

My opinion didn't deter Stanton, who spent nearly thirty minutes trimming the shrubs. Despite being about a hundred feet from his front yard, I still heard the power blade do its work. To my eyes, the bushes looked much the same as when he began. This is why I didn't own anything requiring landscaping. My plot didn't even have any grass to mow, which suited me fine. Stanton disappeared behind his house and returned a couple moments later with a large bag of mulch over his shoulder.

I didn't like Elliot Allen, but I began to sympathize with his position.

The sympathy increased when Stanton again walked away and returned with a second identical large bag. While I've never used one, I've seen enough of them to know they weigh forty or fifty pounds each. Hoisting a couple like Stanton did with a bad back should be impossible—or at the very least, pain-inducing. He dropped the second bag, split it open with a knife from his pocket, and slipped on a pair of gloves. Stanton got down on all fours and scooped mulch from the bag, setting it in even amounts around the bushes he'd recently pruned.

After another half-hour passed—and Stanton carried another heavy sack to the front of his house—he disappeared again. I opened a note-taking app on my phone and entered a few bits of information. Elliot Allen struck me as the kind of man who valued precision. I made sure to capture the time I saw him open the final bag. The other two required some guesswork. So much for precision. I'd try to paper over it in the precious report he expected.

My passenger's side door opened, and I dropped my phone and slid toward my own door. Charles Stanton plopped down next to me, and he didn't look happy.

How THE HELL did I leave the doors unlocked? I'd recently observed the man next to me using a knife to slice open bags. While I couldn't see a weapon, he still could've carried one in his pocket. My seat belt was off, and I'd scooted against the left-side bolster. I didn't have any farther to go without leaving the car. The .45 at my side offered some reassurance. In this small space, if Stanton pulled his knife, I could deter him long enough to shoot him.

If I didn't flinch.

As if sensing my internal struggle, he said, "You all right, man?"

"Yeah." I took a deep breath. "Just surprised."

"Shouldn't leave your door open."

"What do you want?"

"You're sitting here watching me, and you're going to ask why I'm curious?" Stanton said. It was a fair question.

"I didn't walk up to you while you were working."

Stanton stared at me. I returned the favor. He cracked first. "Who you working for?"

"Who said I'm here for you?" I asked. "You must have a high opinion of yourself."

"Ain't nobody else interesting live on this street." He ran his hand down the leather on the S4's dashboard. "You got a nicer car than the last two guys, though."

"What last two guys?"

"You think you're the first guy those damn bean counters sent to watch me? Fifteen years, and this is the treatment I get."

"To be fair," I said, "Your back doesn't seem injured."

Stanton sighed. "Guy who hired you was an accountant, right?" He didn't wait for me to answer. "All they know is their fucking spreadsheets. I got hurt on the job. I shoulda been smarter, but I thought I could lift the guy on my own." He shook his head. "Dumb. I knew I was down for the count right away." Stanton paused. He kept looking straight ahead. I wondered if he needed to tell all this to someone, and I simply happened to be here. "You ever throw your back out real bad?"

"No," I said once I was sure he left me time to contribute to the conversation.

"Don't. It sucks. Took me a couple months to feel better."

We had this in common, but I didn't want to engender Stanton's sympathy. Mostly, I wanted him out of my car. "Are you back to normal now?"

Stanton didn't answer right away. He sat in the passenger's seat staring out the windshield. Finally, he said, "It's too much. I seen too much. Hospitals have been hell for about a year now."

This didn't count as an answer to my question, but I understood his plight better than he realized. Stanton seemed physically able to return to work, but his mental fitness for the job would be a question mark. Gloria basically said the same thing about me, and I couldn't deny the accuracy in her words. "You mentioned the other guys who came to watch you."

"Yeah." Stanton's voice grew quiet. "They were a couple of classic PIs. Looked like former cops who couldn't stop eating donuts when they retired. On some level, I think they understood what I told them."

"I think I understand, too," I said, "but I need to make updates to keep up appearances."

"Want to help me tend to the azaleas?"

"Not a chance."

"You can't blame a man for asking," Stanton said. He got out of my car and walked back to his house. I realized I still sat as close to my door as possible, so I arranged myself normally in the seat. The passenger's door opening gave me a surprise, but I still flinched even if I didn't physically recoil. If Stanton climbed into my car with a knife in his hand, he could have filleted me before I mustered any resistance.

Maybe the other case would rejuvenate me. I fired up the S4 and left Stanton's neighborhood.

* * *

I'D STARTED my inquiry into Suzie Sloan's murder by looking at the police report. It could only tell me so much, and it still managed to come up short. Returning to my office, I looked more into Suzie herself. With the possible exception of people who go to great lengths to live off the grid, everyone leaves footprints online. If I found and followed enough of them, they could lead me to a murderer.

One of the disadvantages of renting the office above a repair shop was the noise. The mechanics talked loudly, used power tools, and banged out dents at various points throughout the day. I needed a viable long-term solution, but for now, I slipped on a pair of noise-canceling headphones. Because I felt especially foolish wearing them with nothing to listen to, I played some quiet classical music. Maybe Mozart would inspire my Facebook searches.

Suzie Sloan was three years out of college, where she amassed friends and accolades in equal measure. She graduated on the dean's list with a degree in communications and worked at a nonprofit for a year. From there, she landed a gig as the receptionist for noted plastic surgeon Dr. Neal Fabian. She toiled there until about a month ago when he fired her. Her online posts expressed frustration and hurt.

Her Facebook profile showed over 1600 friends. I pondered how social media strained the word's definition, then stopped when I realized these musings added a generation to my age. At this rate, I'd be talking to my actual friends about the socks I bought on a good sale. The volume of Suzie's connections didn't mean anything. She'd probably never met a swath of them, and whoever killed her might not even be among the number.

Between what Amy told me and what I gleaned from Facebook and other sites, I assembled a short dossier on Suzie Sloan. Its purposes were twofold. I might be able to determine who killed her, and I could use it to gain access to some of her accounts. I started with Twitter. The *Forgot password?* link asked me a security question. Suzie's high school mascot. As I knew where she went, I had the answer a second later. Next, the site presented me the choice of where to receive a reset link. Without Suzie's phone, I chose the email option. Despite a bunch of asterisks obscuring the details, I knew it referred to her Yahoo account.

The next step involved gaining access to it. After answering the same security question, I was presented another one: the make and model of Suzie's first car. "Shit," I muttered to the empty office. The nuggets of information I assembled only told me about her current vehicle, a Honda Civic which rolled off the assembly line five years ago. Suzie would've been twenty at the time. She stayed local for college and lived on campus rather than commute. Her current car could've been her first. I typed *Honda Civic* into the answer box and pressed Enter.

Bingo.

I reset her password and enjoyed access to her email and her Twitter accounts. I went after the latter first. After a little while scrolling through her timeline, I checked her direct messages, and then ran a few searches. Suzie didn't post a lot, but she liked her share of tweets and used the platform to keep in touch with a few people from high school and college. None of them jumped out to me as killers.

Next, I dove into her emails. Many more correspondences with friends and acquaintances scrolled past. Amy was mostly correct: Suzie was a popular woman with a lot of friends—by any definition of the word—and many more acquaintances. I couldn't find anyone who disliked her. Even her former boss remained cordial after firing her. Suzie sent him an email asking the real reason he let her go. I found her wording curious, but nothing in his answer suggested foul play.

. . .

Suzie,

The reality is my insurance information was incorrect because of your oversight. The effects are twofold: it costs me patients, and it means people who might otherwise need our services go somewhere else. I wish you well, and I'll be happy to overlook this error and give you a recommendation if you need one.

Neal

I DIDN'T KNOW MUCH about whatever insurance problem the doctor experienced, but it must have been serious for him to sack a good employee of nearly two years. I spent another couple hours combing through everything I could, but nothing jumped out at me. Maybe my dossier would prove useful, but at the moment, more questions faced me than answers.

CHAPTER 4

SHORTLY AFTER I WALKED INTO MY HOUSE FOLLOWING A fruitless search through Suzie Sloan's life, my phone rang. I expected it to be Elliot Allen asking for an update. Instead, my parents' house number showed on the screen. Ever since they declined to keep funding my cases, our relationship cooled to frosty, and we'd barely spoken in months outside of a brief thaw for my father's birthday. I pondered continuing the trend before relenting and answering. "I wasn't sure you'd pick up," my father said.

"Me, either." I stopped in the kitchen and leaned against the counter.

"Coningsby, you can't dodge us forever," my mother added.

"I'm younger and faster," I said. "Pretty sure I'll win. Let me guess . . . you two are in separate rooms. The call was Mom's idea. Dad, you're probably sitting in the study, and Mom, I'm going to guess you're in the living room."

"We both want to talk to you, son," my father said. "You're right about the rest, though."

"We don't have much to discuss."

"I know you're upset about what happened. Have you—"

"You got shot, Coningsby!" my mother broke in. "How

could we keep paying you to work cases when something like that happened?"

"It's part of the job, Mom." I sighed. We'd hashed out this ground before. My parents held their beliefs, I held mine, and a great chasm separated them. There was no middle-of-the-road option to be found and no bridge to bring the sides together. "If I were a crossing guard, and I got hit by a car, would you expect me to throw in the towel? Cooks cut their fingers. Hair stylists burn themselves with flat irons. Sometimes, people in my line of work get shot." A memory of the event flashed in my mind. I closed my eyes and tried to push past it.

"You could find something else to do, son."

"I don't want to do something else."

"At least come for dinner," my mother said. "We've been inviting you for months."

"I know," I said. "I thought about going once. When I looked online for the Iscariot residence, though, I couldn't find anything."

"We're not Judases for pulling the plug," my father said. Annoyance crept into his voice. "We did it out of concern."

"I know. The two of you have certainly told me enough times." My mother started to interject, but I talked over her. "I'll come by one of these nights. I don't know when. Trying to get me over by asking Gloria isn't going to work, either. I feel betrayed, and you don't get it. You've both really pissed me off. I need some time not dealing with you for a while."

"Son, we just—"

"I'll call you when I want to talk," I said and hung up. I set my phone on the counter and plucked a beer from the fridge. After I opened the IPA and enjoyed a long pull, Gloria walked in.

"Were you talking to someone?"

"My parents."

She frowned. "Any change?"

"Nope."

She squeezed my hand and sashayed toward the living room. As I watched her with some interest, I felt glad she didn't try to get me to open up about it.

* * *

I LEFT a message with Doctor Fabian's office, explaining who I was and what I needed to talk to him about. Afterward, Gloria and I ordered delivery from a local Chinese restaurant, and she convinced me to watch some show on Netflix a bunch of her friends recommended. After enduring three episodes, I told her their tastes were dubious. She agreed, and we went to bed soon after.

The next morning, my phone vibrating on the nightstand jarred me from my sleep. The time showed 7:25 as I answered the call from a number I didn't recognize. "You're the detective who called here?" a woman asked after I mumbled an incoherent greeting.

"Yes," I said, forcing myself to wake up. "Are you from the doctor's office?"

"Yes, sir." Her pleasant voice almost allowed me to forgive her for calling so early. "We don't officially open until eight-thirty. You could probably get a few minutes with Doctor Fabian before his first appointment."

"Great. I'll be there as soon as I can. Thank you." I hung up, threw some clothes on, brushed my teeth, and hurried out the door. Doctor Fabian maintained an office in a professional building in the shadow of Johns Hopkins Hospital. Maybe he hoped the prestige would rub off on anything nearby. After a struggle with morning traffic, I parked in a nearby garage at eight-thirteen. Four minutes later, I walked into Beleza Plastic Surgery of Maryland.

Three people sat scattered in the waiting room. Posters extolling the virtues of beauty and self-confidence lined the walls. As those possessing both would be unlikely to walk through the door, whoever hung these signs lacked much sense of irony. I walked to the counter where an attractive young woman sat behind the desk. She wore a maroon sweater and kept her dark hair in a neat ponytail. "Are you here for a consult?" she asked as I approached.

"No," I said as I passed a hand over my face. "Not much room for improvement here. I'm the detective who left a message yesterday." I showed the receptionist—Nancy with her nameplate now visible—my ID.

"I'm glad you could make it down. Go through the door to your right, and I'll take you back." I did as she instructed, and Nancy led me a down a hallway dotted with closed doors on either side. Despite the wall decorations in the lobby, this area of the practice looked and smelled as antiseptic as any hospital or doctor's office. Nancy opened the last door on the right and gestured for me to go in.

I walked into the exam room. "Doctor Fabian will stop by in a moment," she said. I hopped up onto the table and waited. Nancy left the door cracked as she walked away. A minute later, a middle-aged man in the requisite white lab coat walked in. For a plastic surgeon, Doctor Fabian didn't look like he'd had any work done. He drew a line at conceding to aging with his hair, though. It was way too brown to be natural at his age.

"Morning," he said as he dropped into a nearby chair. "You're the detective?"

"I am." I showed him my ID. He fumbled a pair of reading glasses out of his breast pocket to get a better look at it. "I'll presume Nancy told you why I'm here."

"She did. I was gutted to hear about Suzie. So unfortunate." The doctor grimaced, and from where I sat, it struck me as sincere.

"Isn't it odd to feel so bad about the death of someone you fired?" I asked.

"I don't think so. I didn't do it maliciously. Suzie made a grave error when it came to insurance, and I couldn't look past it."

"Did she understand?"

"She told me she did," Doctor Fabian said, "but I'm not sure I believed her. She loved working here. It's a prestigious job, after all, especially for a girl so young."

The medicinal smell in the air yielded to the aroma of arrogance. I should've expected it from a plastic surgeon. "What exactly caused you to get rid of her?"

"An insurance misunderstanding. I wasn't listed properly somehow, and because of Suzie's oversight, I didn't appear in several providers' networks."

"How much of what you do is covered by insurance?" I said.

"Mister . . . Ferguson, right?" I bobbed my head. "If this were Los Angeles, I'd probably be awash in tummy tucks and tit jobs. I do a few of those, of course. People need to feel good about themselves, and some can afford to put their visions into action. Procedures like those are cosmetic, and you're right to presume they're not covered. However, I do plenty of surgeries like skin grafts and breast reconstruction for cancer. Those are usually reimbursed by insurance."

"If you're in the network."

"Precisely," he said. "I have no way of knowing how many people were denied my care because of Suzie's mistake. I couldn't see a way past it, though. I didn't think I could trust her afterward, so I had to let her go."

"Are things running better now?"

Doctor Fabian glanced at his smartwatch. My time grew short. "Not really. I've replaced her with two part-timers. Nancy out there works three days a week, and I have another girl who handles the other two."

"Conveniently, you don't need to give them benefits if they're not full-time," I said.

"A happy coincidence," the doctor said. "Now, if you'll excuse me, I need to start seeing patients."

"Of course." I gestured toward the door even though it wasn't my office. Doctor Fabian left. I checked out the exam room. It looked like any other I'd been in. Only a poster on the wall talking about liposuction differentiated it from any other similar space I'd ever been in. I left the back area through the door and returned to the waiting room. One more person occupied a chair now. Nancy typed something on her computer as I approached.

"Did you get what you needed?" She looked up at me with a sincere smile reaching her eyes.

"For now," I said. "I might need to come back if I have any other questions."

"No problem," she said. "Casey is here Monday and Friday. I cover the days in-between. Either of us can get you more time with the doctor if you need it."

Knowing the schedule could help in the future. I hoped I wouldn't need to see the smug surgeon again, but I thanked her anyway.

* * *

I FIELDED a call from Amy Sloan after lunch. As soon as I recognized her number, I dreaded picking up. She would want an update on the case. The police chewed on it for ten days and got nowhere. After a single day, she expected me to make major progress. While I appreciated people thinking me a miracle worker, I found I could never live up to the title. "Hi, Amy."

"Hello, Mister Ferguson."

"Please, call me C.T."

"All right, C.T.," she said. "I was just wondering how the case was coming along."

I moved the phone away from my mouth to mute my sigh. "It hasn't even been a full day yet."

"I know. I just . . . I guess I hoped you could work faster than the police."

"I can," I said, "and I do. But they've been sitting on this for a week and a half. Rome wasn't built in a day, as my grandfather used to say, and most murder cases don't get solved so quickly, either."

"You're right. I'm sorry."

"Don't be. I know you want to put this behind you. I'm working on it." I left out the part about dealing with possible workman's comp insurance fraud. My life was easier when I stuck to one case at a time.

"All right," Amy said. "I presume you'll let me know if you make a break in our investigation."

I took exception to her modifier but kept it to myself. "You'll be my first call. Maybe my second if I have to call the cops first."

"Thanks, C.T." We hung up, and I rolled my eyes. When I worked *pro bono*, I could get away with not updating my clients regularly. With money now changing hands, I couldn't blow them off, and it meant I needed to do more paperwork on the back end. I again pondered how to fit an assistant into my business budget. Solving the two matters in front of me would be a good first step in raising the funds.

Later in the afternoon, Gloria dropped by my office with a

hot vanilla latte. "I'm going to meet a potential fundraising client in the county," she said after a couple delicate sips of her own hot beverage.

"Awesome." I stuck my hand up, and Gloria slapped it in one of the hardest high-fives I've ever received. "Does this mean you're a freelancer now?"

"We'll see. I'd like to find some smaller organizations that could use the push." When we first met about three years ago, Gloria found the idea of working to be an anathema. She took a greater interest in my cases over time, however, and it led to her using her money and connections for charity work. Her best client had been Vincent Davenport, a local businessman, part-time philanthropist, and full-time bastard who ruined a lot of lives other than Gloria's when he won the election for mayor of Baltimore last fall.

"Good luck," I said. "I'm sure you'll do great. I'm glad you want to work with smaller places. They can use the boost."

She smiled. "Thanks. I hope we both find meaningful work."

"I'm trying."

"I know. I just don't want you to end up in a funk."

"I'm so funky I'm going to be on George Clinton's next album," I said.

"Is he related to Bill Clinton?" Gloria asked, and I hoped she was kidding.

"No. Don't worry about me, though. I'm finding my way."

"I hope so." Gloria took another sip of her drink. Never to be outdone, I partook of mine, as well. "I'll probably stay at my house tonight. She's not far from me."

I nodded. "All right." Gloria slept at my house a lot. I occasionally stayed with her. Whatever the configuration, we spent five or six nights a week under the same roof. It didn't count as living together—something we'd never officially discussed—and the arrangement worked for us.

Gloria stood, walked around my desk, and sat on my lap. She put her arms around my neck. "Promise me you're OK."

"Right as rain," I said.

"I'll give you the benefit of the doubt," she said before leaning in to kiss me. This turned into several more kisses before she broke away and stood. "I don't think your landlord would appreciate office sex."

"His workers might," I said.

Gloria slapped me on the shoulder, planted a final lingering kiss on me, and left. It felt nice having someone to worry about me. I was glad she extended me the benefit of the doubt.

Now, I needed to earn it.

CHAPTER 5

I LEFT MY OFFICE ABOUT AN HOUR LATER AND DROVE TO A gym. Suzie Sloan's boyfriend owned and operated the Catonsville Athletic Club a couple blocks past the city limits. From the outside, the place looked squat and long but not deep. A window at the far end was boarded up, though the rest of the exterior appeared in good shape. Automatic doors slid open as I approached.

The interior looked like many similar facilities I'd been to before. The front desk sat to the left, manned by someone whose physique suggested he could pick up the whole thing and carry it around with him if the place ever remodeled. He kept his blond hair short but spiky, and the Catonsville Athletic Club polo he wore strained across his broad chest. I glanced around and noticed several women working out along with a couple other trainers in similarly tight tops.

The main area held racks of free weights. Mirrors lined the walls, and several men monitored their forms while they lifted. A machine circuit beckoned in the next room. The massive desk man assumed his post. "Here for a workout?"

"Not today." I showed him my ID. "I'm here to talk to the owner."

"About what?"

"His murdered girlfriend."

"He didn't do it," the guy said.

"Great. Thanks for your contributions, Detective, but I'd like to talk to the boss all the same."

The blond man leaned down, resting his huge forearms on the counter. "How about I take you back to see him if you can out-curl me?" He raised his right arm and flexed to accentuate the point.

"As long as we can also have a spelling bee and a math contest," I said, "sure. Two out of three."

"Listen here," he said, but an intercom buzzing on the desk cut him off. He pushed a button and grunted.

"It's fine, Jimmy," said the voice on the other end. "Send him back."

"All right." Jimmy mashed the button again. "Go on back. Past the circuit on your left." He jerked his head toward it, even though the path was obvious.

"Thanks." I walked in the indicated direction. Beyond the Nautilus machines, the walls closed in to form a hallway. A basketball court sat on the right side. Two restrooms and a door simply labeled *Office* were on the left. I knocked. "Come in," the same voice bellowed.

I turned the knob and walked through. Like the club itself, the room was long and narrow. Three desks consumed a lot of the carpeted floor space. TVs connected to a security system hung from the rear wall. A man who must have been pushing his late thirties—making him much older than Suzie—sat behind the largest desk. He stood and revealed himself to be in good shape—not like Jimmy, but he clearly availed himself of the equipment in his gym. "You're a detective?"

"Yes." I showed him my ID before dropping into a chair in front of his desk. "C.T. Ferguson."

"Glenn Mathews," he said. "Two Ns, one T." He finished with a much bigger grin than his cheesy line deserved.

I wondered if he put the slogan on his business cards. "I'm sorry about Suzie, but it's why I'm here. Her sister hired me because the police haven't had much luck yet."

Mathews leaned back in his chair and crossed his large arms. "Whaddaya need to know?"

"I guess my first question is did you kill her?"

"What are you, some kind of asshole?" Mathews' brows knitted. I wondered if he employed his musclebound crew as impromptu goons in case someone like me showed up and nosed around.

"No," I said. "If I were, I'd point out how you haven't answered my question." I put my hand to my mouth in mock surprise. "Whoops."

We engaged in a staring contest for a few seconds before Mathews let out a sibilant sigh. "Cops asked me days ago. I didn't kill Suzie. We had a good relationship."

"All right. Any idea who might've wanted her dead?"

"You said Amy hired you?" I bobbed my head. "The police already asked me this. How are you going to figure out what they can't if you come in here with the same questions?"

"I'm smarter than they are," I said. "Besides, I need to start somewhere. Might as well lead off with the basics."

"Hell, I can't think of anyone. Everyone liked Suzie."

"No problems with any of her friends . . . or yours?"

"You got something against my friends?" he asked.

"Suzie got beaten to death with a baseball bat," I said. "I've seen the pictures, and trust me when I say you don't want to. It's a weapon anyone could use, but the brutality suggests a man did it."

Mathews leaned forward and glared at me. "I don't think I like you very much."

"Can I have one of your gym towels to wipe my tears?"

"I don't have to talk to you," he said. "You ain't a cop. You got any real questions for me, or should I have a couple of my guys toss you out of here?"

A few months ago, I would've vigorously disputed the ability of Mathews' employees to evict me from the building. Considering my more recent problems with flinching and confrontations, however, I thought better of it. The humiliation of getting bounced by someone with a camera roll full of gym mirror selfies would cut deeply. Instead, I said, "Sure. Suzie ever tell you of any problems at work?"

"No." He frowned. "Like what?"

"Like with her boss . . . or maybe a patient."

"You think some patient killed her?"

I shrugged. "According to Doctor Fabian, he fired her for some problem with his insurance listing. Someone could've missed out on an important surgery because they didn't know he was in their network."

"Pretty flimsy reason to kill someone," Mathews said.

"People get killed over shit like candy bars every day."

"I guess. Look, I don't know how much more I can tell you. I don't know who'd want to kill Suzie. I loved the girl."

"Someone didn't," I said. "I'm going to find out who." I stood.

Mathews got to his feet, too. "Good luck, but I don't like you. Might be good if you didn't come back here. I'll ask my guys to keep an eye out."

"If I need to ask you something else, I'm going to do it. I guess we'll see if Hans and Franz are good for more than just bicep curls."

I didn't wait for Mathews to escort me out. No one stopped me or encouraged me to leave more quickly. I considered it a win as the automatic doors yielded, and I walked outside.

* * *

I RETURNED to my office and pondered my next move when my phone rang. Rich. We hadn't talked much over the last couple weeks, so I picked up. "I hear you've been diving back into your work," he said.

"*Et tu, Brute?*"

"You should be glad people are concerned about you."

"On some level," I said, "I am. On a few other levels, I find it pretty tiresome."

"You've been through a lot."

I leaned back in my chair and stared at the ceiling. "I'm aware, Rich, since I'm the one who survived it."

"I just don't want you to run before you walk," he said. "I've seen cops push to get back on the streets too soon. It usually doesn't end well."

If I wanted to unload everything on my mind, Rich would make a good sounding board. He followed a decade of service in the army by joining the BPD, where he now worked as a plainclothes sergeant. He'd seen a lot, and while he'd never been shot and forced to dive into a harbor, he'd witnessed his share of death up close. Despite the grief I gave him for being a square, I always thought Rich kept everything together well. "Let me guess . . . you've talked to my parents recently."

"I have. It doesn't make my concern any less genuine."

I understood this, but I also knew they'd be expecting him to provide a report. If I told him something in confidence, it put Rich in a bad spot. He wouldn't betray me, but he also wouldn't want to lie to his aunt and uncle. "I'm fine, Rich."

"I'm not sure I believe you," he said.

"It's a free country," I pointed out.

"Do you have a case?"

"Two, in fact. One is yet another murder I'll need to close

on behalf of the Baltimore police. If the city didn't have budget issues, I might ask for a stipend."

"You sure you're ready for it?" he asked after a short pause. I knew he spent the fraction of a second rolling his eyes.

"I just walked into the lion's den," I said, "and I emerged without getting bitten or scratched."

"Let me know if you're getting in over your head."

"I'll call you when I have an ironclad case. Then, you can make the arrest and get the commendation. You know . . . our usual arrangement."

Rich sighed. "Just remember people are worried about you."

"It's hard to forget," I said. "You all remind me so much." We hung up, and I resumed pondering what to do next. I looked at my watch. A couple hours of daylight remained. Maybe I could hit a couple birds with a single stone.

* * *

I PARKED in the same spot along the curb near Charles Stanton's house. A chill hung in the afternoon air, but if he were still doing some almost-spring yard work, a couple hours of daylight remained. This time, I kept a camera on the passenger's seat. Elliot Allen struck me as the type of man who wanted copious photographic evidence.

Within a few minutes, the nurse was back to it. He walked to a patchy spot in his yard, dropped to his knees, and used a hand tool to till the soil. I snapped a couple pictures while thinking there had to be a better way of doing the work. So far, I'd seen Stanton carrying large bags of mulch. Hoisting them would be a challenge for a man with a back injury. Operating a large power tiller would probably be worse.

After about a half-hour, he stood and wiped his forehead.

Then, he looked up and saw me. As he walked to my S4, he shook his head. After Stanton dropped in on me last time, I made sure the doors were locked. Sure enough, he tried the handle and had no luck. "Sorry, we're closed," I said.

Stanton leaned down and peered into the car. "Didn't know if I'd see you again."

"Here I am."

"You'll have to come back tomorrow to make it as long as the last guy did."

"I'm not here to set records." I pointed to the camera on the seat.

"Right," Stanton said. "My hand tool is really heavy."

"Pretty strenuous work."

He put his hand on the door again. "You mind opening up?"

There seemed little harm in it past getting sweat on the leather, so I disengaged the power locks. Stanton moved my camera to the console as he climbed in. Once he settled in the seat, I locked the door again. "Something on your mind?"

"I told you my story," he said.

"I'm doing a job," I said. "Not all of us can skip work for months and still get paid."

"You should try it."

I'd considered it. Once my parents cut me loose from their foundation's payroll, however, my opportunity dried up. I would've been eligible at the time, since I still had a fair way to go in my recovery. In the end, I think I would've gone stir crazy and probably driven Gloria nuts on top of it. "I don't think it's for me. As much as I might like jabbing my thumb in the system's eye, I'm not a cheat."

Stanton lapsed into silence. "You're gonna keep coming back?" he said after a moment.

"Every day if my other case lets me."

He half-turned in the seat to face me. "What else you have going on?"

Now, I'd learn if he could offer any insights into the possibly shady surgeon. "A murder investigation."

"And you're here wasting your time on me?"

"The good thing about the dead is they're not going anywhere," I said. "They're also not busy in their gardens."

"You got any medical reports to look over?" Stanton asked.

"If I do, I know someone in the ME's office."

"Fine." Stanton faced forward again and slumped in the seat. "You can't blame a fellow for trying."

I baited the hook again. "You've been a nurse for a while, right?"

"My whole professional life."

"Know a doctor named Fabian?" I asked.

He stewed on it for a few seconds. "The plastic surgeon?"

"He's the one."

"Never met him," Stanton said, "but I know him by reputation."

"And?"

"He's an asshole. Another doctor who operates on a few people and gets a god complex. You know he worked at Hopkins?"

"His current office is less than a block away," I said.

"Wait." Stanton frowned. "You said this was a murder case. Someone kill him?"

I shook my head. "His assistant."

"Fabian's a jerk," Stanton said, "but I'm not sure he's killer material."

"Someone is."

"It doesn't sound easy to figure out."

"We all have our crosses to bear," I said.

CHAPTER 6

THE NEXT MORNING, I WOKE UP IN MY BED ALONE. IT happened a couple days a week, but I'd grown used to Gloria sleeping beside me. My eyes lingered on the empty sheets as I rose and changed into my running attire. For the chilly morning, I wore full pants, a base layer on top, and a long-sleeved shirt. Cold air greeted me as I walked outside, but once I got moving, I knew I would soon warm up.

At just past nine o'clock, the street was empty as I made my way toward Federal Hill Park. Downtown Baltimore—visible across the harbor—bustled at the start of a new day. A few shops nearby were already open, and restaurants prepared to be, but I had the sidewalk to myself. Until two car doors opened and a pair of goons stepped out, at least.

They were dressed similarly to me, both decked out head to toe in track suits. I saw muscles swelling through the fabric but no signs of a gun on either man. Both were at least my height but outweighed me by a good fifty pounds. They looked like weightlifters or trainers, and I knew right away who sent them. "Shouldn't you be helping some bored housewife with her deadlifts?" I asked as they blocked the sidewalk ahead of me.

A confused look passed between them. The one on the left

ran a hand through his greasy mullet. "You're causing problems," he said in a squeaky voice which didn't match his frame or profession.

"Sorry, did I interrupt you sucking helium out of a balloon? My bad." I held my arm out toward their Camry against the curb. "If you want to get back to it, I'll understand."

"You've been asking questions," the other said. His short blond hair made me think of the fellow behind the counter at the Catonsville Athletic Club yesterday, but this wasn't the same guy. "We want you to stop."

"What's the problem with a few questions?" I said. "Whoops, there I go again. Can I get a mulligan?"

The banter ended as the mulleted enforcer moved closer. I shifted my feet into a ready stance and glanced at the other goon, who held his position. My eyes returned to the long-haired one. He planted his left foot and drew his right arm back.

I flinched.

His fist clobbered me in the face, and the force of the blow spun me around. The other goon stepped up and shoved me hard in the chest. The punch already unbalanced me, and I couldn't keep my feet. I landed hard on the concrete, and pain traveled across my shoulder blades when they hit.

Nothing like a quick pummeling to get the blood moving on a frosty morning.

They both capitalized on my plight by striding toward me. I sat up with a surge and punched the closer one—mullet man —squarely in the balls. He folded in half and sagged to the pavement. It wouldn't keep him down for long, but I only needed it to create an opening. I didn't have time to get back to my feet before the other guy was on top of me. He launched a side kick. I leaned away from it and used my upper left arm to help turn it aside. Then, I bent forward, grabbed the ankle of his plant foot with my right hand, and pulled for all I was worth.

It was enough. He grunted and topped over backwards. I stood as he went down, and he looked up at me just in time for me to give him a hard right cross to the face. His head bounced off the sidewalk, and he lay still. I stood in time for the long-haired muscle man to regain his feet. "You son of a bitch," he muttered, his face screwed in a mix of anger and lingering pain.

"Sorry, did you call Marquis of Queensbury rules? I must have missed it in all your empty threats."

"I'm gonna beat your ass."

"You might want to get started, then," I said.

He came at me, and I was ready. With my adrenaline flowing, I didn't flinch at his punches. Instead, I turned them all aside. When he sold out for offense, I hit him with a short left in the solar plexus. He backed up and sucked wind. I punched him in the stomach twice, gave him a sharp elbow to the face, and then rammed his head into a nearby signpost. He joined his fellow goon on the sidewalk. While unconsciousness claimed him, I whipped my phone out and snapped both their pictures.

I looked around. No one seemed to be interested in our scrum. It didn't mean someone didn't call the police, however. I glanced at the park, decided to count this fight as my morning constitutional, and walked back to my house.

* * *

AFTER A SHOWER and simple breakfast of oatmeal and sausage, I pondered where I stood with my dual cases. Two enforcers just tried to discourage me from pursuing one. The nurse sending a pair of weightlifters after me seemed unlikely. Therefore, they menaced me over the Suzie Sloan investigation. Either Doctor Fabian or Captain "Two Ns, One T" could have sent them. I favored the latter but couldn't say for certain.

On top of not knowing who paid the two goons, I flinched when the confrontation turned physical. It was bad enough doing it against portly executives in parking lots. I'd hoped a threatening situation would kick me back into gear. Not so much as it turned out. Once I took a good punch—from which my face still ached—and a shove to the sidewalk, I recovered and fought like I knew what I was doing. Which I did. Opening every altercation by getting clobbered first, however, would not be conducive to a long career. Or life.

I needed to get a handle on this . . . whatever it was. When I convalesced from my injuries at the facility in Arizona, I made a mostly complete physical recovery. Some time and training here got me back more or less to where I'd been before, though I lamented the last bits of my missing stamina. Mentally, however, I was obviously a mess, and I wasn't used to the feeling. I waded into situations knowing I had the facts right and understanding what needed to be done. Now, the memory of getting shot and nearly dying betrayed me.

Years ago, I spent time seeing a psychiatrist at the urging of my parents. My older sister died when I was sixteen. At the time, I thought natural causes claimed her life so soon. My parents foisted Doctor Janishefski upon me. He was nice enough, and he nodded in all the right places when I talked and wailed, but he didn't make a damn bit of difference to my mental health at the time.

I'd remained off the couch until recovering in Arizona. There, Doctor Parrish actually helped me begin the process of moving past what happened to me. Leaving must have interrupted things. She worked two thousand miles away, but I needed to ask if she would see me over Zoom or Skype. I looked her up at the facility and dialed her office.

A recording picked up after four rings. When the beep chirped in my ear, I left a message. "Doctor Parrish, this is C.T. Ferguson. I hope you remember me. I checked out a few months ago. At the time, I thought I was OK, but now I flinch every time a situation turns physical. So far, no serious outcomes, but it could catch up with me at some point. I know you're far away, but if we could do virtual sessions, I'd appreciate it. I'll pay you whatever your rate is. Please let me know." I left my cell phone number and ended the call.

Gloria would be proud of me for taking the step but also worried because I felt I needed to. I debated whether I should tell her.

* * *

I DROVE TO MY OFFICE, nodded to the mechanics working in the bay, and hoofed it upstairs. I wanted to know who sent the goons. Doctor Fabian probably had the resources to hire a couple of idiots to menace someone. Did it make him guilty? It certainly painted him in a negative light. What about Glenn Mathews? Either of the enforcers could have tossed a barbell down and driven to my street.

A couple years ago, the BPD upgraded their facial recognition program and tied it into the one operated by the state police. I uploaded the photos I snapped of the fallen goons, dropped both into the app, and waited for a result. It wouldn't take long. The second fellow I dispatched was Karl Blair, a semi-professional miscreant well-known by local law enforcement.

Starting at age seventeen and continuing for the next dozen years, Blair showed a pattern of assault. He got arrested eight times, charged five, and spent three years in jail over two trips. Most of his issues were with other men, but he got popped once for hitting a girlfriend, leading to his first time behind bars. For whatever reason, prosecutors could never seem to make a lot stick to this asshole.

I couldn't find anything linking him to Doctor Fabian. They didn't live close to one another, and I didn't find any friends, followers, or acquaintances in common across several social platforms. This didn't prove the surgeon didn't send this guy and his friend after me, of course. Picking someone who can't be tied back to you was smart.

As usual, I needed more information, so I dug deeper. I found Blair's email address and a corresponding password in a massive data breach. He never changed it. I scrolled through his messages and didn't notice anything from Doctor Fabian. Blair subscribed to some newsletters I would only call interesting on my most charitable day. He received a lot of mail from adult sites, much of which was probably spam. This was the likely cause of him winding up in the data breach.

Someone else's poor cyber hygiene, however, usually turned into my good fortune. Karl Blair's would be no different. On the second page of his inbox, however, I saw a personal training appointment reminder.

It was at the Catonsville Athletic Club.

CHAPTER 7

I DROVE BACK TO THE CATONSVILLE ATHLETIC CLUB. THE lot was mostly empty. When I walked inside, the same fellow manned the desk. "Can I help you?" he asked as I blew past his station.

"Nope," I said and marched farther into the building.

"Sir, this is for members only." He didn't move to stop me, though. Normally, I would have welcomed the challenge, but I tried to focus on staying in the moment and not flinching in case Glenn Mathews tried to get physical with me. Once he saw his goons failed to keep me off the case, who knew what he would do?

I reached Mathews' office and found the door closed. A quick check of the knob revealed it wasn't locked. I threw the door open and strode in. Mathews looked up. Recognition lit in his eyes, and he frowned. "Hi, Glenn with two Ns." I sat in one of his guest chairs without waiting to be invited. "Surprised to see me?"

"Yes," he said. "I didn't think we had anything else to discuss."

"Turns out we do." I leaned back and kicked my feet up, toppling a stack of papers in the process. Mathews scowled but did or said nothing else. "You sent a couple of supposed tough guys to keep me off the trail. By the way, I'm not sure Karl is going to make his next physical training appointment. He probably has a concussion."

"What are you talking about?"

"Don't sit there and plead ignorance. You may not be very bright, but you know what happened, which makes you an asshole--with two esses."

Mathews' left hand rubbed his temple. "You think I sent a couple guys from my gym to threaten you?"

"I do," I said. "They weren't wearing the official merch, but I learned who Karl is. He's a member here. Stands to reason the other guy is, too. Maybe you offered them a free month of dues if they got me to stop my investigation."

"I didn't do anything!" Mathews' right hand slapped his wooden desk, and I'd be surprised if he didn't crack it. I recoiled again and took a deep breath as he jabbed a finger at me. "Listen, you son of a bitch. I sat here and listened to your questions about Suzie. You didn't know why she would be with me. I could see it on your face. I'm older. She was young and pretty. I heard it all before. We had a good relationship. I didn't have anything to do with her getting killed, and I didn't send any guys to try and beat you up. I'm pretty sure I could do it myself."

"You might want to ask Karl and his friend how easy it was." I kept controlling my breathing. I hated flinching, but a man slapping his own desktop would surprise a lot of people.

"And maybe you might want to ask Suzie's boss some questions," Mathews said.

Now, we were getting somewhere. "I've talked to him already." I offered a noncommittal shrug to see if Mathews would keep talking.

"Well, go back and talk to him again. The guy's a prick."

"Maybe," I said. "Doesn't mean he had anything to do with Suzie's murder, though."

"He fired her over some insurance bullshit. You ask me, he was looking for a reason. Probably tried to get in her pants, and she turned him down. Men have killed women who work for them over less."

His point made sense, so I said, "True." Mathews became my top suspect because Karl belonged to his gym. It could have been a coincidence, though. Nothing in Mathews' words or actions led me to believe he told me any lies. "You might want to revoke Karl's membership. He's giving your club a bad name."

Mathews grunted. "Anything else you want to accuse me of?"

"Maybe tomorrow," I said. I stood and left his office. The guy behind the desk watched me the entire time as I walked out the front door.

* * *

* * *

BACK AT MY OFFICE, I ruminated on the chat with Glenn Mathews. If he told the truth, maybe I'd been too quick in dismissing Doctor Fabian. I couldn't imagine the surgeon beating a young woman to death over an insurance misunderstanding, however. Despite doing work covered under policy, he could make a very good living performing elective boob jobs, tummy tucks, and facelifts. Baltimore was a long way from Los Angeles in the number of rich, vain citizens, but every city housed people who wanted to look better and could pay for the privilege.

My cell phone doing its vibration dance on the desktop

shook me from my thoughts. Rich again. "'Twice in as many days," I said when I picked up. "Need me to help you earn another ribbon for your trophy case?"

To his credit, Rich took the barb with a chuckle. We disagreed about my role in his commendations, but it was always good-natured. "I actually have an offer for you."

"I don't need any overpriced weight-loss shakes."

"What?"

"I'm also not interested in joining your pyramid scheme."

"This is serious," he said. "I . . . posed some hypotheticals to a police psychologist I know." I rolled my eyes but didn't interrupt. "He normally only treats members of the force, but he said he'd be willing to see you after normal business hours."

"You think I need to see a shrink?" I asked. "Really?"

"I think it could help you."

"Who says I need help?"

"You still flinching when a situation gets physical?" Rich said. "Against a couple random muscleheads, you'd probably be fine. But if the next two know what they're doing, you could be flat on your ass before you know it."

I pretty much was the last time against the unskilled goons my mystery adversary sent to dissuade me. Reaching out to Doctor Parrish constituted a huge olive branch for me. I'd written shrinks off after the bad experience following my sister's death. "I appreciate it, Rich."

"But?"

"But I'm going to decline. Give the doctor my thanks. You remember the facility in Arizona?"

"Sure," he said. "You saw someone there, right?"

"Yeah. I called her and left a message. I know she's two thousand miles away, but if I can talk to my general practitioner six blocks away over Zoom, the same should be true for her."

"I hope she says yes."

So did I. Rich was right—recoiling in the wrong encounter could lead to me catching a beatdown . . . or worse. I needed to keep working my twin cases, but I also needed Doctor Parrish to help me get back to where I was before two bullets changed my life for the worse.

I didn't know what I'd do if she failed.

* * *

DESPITE MY DISLIKE of Glenn Mathews, his viability as a suspect--in both the murder of Suzie Sloan and ordering my assault--teetered at the edge of a cliff. I broadened the pool by looking into Doctor Neal Fabian. Short of uncovering someone with a grudge against Suzie, he was my best shot to make progress in the case.

Beleza Plastic Surgery of Maryland opened five years ago. It thrived for a while, and the doctor expanded, taking on an additional suite—and the associated rent—and obviously hoping to make up the expense in patient volume. Economic downturns come for everyone, however. Elective surgeries declined across the country, and this must have left Fabian holding the bag. He didn't look overcapitalized to my non-accountant eyes, but I wondered if he enjoyed an infusion of cash about a year ago to smooth things out.

Before venturing out on his own, Doctor Fabian served as the chairman of the plastic surgery department at Johns Hopkins Hospital, the building in whose shadow he now operated. My experience with hospital bigwigs is they earned their positions due to visibility in things like journal publications and fundraising over pure surgical skill.

I navigated to the home page for Doctor Fabian's former department. Most enterprises maintain a variety of documents in addition to web pages. While they're not normally viewable, a simple Google search including file extensions will often reveal them. I sought Word documents around the time of the good doctor's departure. A few popped up at me.

One happened to be a resignation letter.

I read it. Fabian stepped down to pursue private practice. He was unabashed in seeking more money, fewer insurance claims, and greater independence. I wondered why he stayed in Baltimore. A place like Los Angeles or New York would offer many more potential clients even allowing for greater competition in the profession. I found his desire for fewer insurance claims especially interesting in light of his reason for firing Suzie.

Neal Fabian was born in Baltimore fifty-two years ago, and he remained in and around the city his entire life. This explained why he never left. Despite a smaller client pool, he seemed to be doing very well for himself. He drove a late-model Jaguar SUV, lived in a large home in a posh neighborhood, maintained a beach house, and owned a boat. He lived alone, having never been married.

While I learned quite a bit about the man and his past, none of it made him a killer. Unlike other doctors, I saw no evidence of charity or volunteer work. This contributed to the narrative Fabian was impressed with himself, but it wasn't nefarious.

Most murder victims die at the hands of someone they know. Those beaten to a pulp with a baseball bat are almost always killed by an acquaintance. Suzie Sloan spent most of her time with Neal Fabian and Glenn Mathews. This made them the most likely suspects, but I couldn't muster any good evidence pointing at either. I sighed and leaned back in my chair.

It was rare for me to sympathize with the police, but I did right now. I was stumped, too.

CHAPTER 8

I WAS ABOUT TO CALL IT A DAY WHEN AN EMAIL POPPED onscreen. Doctor Parrish said my request to talk to her was indeed irregular, but she agreed to do it, anyway. She sent me a Zoom link and a suggested meeting time in fifteen minutes. I let out a deep breath in relief. I'd actually liked talking to Parrish during my rehab in Arizona, and while I didn't expect her to be a miracle worker, I hoped the rapport we built up while I convalesced would help me now.

At the appointed hour, I clicked the Zoom link and joined the call. Parrish sat in her office, which I remembered from my visits there. A tall shelf full of both psychological and science fiction books dominated the background. Parrish herself hadn't changed. Her short blonde hair might have been a tiny bit longer. She still looked serious and professional. A small smile played on her face when I hit the room. "Hello, Mister Ferguson."

"Thanks for seeing me, Doc. I know this is unusual."

She shrugged. "Our patient load isn't as high right now, so I'm already seeing a few people remotely." I started to feel better about the situation before she added, "Of course, they're not two thousand miles away."

"It's important for me to talk to someone I trust," I said.

"I understand. It's a lot more important than distance and time zones." She paused. "I would ask how you're doing, but I think I can guess the answer."

"Not as well as I'd hoped." I frowned. "I feel fine physically. My stamina is a good part of the way back. I'm as strong as I was before. Losing my spleen hasn't mattered these last few months . . . no flu or anything." It was my turn to pause, and I filled the time with a sigh. "Mentally, though, I'm not completely where I was before."

A pen appeared in her hand. I found something comforting in the fact she still took old-school notes on a virtual session. "Tell me what's happening."

"My job requires me to get into the occasional altercation," I said. "I don't go out and seek violence, but I also don't run away when it finds me. I expect it. I've dealt with it for a while. I know how to handle myself, so I'm rarely worried about a goon or two trying to keep me off a case."

"I take it these altercations aren't going in your favor?"

"So far, only one has really gotten past the tipping point. Basically, I'm flinching at the first sign the confrontation is turning physical. Someone draws their fist back, and I cringe."

"Doesn't sound beneficial to your work," she said in a deadpan tone I became familiar with during my stay.

"It's not." I recalled dealing with the two goons sent by a still-unknown person. "It caused me to get hit in the face and shoved to the ground. Once I did, I was all right. Maybe adrenaline kicked in then . . . I don't know. I ended up fine, but against a couple people who know what they're doing, the outcome could've been a lot worse."

"Or if one of them produced a gun."

"Yeah," I said. "I'd rather not get shot again."

"Understandable."

"What do I do?"

"I'm afraid you've come to me looking for a panacea, Mister Ferguson. There just isn't one. You're fundamentally no different today than you were the morning you got shot."

"Sounds like you're telling me it's all in my head," I said.

Parrish showed a gentle smile. "You've read Harry Potter, I presume. Dumbledore was right. It can be in your head and still be real."

"What's this mean for me?"

"You underwent a great deal of trauma. Your body may be fine, but your brain needs to process it. I hate to rush into a diagnosis, but I don't think you want to drag this out. You probably have post-traumatic stress disorder."

"PTSD?"

"Yes," she said.

"I guess it shouldn't surprise me to learn PTSD doesn't only happen to soldiers."

"You're right," she said. "While the disorder is common among the military, Anyone can get it. As in your case, all that's needed is sufficient trauma."

"So how do I get past it?"

Parrish jotted a note before she spoke again. "Again, I think you're looking for a panacea."

"I'll put in the time." I pulled my wallet from my jeans and held it up. "And the expense. I'm not expecting a miracle pill."

"Good thing," she said.

"If you have one, though, I'll send you my address."

"You'd need to get in line," Parrish said with a chuckle.

"If there's no magic elixir to get me past this," I said, "what can I do?"

"My main suggestion would be working up to what you need to do." She paused and frowned. "You flinch when things get physical?" I bobbed my head. "Not the easiest thing to build toward. Someone yelling at you isn't quite the same. It doesn't provoke the necessary reactions."

I decided not to mention I'd turned away when Glenn Mathews shouted at me. "Should I take up boxing?"

"You said you can take care of yourself?" Parrish asked. I nodded. "Training?"

"Since I was in middle school," I said.

"Your boxing comment may have been glib, but it was insightful. Have you tried sparring recently?"

I hadn't, and I chided myself for not thinking of it sooner. Since returning from Arizona and continuing my recovery, I'd worked out on my own, including practicing strikes, kicks, blocks, and forms. Going to the dojo never crossed my mind. "I should've thought of it on my own. I'll definitely look into it."

"I think it'll be good for you." Parrish turned her attention to her notebook for a few seconds. "It should simulate getting into an actual altercation. Give it time, though. Just because you flinch on your first couple attempts doesn't mean it's a failure. You've been through a lot. Your brain needs to catch up to your body."

"I wish it would hurry," I said.

We chatted for a couple minutes before I thanked Parrish for her time. She told me she'd be happy to talk again. I hoped my new insurance would cover our conversations. I ended the call and felt hopeful. If sparring could get me back into form, I could clear the biggest hurdle remaining when it came to doing my job effectively.

"Come at me, goons," I said to my empty office.

* * *

WHEN I ARRIVED HOME, Gloria's red rocketlike coupe waited on its concrete launch pad at the rear. I pulled in beside her car and walked inside. She padded into the kitchen from the living room and embraced me. "You all right?"

"Sure," I said. "Why wouldn't I be?" We kissed.

"I'm worried about you."

I took off my jacket and flexed my biceps. Despite being in good shape—and hoisting the iron a couple days a week—no one would confuse me for a weightlifter. "The miscreants of Baltimore can't handle all this."

Gloria rolled her eyes, and her short laughter played off the walls. "You're such a dork. I love you."

"I talked to Doctor Parrish."

"The woman from Arizona?"

I bobbed my head. "Just finished before I left the office."

Gloria cocked an eyebrow. "And?"

"She thinks I have PTSD."

"You probably do." Gloria squeezed my hand. "How could you not?"

"A diagnosis is fine," I said. "My bigger concern is how to get past it. Enforcers aren't going to leave me alone if I tell them I'm dealing with post-traumatic stress."

We talked about a way to try and get me past my problem as we pondered dinner. I wanted to cook, Gloria preferred to order in, and I decided sitting on the couch was better than standing at the stove. Forty-five minutes later, Maria D's delivered Italian food to my front door. We ate in the living room, watching a different show Gloria heard about from a friend after our lukewarm reception to the first. It wasn't my cup of tea, but I indulged her as I pondered getting back into sparring.

We went to bed early, and Gloria wasted little time reminding me why nights are so much better with her beside me. Afterward, I slept like a rock, and only bright sunshine pouring in past my curtains woke me around nine. I let Gloria remain in dreamland, changed into warm running clothes, and pounded the pavement. After about thirty-five minutes, I walked back up my street breathing heavier than I used to. I kept telling myself the stamina would come back, and I believed it. I also wished it would hurry up and get here.

Once the coffee brewed and bacon sizzled, Gloria joined me in the kitchen. We enjoyed a simple breakfast and light conversation. Then, I showered and got dressed for work. Gloria kissed me goodbye several more times than necessary—not so I would ever object—and I left for the office. Twenty minutes after I arrived—and eighteen after my last productive thought—Charles Stanton walked in.

I frowned as he plopped into a guest chair. He cast his eyes around the room, taking in the incomplete decorations. "I was wondering if you forgot about me."

"Did I leave you a business card?"

"Naw. I thought you looked familiar. Turns out you were in the paper a couple years ago." This is why I tried to avoid being photographed. Even in my days as a *pro bono* PI, I insisted stories of my exploits run without an accompanying picture. The first couple articles about me included one, however, and if Charles Stanton could find it, an enterprising criminal could, too.

"Sorry," I said. "I only sign autographs on weekends."

"Insurance man on your case?" Stanton asked.

"He actually hasn't been for at least a day or two."

"He will be. Billion-dollar companies don't like spreading a few thousand to folks who might need it."

"You're nurse Robin Hood now?" I said. "Elliot Allen might be a prick, but I wouldn't cast him as the sheriff of Nottingham."

"He doesn't care about me. He doesn't care about you, either." He punctuated his statement by pointing at me several times.

"I'm not expecting a Christmas card in ten months. Just a check when I'm finished."

"You're in it for the money?" he asked with a sneer. "Not what's right?"

"Tell me what's right about milking workman's comp."

Stanton stared out the window. "I need a break." His head wagged from side to side. "It's too much. This last year has been way beyond. I know being a nurse ain't gonna mean sunshine and puppies all the time, but god*damn*."

"Maybe you have PTSD," I offered. There seemed to be a lot of it going around.

"Maybe I do."

"I'm not a qualified professional, but I'm sure you could see one who could confirm it for you." I watched Stanton while he kept staring out my window. He'd been doing his job for a long time. In the last year, it became much more challenging in ways I couldn't understand. I'd come to understand a little bit of PTSD and its effects, however. "Go home."

"What are you going to do?" Stanton asked, his eyes fixed on something outside.

"Nothing for now. Maybe I'll ask you some more questions about Fabian and doctors in general."

"He's a prick. However I can help."

"Right now," I said, "you can help by going home and staying out of my office."

He nodded and stood. "I hope you'll do the right thing."

I wished the right thing weren't so amorphous.

* * *

A COUPLE HOURS LATER, I got a text inviting me to lunch. Melinda Davenport said she had some news to tell me. I offered to pick up Brick Oven Pizzeria, and we would share it at my desk. She agreed. I met her on one of my cases when she worked as a prostitute with the *nom de rue* of Ruby. I solved her stalker problem, and she got her life in order and even reconciled with her estranged father—the prick who happened to be the current mayor of Baltimore.

I walked a few blocks, picked up two piping-hot pies, and carried them back to my office. No sooner did I set the boxes down than I heard footsteps coming up the metal stairs. A moment later, Melinda poked her head in. "Hi, C.T.!" She entered the office and wrapped me in a tight hug. "It's good to see you."

"You, too." It was always good to see Melinda. She was an unfailingly gracious person, and she possessed brains and beauty in equal measures. Since getting off the streets, luster returned to Melinda's skin and fiery red hair, and she could have a long line of suitors if she wanted—or if her time running a foundation allowed. I set out a pair of paper plates and opened the boxes.

"A pepperoni and a mushroom?" Melinda wrinkled her nose before grabbing two slices of the vegetarian option and putting them on her plate.

"You didn't specify," I said as I took one of each.

We both devoured our first two pieces before going back for more. Only when she'd polished off a third did Melinda look ready to share whatever she came to tell me. "I have some good news, and I figured you'd want to be among the first to hear it."

"Sure," I said. I grabbed two bottles of water from the fridge and set one in front of Melinda. "Lay it on me."

"T.J.'s been in a program to learn office work." Melinda smiled, and her whole face lit up. "She's about to complete it."

"You must be proud of her." T.J. had been another young prostitute until Melinda met her. Through the Nightlight Foundation, she'd rescued a bunch of girls from the same streets she used to walk. T.J. counted first among this number, and even though I'd helped get her to safety, I was happy to let Melinda take the credit for it. "She's come a long way."

"She really has. She's almost twenty now, and she has a GED and this program. She just needs someone to take a chance on her."

Melinda didn't say anything else, and I didn't offer a response. I got the feeling she wanted me to be the risk-taker in this scenario, and I wasn't ready to have an employee. With my current caseload, I didn't know if I could pay myself every week, let alone someone else. I ate a bite of pizza to pass the time. Melinda waited me out. When I picked my slice up again, she crossed her arms and smirked. "I get the feeling you want something from me here," I said after wiping my mouth.

She made a show of looking around my office. "I don't see anyone else here. Maybe you need an assistant."

"Having someone to do mindless paperwork and answer the phones would be great. I hate both. I also don't know if I can afford to hire someone."

"I'm sure the director of the foundation can work some-thing out with you." She flashed her best sweet smile. It was a good one.

"I don't know, Melinda. Two guys tried to beat me up just yesterday."

"Here?"

"No, near my house, but it's pretty easy to find this address. I wouldn't want someone to come here and threaten T.J. to get to me."

Her smile remained in place, but the sweetness vanished. "Remember when you used T.J. as bait to catch a pedophile?" I had a feeling I knew where this was going, but I bobbed my head to play along. "I didn't want you to do it. I was *so* mad at you for even thinking about it." Her face darkened as she talked about it, but the storm passed quickly. "What did T.J. say? It was her choice, and she chose to do it. I'm sure she'd say the same if you asked her now."

It became clear Melinda wouldn't be taking no for an answer. I couldn't get to yes, though, so I opted to delay. "I'll think about it." Melinda's happy expression returned, but I held up my finger. "In the meantime, you might want to ask someone you know who might not see gun-toting goons walk through the door."

"You ever think having someone here would be good for you?" Melinda said.

"I've considered bringing Gloria here, but then I'd never get any work done."

Melinda shook her head. "You're here all alone. You probably talk to yourself."

"Talking to yourself is fine," I said. "When you start to answer, you're in trouble."

"All right." She put up her hands. "I hoped for a yes, but at least you're going to consider it."

"I will." My concerns were legitimate, even if someone like T.J. could take over the work I hated doing. My life was complicated enough at the moment. I clung to what simplicity I could.

* * *

I DIDN'T KNOW who killed Suzie Sloan yet. Instead of continuing to poke around my two primary suspects, I turned my attention to the victim. She was young and pretty, and like many similar people, created a large online footprint. After not seeing much on Twitter—including a surprising lack of direct messages from desperate men—I focused on Facebook, Instagram, and LinkedIn.

A while ago, I wrote a script designed to scrape social

media profiles and gather information. It works a hell of a lot faster than I could. I've tweaked it over time as the platforms changed things here and there. The tool focused on interactions: friends, contacts, posts, direct messages, and even reactions. If someone stalked Suzie online, I felt confident my script would uncover it.

I pointed it to her profiles and let it run while I made a cup of coffee in the Keurig. Before I took my first sip, my screen showed a message telling me data gathering and analysis finished. The tool dumped its output into a file. I opened it and hoped for insight.

The first thing it pointed out was closest connections. Anyone appearing on multiple platforms would go here, the same for any users Suzie interacted with most often. Most of the people here were women, and the men who showed up looked like hipsters who would rather prattle on about some unknown album they bought on vinyl than bludgeon someone with a bat. My script judged Daniela Gallo to be Suzie's closest acquaintance.

I looked at her profile. She lived and worked in Baltimore. Daniela was a year older than Suzie, and their shared social media history told me they met at Goucher College. Her Facebook wall featured three posts in memory of her late friend. I reached out and sent her a private message.

D*ANIELA*,

I'm sorry for the loss of your friend. Suzie's sister Amy hired me to look into her murder since the police haven't made much progress. I'm wondering if you can tell me anything. You can reply here or call or text me at 410-555-7690.

. . .

I SIPPED some coffee while I waited for her to reply. It was more warm than hot now, and right when I decided to refresh it in the microwave, a PM appeared in my inbox.

I REALLY WISH I could tell you something. Suzie was the best. Everyone loved her.

WE WERE BACK to Suzie being universally revered again. I didn't want to point out again how one person clearly didn't love her—I'd already made this case to Amy Sloan, and it struck me as a low-value play here. I replied.

I'VE HEARD this from a few people. What I need is information I can't find online, and Suzie's friends are the best sources of it. Someone needs to speak for her. Right now, it falls to me, but I need your help.

I WAITED. I even finished my coffee and made a mug of tea. No reply came.

CHAPTER 9

I REVIEWED MORE DATA WHEN MY DOOR OPENED. GLENN Mathews stormed in, and his red face and sour expression combined to put me on edge. He stood behind one of my guest chairs, his hands balled into fists. I took a deep breath as quietly as I could. If he decided to throw down with me, I knew what I was doing. I could take him. I told myself this a few times in the hope it would sink in. "You son of a bitch," he growled.

"I'm not getting along too well with my mother right now," I said, "but there's no reason to impugn her character."

"You think this is funny?"

"I still don't know what *this* is. You barged into my office and started yelling. What the hell are you going on about?"

"Like you don't know?" He spread his beefy arms wide. "Don't sit there and play dumb."

"I'm far too smart to play dumb," I said.

Mathews glared at me. I stared back at him. I tried to focus on not flinching if things escalated. It was a bit like not trying to think of an elephant. After a few seconds of this standoff, Mathews grumbled and dropped into a chair. "The fucking cops are onto me. I think you put them there."

"Why the hell would I?"

"I know I'm a tough nut to crack," Mathews said. I fought the urge to roll my eyes. "You couldn't break me, so you passed me off to people who could try better."

I blew out a deep breath before answering. "Here's an alternative theory . . . one which doesn't require a tinfoil hat. You were Suzie's boyfriend. The police always investigate a victim's significant other, especially when he's a musclehead. You're not special."

"I read up on you."

"I didn't know I'd been featured in a paper dedicated to using small words."

Mathews glowered before closing his eyes. His hands clenched and unclenched. "You think you're hot shit. I can tell from the interviews. The cops get stuck, and you come in and save the day." He snorted. "What a fucking crock. You took a couple-three runs at me, couldn't find a hole, and punted back to the police."

"I haven't talked to the cops about you," I said.

"Bullshit!" Mathews' right hand went up. I leaned back in my chair as he slapped the top of my desk. "You probably didn't think I deserved someone like Suzie. A lot of her stuffed-up friends thought so. Fuck them, and fuck you. We were in love."

"If the BPD is sniffing around you, it's not because of me. I've been looking into Doctor Fabian and Suzie's friends for the last day or so."

"No shit?"

"No shit."

Mathews jabbed a finger at me. "You better not be lying."

"I'm not," I said.

He stood, shoved my guest chair into my desk, and stormed out.

* * *

I CLOSED THE OFFICE EARLY—THIS being a relative term, as I didn't exactly post fixed hours—and drove toward downtown. My phone buzzed on the passenger's seat after I left Fells Point. The display between the speedometer and tach identified the caller to be my father. I pushed the button on the wheel to decline the call. This solution proved temporary when he called back right away. I let him have this round. "Hi, Dad."

"Are you busy?"

"Yes," I said, though driving—even with a manual transmission—hardly counted.

"Well, I won't take up too much of your precious time," he said.

"I recognize this particular guilt trip from Mom's playbook. You've been copying off her."

"We want to see you, son. I understand you're upset, but—"

"No," I broke in. "You don't."

"Then, talk to us about it," he said. "In person. We'll all go to dinner."

I stopped at a traffic light. "I'm working a couple cases at the moment, Dad. Call it a product of needing to charge clients for my time."

"Now who's employing a guilt trip?"

"We both learned from the best."

"This isn't a new thing, you know," my father said. "I feel like you've been mad at us for a while, and you've just kept it low-key."

He wasn't wrong, but I also didn't want to tell him. The light turned green. I put the S4 into first gear and continued into downtown. "I guess it depends on how you're defining a while. When did you renege on our deal?"

"I'm not getting into this with you again," he said, and his voice took on the stern tone I got used to in high school. "We want to see you because we're your parents, and we love you despite the fact you're a pain in the ass sometimes. When you're ready to talk to us, let me know. I'm not going to beg." He hung up before I could answer. At some point, I needed to deal with my parents. For now, I was happy to let the frost keep its icy edge.

A few minutes later, I lucked into a parking spot near the station. After waiting for a couple of uniforms to escort someone inside, I walked into Rich's precinct house. My cousin sat at his desk. It butted up against the one belonging to his partner of a few months, Detective Paul King. They were a contrast in styles. Rich valued neatness and professionalism from his time in the army. He always wore a pressed suit, and I thought he kept a schedule for which to wear on a given day. King, on the other hand, looked like a rock singer who just got out of rehab and dressed to fit the part. "How are my two favorite detectives?" I said as I approached their area.

"It's nice to be recognized," King said with a grin. "You bring us coffee?"

"Not this time."

"You want something?"

"Yep."

"You take economics in college?" King said.

"Unfortunately."

"We're probably his favorites by default, anyway," Rich added.

"Now I wish I'd stopped for coffee," I said. "I'd raise my cup to you for your sage observation."

King looked into a mug on his desk and frowned. "What brings you by?"

I dropped into a guest chair beside Rich's desk. "The Sloan murder."

"Still not our case," my cousin said.

"You've probably looked at the report, though." Rich

offered no reaction. "Once I asked, you knew you'd want to help your favorite cousin." Still nothing. I expected an eye roll at least. "Of course, you're a dutiful and concerned sergeant, so I'm sure you want to stay up to speed on cases requiring the intervention of handsome private investigators."

"All right, I might've looked at it."

I spread my hands. "And?"

"I wish I could tell you something of substance," Rich said. "It hasn't even been two weeks yet. You know not all cases get solved quickly. Sometimes, pinning a murder on someone takes a while."

"I understand."

"Does your client?"

"Probably not," I admitted.

"I'm going to get some caffeine," King said. He stood with his mug. "Let's hope someone made a fresh pot sometime this week."

When he walked away, I leaned in a little and lowered my voice. "Did you see O'Malley made an entry in the report?"

Rich nodded. "Be kind of hard not to."

"It didn't surprise you?"

"Should it?"

"How often does he add his own notes?"

"He's my lieutenant," Rich said. "I don't get to spot-check his work."

"It just seems unusual," I said. "I expect him to review these sorts of things, but I've never seen him make an entry before."

"Sometimes, lieutenants and captains are among the first to arrive at a scene." Rich shrugged. "Just because something doesn't happen often doesn't mean anything's wrong when it does."

"I guess." I resumed my normal posture when King returned.

He raised a Spock eyebrow toward me. "What are you two ladies gossiping about?"

"Grooming standards," I said.

"Good thing I'm an expert," said King.

A voice behind me bellowed. "What are you doing wasting my detectives' time?" O'Malley. I'd hoped to avoid seeing him. He didn't like me—I thought he was a boorish overpromoted buffoon, and he knew my opinion. Not like I'd taken any steps to hide it.

Despite my distaste for the man, I tried to remain pleasant. "Talking about a case."

He narrowed his eyes. "We're not the information desk. You want answers? Go hit the streets."

"Hang on," I said. "I want to take notes if you're going to drop these nuggets of wisdom."

King snorted, and O'Malley glowered at him briefly before returning his attention to yours truly. "You done?"

"I don't know. I'm curious what to do if I run into a loud-mouth who doesn't like me for some reason. You have experience being unpopular. What's your advice?"

O'Malley stewed quietly. I suppressed a smile as I watched his face redden. "See yourself out," he said in a measured tone before returning to his office and slamming the door.

"I don't think he likes me," I said.

"Can't imagine why," Rich said.

"He doesn't enjoy being called out for his many shortcomings." I stood. "I understand why you can't do it. I got your back."

Rich smirked. "Lucky me."

"Gentlemen." I tipped an imaginary cap in their direction. Then, I headed back toward the door. I got the feeling Rich also found O'Malley making a case entry unusual. He tried to play it close to the vest like he did with many things. On some level, though, he knew his lieutenant was an asshole who didn't deserve the title or the office.

It created one more complication in a case already over-flowing with them.

CHAPTER 10

AFTER SAMPLING A SOUR TASTE AT THE PRECINCT THANKS to O'Malley, I cleansed my palate by stopping for a vanilla latte. I also snagged a chai for Gloria, which I handed to her when I walked in the back door of my house. She received it with a smile and a kiss, and I told her I needed to do a little work. It was time for a deeper dive into Neal Fabian.

The more I talked to Glenn Mathews, the less I liked him. How he landed an apparent saint like Suzie Sloan was a mystery my considerable skills couldn't solve. However, despite my antipathy for the man, I found him an unlikely killer. Absent any of Suzie's friends, her boss—who fired her for costing him patients and thus money—made the best suspect.

Earlier, Charles Stanton told me Doctor Fabian was an asshole. I got the feeling he would reach this conclusion about a great many individuals in the profession. Regardless, I couldn't find anything to tell me he was wrong. Reviewers of the practice commented on the surgeon's skill but panned his lack of empathy and bedside manner. A couple women even said they found him a little creepy.

I went back to Doctor Fabian's tenure at Hopkins. He volunteered very little of his time for charity. Up until a few years ago, he performed an occasional procedure for a local foundation *pro bono*, but he abandoned this when he ventured out on his own. The charity's web page made no mention of him, though an archived version of their site listed Fabian as a provider.

I called Surgeons for a Healthier Maryland, but there was no answer. No other similar organizations claimed any involvement with Fabian or Beleza Plastic Surgery. For someone who loved to toot his own horn, I found Fabian's lack of online presence puzzling. No charity in the last few years. No articles in medical journals. No Facebook page. Nothing on Instagram. A LinkedIn profile he abandoned after opening Beleza. The practice's Google page contained only the most basic information.

He didn't belong to a generation which lived its life online, but he was a sought-after professional in a competitive business. Being a doctor was fraught with peril about protected data and healthcare privacy laws, but even in this context, Fabian's tight lips made him stand out. Three other plastic surgeons within a couple miles of him boasted of much larger online footprints, not to mention better reviews. Suzie could have helped here, as could either of the two current assistants.

It all made me wonder what the good doctor was hiding.

In my earlier visit to his office, I learned he replaced Suzie with two part-timers. I met Nancy. Her colleague would be in the office today. She didn't know me. I glanced at my phone—3:45. By the time I got there, the practice would be closed. I needed another option, and I had plenty at my disposal.

I embedded a common malware exploit into a PDF. Fabian's office didn't strike me as the most savvy when it came to technology. Still, I modified the document, setting it up to look like it came from a consumer advocacy group. I hurried to rejigger the questions for a doctor and sent everything to the contact information on the practice's Google page.

Then, I waited.

I'd find out soon enough if everyone left for the day. If the receptionist remained, and she opened the attachment, her PC would appear in my console. Presuming everything worked—and it did when I'd used the same exploit before—I would establish a persistent connection and be able to browse the contents of her PC. If Fabian stashed hidden files somewhere, I would find them. I didn't care about his legitimate patient records. They'd be easy enough to ignore.

A few minutes later, a computer name popped up under the *Remote Hosts* header. Bingo. Thanks to the malware, the admin assistant wouldn't know I nosed around her hard drive. The first thing I saw in my command prompt was a laundry list of folders. Who the hell could organize anything this way? I didn't even know where to begin. It would take me an hour or more simply to try and make sense of it all.

I wouldn't get the chance. My command and control suite told me the remote PC was shutting down. A few seconds later, the connection went dark. If I needed to, I could wake it up over my connection and get back to my search. For now, I was happy knowing it worked.

* * *

GLORIA and I were perusing menus and considering our dinner options when my phone rang. It was my longtime friend Joey Trovato. "Perfect timing," I said when I picked up. "We were thinking about food."

"My ESP must have kicked in." Joey was a black Sicilian of good humor and better appetite. He stood a little shorter and outweighed me by a hundred pounds, but his size belied some real athleticism. "What are we having?"

"Gloria and I haven't decided yet."

"Hi, Joey," she said.

"I also wanted to see how you were doing," said Joey.

"I'm good. I appreciate people's concern, but I'm honestly getting a little tired of answering."

"I probably would be, too, in your place."

Gloria tapped my shoulder. "Hang on, Joey." I held the phone against my chest.

"Why don't you invite him?" she said.

"I'm on a budget now. It doesn't fit Joey's appetite."

"Could he spar with you?"

I frowned and considered it. "I guess. Not here, though. I don't have the room."

"Invite him to my house. I'll pick up some Italian food."

"Thanks," I said. I put the phone back to my ear. "Want to help me with something?"

"Sure."

I paused. "You're not even going to ask for food?"

"As long as we've known each other," Joey said, "I figured it was implied."

I filled him in on the plan. Joey told me he'd be happy to help, and he'd meet us at Gloria's in about forty-five minutes. My girlfriend and I took separate cars to her place. Her faster model led our mini convoy, and we made it from Federal Hill to Brooklandville in good time. Gloria owned an average-sized house in the tony neighborhood, which meant it could hold three of mine. Her yard—she actually had one—required a team of landscapers to maintain. Shrubs and trees were plentiful in the area, creating a lot of privacy for each home. It was the exact opposite of a rowhouse. Despite being a city boy, I appreciated the differences offered in this area.

A few minutes after we walked inside, Gloria zoomed away to get carry-out. Joey arrived a short while later. He wore loose-fitting sweats. We bumped fists, and I went upstairs to change. A running outfit would do the trick. We headed to the basement. Down here, Gloria setup a spare bedroom, but much of the unused floor space became a home gym. She owned a treadmill, a stationary bike, and some little-used weight bench monstrosity with flexible bands. Plenty of square footage remained open ostensibly for stretching and yoga. Gloria's dedication to staying in shape for tennis impressed me.

"Why do you need to spar?" Joey asked as we both loosened up.

"I'm . . . struggling with confrontation." I drew my right fist back. "Every time it gets physical, I flinch."

"What happens then?" Joey slipped on a piece of headgear. I frowned. He pulled an extra one out of the bag and tossed it to me. "You'll need it. Sounds like I might ring your bell."

I appreciated his attempt at humor. "I dealt with a couple goons recently. My hesitation got me knocked on my ass. Once I got back up, I was fine."

"Not a good long-term plan, though," Joey said. He threw a few punches at the air. Joey may have lacked my training, but he took kickboxing for a couple years, and he'd survived his share of scrapes. He could hold his own.

"Definitely not. Hence, sparring here with you."

"And feeding me afterward."

"It's the least I can do after the beatdown coming your way."

Joey grinned. "Good to go?" I nodded. He took a ready stance, and so did I. "Want me to strike first?"

"Yeah," I said. "I need to see if flinching will be an issue."

I took a deep breath. My balance was good. I carried my weight on the balls of my feet. My arms were bent and loose, ready to turn aside a punch or a kick. I'd trained for this for years—about twenty now, in fact, since my mother enrolled me in martial arts after a bully got the better of me in sixth grade. Joey's weight shifted. His meaty fist went back.

I flinched.

My head turned in, my torso rotated, and I raised my left arm in an attempt to cover my face. "Shit," I muttered and backed away. Joey, who could have laid me out, frowned as he watched me.

"Don't sweat it," Joey said. "We got time to figure it out."

"I hope so."

We took our stances again. Joey loaded up another punch, and I reacted again. He backed off. "Keep coming at me next time," I told him. "I need to see how quickly I can snap out of . . . whatever this is."

"All right." Joey sounded unsure but raised his hands. I set my feet. His fist went back, I felt myself recoil, and this time, Joey completed the punch. He pulled it, so it didn't hit me as hard as it could have. My jaw stung a little, but against an opponent trying to hurt me, it would have gone much worse. To his credit, Joey didn't back off after the opening salvo. He also didn't take it easy on me. His next strike came in at full power, and I turned it aside. Joey pressed the attack. I fell into a rhythm on defense, and when he overextended, I grabbed his arm and pulled. It wasn't hard enough to take him down, but Joey stumbled forward.

"Nice," he said. "You recovered well."

"Only because you let me."

"I didn't think laying you out before dinner would endear me to Gloria."

I grinned. "Probably not."

"You wanna go again?"

From upstairs, I heard the front door open. Gloria would need a few minutes in the kitchen. "A couple more times. You bust my lip, though, and I'll make sure you don't get a meatball."

"You're a monster," Joey said.

* * *

JOEY STAYED for dinner and ate as much as Gloria and me combined. When he left, he offered to spar with me as much as I needed to get back into form. We bumped fists again, and he headed off into the night. Over dinner, we'd avoided the topic, but Gloria asked me how it went now. "No better," I said.

"It was just one time." She offered a supportive smile. "Rome wasn't built in a day."

"It also wasn't defended by people who flinched at the sight of a sword."

"Go easy on yourself."

Implicit in there, I felt, was also a suggestion to take less challenging cases . . . the kind which wouldn't leave me trying to fight off a pair of goons. "I'm trying."

Gloria grabbed my hand. "Why don't you come upstairs?"

"You going to go easy on me?"

A lascivious smile played on her lips. "Definitely not."

She was a woman of her word. Later, I slept like a stone until about eight. Early to bed, early to rise. I walked downstairs and again grew envious of Gloria's kitchen. The entire back half of my house could fit in it. She did little of her own cooking, however, so it was something of a waste. Still, she owned a nice stainless steel coffee maker, so I brewed a pot while I rummaged through her fridge.

I'd already flipped the omelet by the time Gloria came downstairs. Her supplies were well stocked, and I combined eggs, spinach, and provolone into a meal for both of us. Two English muffins popped up from the toaster. Gloria buttered them while she poured her coffee. A few minutes later, we ate at her expansive dining room table. A family of eight could have used it for Thanksgiving dinner.

After breakfast and light conversation, I pondered what trouble to get myself into today. Fabian's receptionist might be in the office, and even if she took the weekends off, I could still remotely power up her PC and browse her files. Glenn Mathews was a worse suspect but also more likely to screw up if he were guilty. Instead of surrounding himself with smart assistants, he employed dumb muscleheads. I called his gym, and whoever answered told me he usually didn't come in on the weekends.

I kissed Gloria goodbye and drove to Mathews' house. He lived in a rowhouse in Pigtown, not far from the stadiums and Horseshoe Casino. I curbed the S4 across the street and a few houses away. One of my least favorite parts of the job involved sitting outside someone's home waiting for something to happen. Rich chided me for my lack of patience. He was probably right. It didn't feel like doing anything to me. As much as I avoided hard work, I wanted to be productive when I put the time in. I figured I would give it a couple hours. If nothing happened by then—or my bladder threatened to burst—I would pursue something else.

About forty-five minutes into my vigil, three police cars rolled down the street with their lights flashing. I sank a little lower in my seat. All three cruisers stopped near Mathews' house. Six uniformed officers of the BPD climbed out. Two ran around behind the row of houses. One waited near the cars. The remaining three walked up to Mathews' front door and knocked. I could hear the exclamation of, "Police! Open up!" even with my windows closed.

Mathews' front door swung open, and the three officers disappeared inside. Were they arresting him? Did I miss something obvious which would have told me he was the guy? A few minutes later, two of them marched the gym owner out in handcuffs. The third officer carried a large evidence bag which held an aluminum baseball bat.

"It ain't mine!" Mathews insisted as they herded him into one of the cruisers.

His protests fell on deaf ears. With a roar of engines and more flashing lights, the three squad cars drove away.

I DROVE TO POLICE HEADQUARTERS AFTER MAKING A STOP for coffee. Rich and King both sat at their desks. "Just the men I wanted to see." I dropped a cup off for each of them. They both remained silent. "I'm sure you're not used to hearing someone wants to see you, but I'd hoped for a little engagement here."

"Thanks for the coffee," King said. He lifted his cup and took a sip.

"What do you want?" Rich asked without looking away from his monitor.

"Can't I just be dropping off some caffeine to my two favorite cops?" Rich stared at me. "Fine. I want to know what's going on with Glenn Mathews."

Rich moved his coffee to the other side of the desk. "Don't know."

"Oh, come on. You're a homicide sergeant, and you're too smart to play dumb."

"Wow," he said. "An actual compliment. You must want something."

"Don't get used to it," I said. "I'm probably going to tell you how you arrested the wrong man, and I'll need to come in and clean up your mess again."

Rich rolled his eyes. "We get it right a lot of the time. I think we did here, too."

"What made you arrest Mathews?"

"We're pretty sure he killed his girlfriend," King said. "You should be happy. The case is closed, and you didn't even have to do a lot of work."

"I doubt it's closed," I said. "For almost two weeks, this guy cruises along. Now, suddenly he's the prime suspect and gets hauled away by three cops. Something doesn't add up."

"It was an actual investigation," Rich said. He took his first sip of coffee. I wished I hadn't drained my entire latte on the drive over. "We got an anonymous tip."

"An anonymous tip?"

"Sometimes, this is how cases break," King said. "We put in a bunch of work, but it takes something like this to really put it over the top."

I shook my head. "I'm not buying it. Mathews may be a prick, but I don't think he's a murderer."

"Someone told us the bat would be in his house," Rich said. He still looked at his monitor. "We got a warrant. Sure enough, we recovered the murder weapon."

"How do you—"

"Her blood was on it." Rich looked at me now, and his expression told me how useless he found this conversation. "So we found the likely murder weapon with the victim's blood in her boyfriend's house. You're telling me we shouldn't arrest him?"

I didn't have much of an answer. Given the evidence Rich cited, I understood why the police put the cuffs on Mathews. My thinking he didn't do it wouldn't get us very far. All I could do was keep working the case and try to find who actually did it —presuming Mathews didn't. "I don't think he did it. I'm going to prove it."

"Good luck," Rich said.

With an arrest made, I knew I would need it.

* * *

* * *

I DROVE TO MY OFFICE, plopped down in my chair, and stared at the ceiling. Mathews remained a poor suspect. I was convinced of this regardless what the police found in his house. Rich and King should have been more skeptical of the anonymous tip. It would be easy for someone to plant evidence and then lead the cops right to it. As much as I didn't like Mathews, I didn't think he beat his girlfriend to death.

While I felt Doctor Fabian made a better suspect, I could uncover no evidence tying him to the murder, either. Unless I could—or discover who really did it if he didn't—Glenn Mathews would go down for Suzie Sloan's murder. I fired up my laptop and checked the command and control suite for my remote access malware. The receptionist's computer was off. I sent the instruction to wake it up.

While I waited, noisy footsteps climbed the stairs outside my office door. Elliot Allen entered and sat in one of my guest chairs. I wondered when the universe started hating me and when it might stop. "Mister Ferguson."

"What can I do for you?"

"You haven't made a lot of progress with Mister Stanton's case. I admit I'm surprised to find you here on a Saturday, all things considered."

"Just because I'm not writing you an hourly report doesn't mean nothing is happening," I said.

"All right," he said. "Tell me what you've learned. Is Mister Stanton cheating us?"

He was, of course, but I didn't want to tell this prick about it. Especially not after he dropped in on me and demanded an update. I needed to string him along and keep him off my back for a few days. It would give me time to decide what to do about the nurse, plus hopefully figure out who killed Suzie Sloan, which was much more important. "I haven't seen any evidence of it yet."

Allen frowned. I got the feeling he wanted to curse me as some sort of imbecile, but he'd spent too long confined to the walls of a cubicle. "What have you seen?"

"Mostly, he stays inside," I said. "Sometimes, he does some light work in the yard."

"You don't find it unusual?"

"What activity level should I be on the lookout for, Mister Allen? Maybe I should sneak into his shed and weigh his hedge trimmer when he's not using it. What weight is too heavy?"

He crossed his arms. "You're mocking me."

"I'm treating your concern with the seriousness it deserves," I said. "In addition to dropping in on Charles Stanton, I'm trying to figure out who killed a young woman, and I'm pretty sure the police arrested the wrong guy. Want to guess which case takes priority?"

"I'd hoped you'd be working on our matter exclusively," he had the gall to say.

"And I'm going to hope for a new Porsche under my Christmas tree this year. Let's compare notes on December twenty-sixth."

Allen showed a humorless smile. "Very well, Mister Ferguson. I suppose I understand competing priorities. I don't work one thing at a time, either." He stood. "We do expect results, though. I'd like to know where you stand on Monday. It's two days from now."

"Thanks," I said. "I'm pretty sure I learned how the calendar works a long time ago."

"Good day, then." He left my office to clomp back down the stairs.

I locked my exterior door and tried to get back to real work.

* * *

GLENN MATHEWS MADE a convenient but poor suspect. I knew this despite what alleged evidence the police found in his house. My problem lay in developing a better one. Charles Stanton told me Doctor Fabian was a jerk. My one meeting with him confirmed the nurse's take. Plenty of people are jerks and don't commit murder, however.

I looked back into Suzie's life, bringing forth the results of my social media deep dive. For phase one of the latest effort, I searched for people who would have crossed her path at work. It turned out to be a short list. Doctor Fabian employed a small staff. Suzie toiled away as the main receptionist. She had help two half-days per week. Three nurses also worked for the practice. From what I could glean, one mostly helped with surgery, and the other two tended to patients while they waited for the doctor.

I spent a few minutes on a brief investigation of each woman, but nothing turned up. Four ladies, zero arrests, no indications of being a murderer. I moved on. Suzie's inbox collected a bunch of junk over the last couple days. I dug for anything related to her job. Hundreds of messages matched the filter.

Suzie found her job through a temp agency. Once she started in the office, though, the communications dried up. I called the firm, was relieved to have someone answer on a weekend, and asked to speak to Donna Sable, the woman who placed Suzie in Doctor Fabian's office. After I spent a few minutes on hold, she picked up. "I'm a private investigator," I said after the initial intro. "I'm looking into the murder of Suzie Sloan. You worked with her a few years ago."

"My gosh. She's dead?"

"I'm afraid so."

"Suzie was terrific," she said. "One of the easiest placements I've had. I'm not sure how much I can help you, though. I only knew her professionally."

"I talked to Doctor Fabian." Donna Sable grunted. "It sounds like you did, too."

She sighed. "He . . . I didn't like him."

"I understand you're trying to be diplomatic," I said. "Suzie's dead, though, and the good doctor is on the short list of people who might have killed her. Anything you can tell me might be useful."

"He's a creep," she said. "I visited his office a couple times to interview him. He never said anything untoward, but I always felt like he was checking me out. Like he wanted to see if I wanted a boob job but never asked me." She paused. "I'm not trying to sound immodest."

"Don't worry," I said. "I come by it naturally, too."

She chuckled. "I've had my share of leers and catcalls over the years. When he checked me out, though, it was different. I guess because of his job. It was clinical but still unnerving."

"But you still sent Suzie to work there."

"Yes. It wasn't an automatic decision, but he never said anything to suggest he would be a problem. Suzie was young. Recently out of college. Not much need for plastic surgery. I figured putting her there would be harmless. I hope it was."

"I hope so, too," I said. "Was Suzie the only person you considered for the job?"

"No," she said. "There one other young woman.

Brenda . . . Brenda Wolfson, I think is her full name. She thought she was better qualified, and she might've been right. Suzie nailed her interview, though. I remember the doctor telling me."

"Sounds like Brenda might have been angry."

"She was, but I don't think she'd kill someone over it nearly three years later."

"It does seem unlikely," I admitted. I thanked Donna Sable for her time and hung up. On a lark, I looked into Brenda Wolfson. The first thing to jump out at me was her college softball career. She had plenty of experience swinging a bat. Combined with simmering anger or jealousy, she could have been the killer.

A few more seconds of digging, however, told me this wasn't the case. Last summer, Brenda suffered terrible injuries in a car accident. She ended up a paraplegic and moved back in with her parents in Ohio. She couldn't be the killer. To borrow a softball metaphor, another swing and miss in this case.

Another dead end.

CHAPTER 12

THE PC IN DOCTOR FABIAN'S OFFICE REMAINED ONLINE. When I poked around it initially, I thought the organization of the files and folders would give me a headache. Another look confirmed my initial thoughts. I didn't even stock any Tylenol at my office yet. Undeterred, I tackled the rats' nest.

It would have been easier with a graphical view of the folders, but my program only provided a command prompt. Considering the privacy concerns and issues like ransomware plaguing the medical community, the filing system Fabian's office used was a disgrace. If malware locked him out, it might take him days to discover it. I hoped Suzie wasn't responsible for this mess, but it seemed unlikely things went to hell in a handbasket so quickly after she left.

The more I hunted around, the more I thought an animal, vegetable, mineral approach might have worked better. Months and years were scattered over multiple folders. Some containers were named after patients or insurance providers instead. I harbored no envy for anyone who tried to navigate this atrocity every day.

It took a few minutes, but I found the last few files Suzie Sloan likely worked on before her death. They were scattered, and I needed to keep swapping between directories, but I didn't find anything unusual. Despite Doctor Fabian griping about Suzie messing up his ability to take insurance, a few of the cases were billed to company names I recognized.

Curiouser and curiouser.

I explored a while longer but only succeeded in increasing my levels of eye strain. On a lark, I tried a search for hidden files and folders. They're easy to create in Windows but hard to setup accidentally, so their presence meant someone deliberately created them to conceal information. I found a single file and opened it.

Six women's names appeared on my screen. I made a note of them. Tara Mayfield. Shannon Getz. Cecelia Henry. Kate Watson. Peggy Nichols. Eva Valdes. It took me a few minutes, but I located each woman's individual file. When I tried to open one, however, the document window on my screen filled with gibberish.

The file was encrypted.

Sure enough, a prompt appeared asking me to enter a key. Naturally, I didn't possess the key, and if it were hidden on the hard drive somewhere, the heat death of the universe would occur before I found it. I searched for text files only a few kilobytes in size but came up empty. The rest of the women' files produced the same result.

I needed to decrypt those files. Even if they didn't help my case, knowing their contents would allow me to keep looking somewhere else. My malware got me only so far.

For the rest, I would need good old-fashioned social engineering.

* * *

To GAIN my initial foothold on the assistant's PC, I emailed her a piece of malware cleverly hidden in a PDF. I could do the same for Doctor Fabian, though with a different payload. The challenge would be making sure he opened it on his actual computer as opposed to a phone or tablet. Sending it on the weekend just about ensured he'd read it on a mobile device.

I hated waiting a couple days to try again. My options were few, however. Beleza Plastic Surgery was a locked, alarmed suite inside a locked, alarmed building which might even employ a guard or two on weekends. I felt confident in my ability to bypass one or two layers of security, but not all those.

I passed time configuring a new payload for the email I would send to Doctor Fabian. The files I wanted were encrypted. It was possible the assistants could open them, but they resided on a shared hard drive for convenience. Doing what was easy compromised security and enabled people like me to ply our trade with less resistance. My guess was the surgeon alone held the decryption key, and he would enter it from his own computer.

This time, I would send a keylogger. As long as it installed successfully on Doctor Fabian's laptop, it would record every letter and number he typed. Much of this would be useless to me, and I'd have a lot of junk to filter through. A few tools in my arsenal would make the process easier. Once I extracted the key, I could open the files and see what was so special about those six women.

Once I finished setting up the PDF, I went back to the receptionist's computer. If my malware plan didn't work, I needed a backup and physical access to the office and its equipment. This was simply a different form of social engineering. Doctor Fabian's assistant maintained an address book. I perused it and found the company they used for their tech support—a local outfit named Digital Sales with which I became familiar during my first case.

I checked their website and looked for photos. While the company held very few events in the last year, they still snapped a few shots of employees working around the office. Included in those pictures were the official company ID. I grabbed a screen capture of the clearest one I could find and spent about a half-hour duplicating it, using my own photo to become the firm's most handsome unofficial employee. After adding the fake persona of Trent Fergus—the former being my actual middle name—I printed my phony ID and ran it through a laminator I bought for just such a purpose.

Plan A was still the malware, but if it didn't work, I would be ready with an alternative.

* * *

I spent a relaxing Sunday morning with Gloria. As usual, I woke a little before nine, but I fell back asleep until ten. Gloria then kept us in bed until eleven, when I finally wandered downstairs. The usual pang of envy gripped me as I walked into her kitchen. I put coffee on and made a pot of oatmeal. Gloria joined me, and we again ate at her needlessly large dining room table.

Afterward, she invited me to capitalize on my day off and play tennis with her. I agreed despite knowing I would be taking a whipping on the court. Gloria was very good. She wouldn't beat a top pro, but she'd competed regionally for years and won a few tournaments along the way. After changing into appropriate attire, we drove to a fancy country club where Gloria's family maintained a membership.

I loosened up for a couple minutes and then stood around the center of my side of the net. "Volley for serve?" Gloria asked. I knew how it would turn out, but I nodded anyway. I don't think I'd ever served first in all the times we played . . . for all the difference it would have made. Gloria tossed the ball into the air, and instead of hitting a leisurely shot for me to return, she whacked the ball at me as hard as she could.

I ducked and deflected the fuzzy missile with my racket. "Jesus Christ!" My exclamation drew curious looks from the people playing on the next court.

"You need to be ready for anything," Gloria said with a shrug. "Let's try again."

"All right." She tossed another ball a few inches in the air and again hit it as hard as she could in my general direction. This time, I simply moved my racket and let the ball hit it. It actually went back over the net, bouncing in bounds once before skittering toward the fence. "All right, I get what you're doing."

"You didn't flinch that time," Gloria said.

"I also won the serve," I pointed out.

"It's not going to help," my girlfriend said with a grin.

She was right. I lost the first game and every other one which followed. Somehow, I lucked my way into a handful of points along the way, but the game count showed me down ten to zip. Gloria could have completed the two-set sweep, but other people were waiting for the court, so I accepted my shellacking, and we called it a day.

"Thanks," I said as we drove back to Gloria's house in her car.

"For beating your ass up and down the court?"

"You know what for. Was it part of your plan all along?"

"No," Gloria said. "It came to me when we walked onto the court."

"Good thing my reflexes are sharp." I rubbed my chin. "Can't ruin the moneymaker."

"You think it helped?"

"I don't know," I said after a few seconds of thought. "Despite the velocity of your serves, I'm sure it didn't hurt."

At Gloria's house, we both showered. She joined me under the hot water, said she was sorry for hitting the ball a hundred miles an hour at my face, and offered to make it up to me. I certainly didn't decline. After lunch, my phone buzzed. Elliot Allen texted and wondered about my progress with Charles Stanton's case.

I ignored him.

* * *

MONDAY MORNING ROLLED AROUND, and I checked the inbox I'd setup specifically for my latest email campaign. Someone read my message and even replied. Sometimes, things turned out to be easy. As I opened the response, I realized this would not be one of those times. Casey, the more part-time of Doctor Fabian's two assistants, thanked me for my note and said they would be in touch. She didn't open the attachment.

"Shit," I said to my empty office. It didn't answer. I didn't expect the secretaries to have access to the boss' email. Most enterprises discouraged or outright forbade this sort of arrangement, but when it happened, it rarely turned up in small medical practices. Good thing I made the Digital Sales ID.

I'd dressed for the part in case I needed to look like an office drone sent out to do some maintenance work. Instead of the usual jeans, I wore a pair of pressed chinos. In lieu of a hoodie or sweater, I sported a long-sleeved Polo. A pair of comfortable brown Clarks completed the look. I was so business casual my picture could appear next to the term in the dictionary.

I drove to Beleza Plastic Surgery, parked in the same garage as last time, and walked into a mostly empty waiting room before nine. Casey worked the desk. Her blonde hair featured blue highlights on the side, and I saw a tattoo peeking out from under her left sleeve. She blew a bubble as I approached but popped it in time to offer a rote smile. "Welcome to Beleza. Do you have an appointment?"

"Sort of." I showed her my faux company ID. "I need to do a hotfix on the doctor's PC. We're concerned about recent ransomware coming out of eastern Europe, and he'd be vulnerable without a patch."

Casey frowned and looked at her screen. "I don't have anything on the calendar."

"No, this is an out-of-cycle thing. Due to the criticality of the patch, we're trying to roll it out as fast as possible." All of this was plausible. I only needed her to believe it.

"You couldn't do it remotely?"

"We tried," I said. "I guess the doc left his computer off." I shrugged. "I just go where they send me. It won't take long."

She scrutinized Trent Fergus' corporate ID. It must have passed muster because she nodded a second later. "All right. Doctor Fabian is doing a minor procedure at the moment, so he won't need access to his office or computer."

"Thanks." I followed her into the bowels of the suite. Past all the exam rooms, a door simply marked *Private* opened into Doctor Fabian's office. Casey left me to my work. The room was small, probably about ten feet square, with a simple wooden desk and a large bookshelf packed with a plethora of medical tomes. A small mini-tower computer lay on its side atop the desk. A smallish flatscreen monitor sat next to it.

For such an allegedly prestigious practice, I expected a fancier setup. My dorm in college looked better than this. I put my disdain aside for now and focused on the task. Casey getting nosy about what I was doing could put a crimp in everything. I sat in the leather chair and counted it as the nicest thing in the room.

My previous malware attack on the receptionist's PC allowed me to access the hard drive and a few choice bits of system information. One thing it did was collect the password hashes when someone signed in. Rather than forward the identifier in plain text, operating systems use a one-way function to encrypt and obscure it. The good thing about these values is they can't be reverse engineered to resolve the password.

The bad thing is certain operating systems—including the version of Windows Beleza used—will accept them in lieu of the actual password.

I entered the user name Digital Sales established—cleverly hidden as *digitalsalestech*—and the thirty-two alphanumeric characters which would give me access. They did. I plugged in a flash drive, executed the keylogger file, and installed it. After a minute of configuring where it would send data and ensuring the system firewall would cooperate, I removed my drive and logged off.

As I left, I thanked Casey for her time. Now, I just needed to wait for Doctor Fabian to use the password.

A COUPLE BLOCKS away from the doctor's office, I noticed the tail.

A dark sedan hung a few cars back. Every other vehicle in my rearview was an SUV. When I changed lanes, the sedan mirrored the move a few seconds later. Whoever tailed me must have dropped halfway through the intro course on following someone. Rich chided me a few times for not being observant. While I've gotten better in this area as I've worked more cases, my semi-competent shadow made it easy.

I stopped at a light. The four-door remained to my rear right behind a Honda SUV whose driver stopped close enough to read the fine print on my registration sticker. When we got going again, I drove slower than normal. A minivan passed me on the left, and my pride took a small hit at the indignity. I held strong. Some things were more important than beating a soccer mom to the next intersection.

Traffic turned out to be minimal headed down Light Street toward Federal Hill. When the signal where Light continues as Key Highway went yellow, I downshifted and got on the gas. The S4 surged ahead. I wanted to see how dedicated my pursuers were. If they stopped, they could lose me in the network of streets ahead. If they increased speed to barrel through the junction, the jig would be up. Neither outcome was good for them.

I zoomed through. The light turned red, and the sedan stopped. I rounded the bend, raced past the Maryland Science Center, and made an illegal right turn onto the one-way William Street. No traffic came at me, and I turned the car around and parked against the curb. A minute later, traffic moved again. The sedan which pursued me drove by on Key Highway.

It was a late-model Dodge Charger with clean gray paint, shiny wheels, and glossy black tires. As it drove on, I noticed the telltale lights in the rear window. An unmarked BPD car.

Why the hell were the cops following me?

CHAPTER 13

No hits from the keylogger came in throughout the day. Maybe Doctor Fabian was busy doing procedures and seeing patients. He could answer emails on a phone. I closed the office around mid-afternoon and drove by Charles Stanton's house. His car was gone, and no one appeared to be around. Oh-for-two today. To complete the crappy trifecta, I only needed Elliot Allen to call and demand an update. I steered toward home before the worst happened.

As the sun set, Gloria handed me a cashmere sweater on a hanger. "We're going out," she said with a grin. "You're underdressed."

Like me, she still wore jeans and a sweatshirt. "If I need to wear this, then so are you."

"I'm going to change, too." I noticed she'd already styled her hair. This would save us a lot of time getting out the door. Unless we went somewhere really fancy, the process of getting dressed didn't take Gloria much longer than it did me. Her hair and makeup took forever, however, and even threatening to time her with a sundial didn't make the process go any faster. Fifteen minutes later, we were both ready save the final bits of Gloria's makeup routine.

"You look great," I said while she examined her face in a mirror.

"Thanks," she said, fingering an area under her right eye. "I can't believe I'll be twenty-nine soon."

"It's only one year from thirty. You're almost over the hill. Might as well throw in the towel now and save strength you'll need later."

She grinned. "You seem to be doing all right." I smirked as she checked me out in the mirror.

"I have a girlfriend who fires tennis balls at my head," I said. "It's one of the keys to staying young and fit."

Gloria stuck her tongue out at me and finished applying some powder to her face. We walked downstairs, she handed me the keys to her AMG coupe, and I happily accepted them. "Pier Five," she said once we were in the car. "Ruth's Chris."

"I could have worn jeans," I said as I fired up the engine. We were on our way a few seconds later. I lamented the short drive not giving me much time to get on the throttle. Gloria's coupe was one of the few automatics I enjoyed driving. We parked in a garage a few minutes later and walked into the restaurant from there. The dining room and its strategically-placed tables were about a third full. Ours was a small one in the right rear corner of the room. The white tablecloth was covered with place settings for four, and the hostess didn't remove any when we sat. I frowned but didn't say anything.

When a waiter dropped off a quartet of menus, I still remained silent. Gloria could have invited Rich and his girlfriend Jeanne, though I couldn't imagine why she'd be cagey about it. I was going to break the silence and ask her, but then I saw my parents reflected in the long mirror mounted on the opposite wall as they headed our way. "Goddammit," I muttered.

"Be nice," Gloria said.

"To you or to them?"

The approach of my mother and father prevented her from answering. Gloria smiled at the pair. I looked up and kept a neutral expression. I didn't want to see them, but they raised me to be polite, so I wasn't going to storm out of the restaurant. "Coningsby, dear," my mother said. "It's good to see you. Hello, Gloria."

"I'm glad you could join us," she said.

My father squeezed my shoulder as he walked past. "Son." With all our party present, the waiter returned, filled our waters, and collected appetizer orders. I didn't choose anything, and Gloria shot me a curious look from across the table.

"I don't think we've been to this new location," my mother said, looking around. "Did the other one close?"

I nodded. "If you mean Water Street, yeah. A few years ago."

"You look well, son," my father said. "You back to running four miles in a half-hour?"

I wasn't sure I could sustain such a pace before getting shot, but doing it now would be out of the question. "I'm a little slower these days," I said, "but I'm still getting my laps in."

The waiter dropped off a dish of calamari and a large order of shrimp cocktail. We all made our dinner selections. With my parents here, I figured I wasn't paying, so I went with the most expensive steak on the menu and added a side of fries. We all speared some seafood onto tiny appetizer plates.

I glanced across the table. Gloria smiled at me. I didn't return it. I'd be polite to my folks, but I didn't want to sit here and engage them in conversation. They burned the bridge and scattered the ashes. Let them rebuild it. My father made the first attempt. "I know you weren't expecting to see us tonight. Gloria invited us and said she wasn't going to tell you."

"She loves you, Coningsby," my mother added.

"I, too, often show my love by meddling," I said. This earned me a trio of sour looks, but I remained undeterred.

"Just because the foundation thing is over," my father said, "doesn't mean we don't want to be a part of your life." I'd hoped the heavy talk, if it happened at all, would be confined to dessert, but here we were. "We'd like to get back to how things were before."

"How far into the past do you want to go?" I asked. "Before I started doing this job, I was in Hong Kong for three years and change. Are we turning the clock back to grad school?"

"Coningsby, you're being difficult." My mother's tone reminded me of one I heard frequently in my younger days. "We know you've been upset. We're trying to understand why. Your father's attempting to say we were your parents before we sponsored your detective work. Let's simply go back to that."

"Fine," I said. "Can I borrow the car?"

Gloria rolled her eyes. The waiter spared me any more chiding by emerging with our food. We all got steaks, though mine—as the most expensive in the place—took up the most real estate on a plate. My parents split an order of fries. Gloria opted for the much healthier asparagus. The conversation blessedly ceased as we all went to work with our knives and forks. My girlfriend shot me a glower. She probably thought I was being a jerk to my parents. I might have been. She'd arranged this with them, and even though dining with the folks wasn't high on my list of things to do now, I needed to make the best of it.

Our devil's bargain—as I called it three years ago—ended when I solved my own attempted murder. Before then, my mother and father were kind, supportive parents. They lost my older sister Samantha when she was nineteen. Burying their only remaining child factored into their decision. While I missed Samantha every day, I could never understand their pain and loss.

When everyone's eating pace slowed, I picked up the conversation. "All right. *Détente*, then?"

"Are you trying to make us out to be the Soviet Union?" my father said with a smirk.

"I'm certainly not going to cast myself as a failed communist regime," I said.

"Fair enough. I think a thaw in the current state would be great. June?"

"Of course," my mother said. "Let's start by not being strangers. Coningsby, you come for dinner next weekend. None of your foolishness about having to work a case instead. You're invited, too, Gloria, dear."

"Thank you," she said with a smile, though I think we both knew the invitation covered her already. "We'd love to come."

I spread my hands. "I guess it's decided, then." We would see how the dinner next week went, but getting us all in the same room a couple times counted as progress.

No one left any space for dessert. My father picked up the check, handing the waiter his card without even looking at the total. In the garage, Gloria and I said goodbye to my parents. My father and I exchanged our usual warm handshake, but my mother pulled me in for a hug. It felt right.

On the short drive back to Federal Hill, Gloria asked, "If you knew they were going to be there, would you have come?"

"I doubt it."

"Are you glad you did?"

"Yes," I said.

Gloria flashed a satisfied smile. "Isn't it nice to have such a wise girlfriend?"

"What answer keeps you from blasting tennis balls at me again?"

She chuckled. "Just nod."

I did.

* * *

THE NEXT MORNING, my keylogger still showed zero results. I was running out of patience for the mills of justice to complete their slow grind. The admin assistant's PC—Nancy would be back on the desk today—also showed nothing new. The encrypted files still bothered me. Did those women sue Doctor Fabian after procedures gone wrong? Even if they did, how did it connect to the brutal murder of Suzie Sloan?

I came back to the names in those problematic files. Tara Mayfield. Shannon Getz. Cecelia Henry. Kate Watson. Peggy Nichols. Eva Valdes. A quick look into each showed no connections to Doctor Fabian, Suzie, or the practice other than them likely being patients. This made no sense in light of their files being the only ones encrypted. The shady surgeon didn't want other people to know what was going on.

Next, I checked all six women out on social media. They all maintained active profiles, and I set my script on the task of scraping them for all the information it could find. A pile of data awaited me once it finished. A few were connected to one another, but not all of them. While none of the women included their birth years in their profiles, all looked to be somewhere in their late twenties or early thirties. I searched my trove of information for common plastic surgery procedures.

Bingo. All six underwent breast enhancement procedures, and based on what I could glean, none of them appeared medically necessary. Doctor Fabian performed them all, of course, and each woman raved about the surgeon, his staff, and his practice online. Eva Valdes even mentioned Suzie by name and thanked her for her referral. Interesting. I wondered if Suzie maintained any data on Eva on her computer.

She didn't. Even searching for any string involving Eva's name within file contents yielded no results. Whatever reasons Suzie had for referring someone she knew—and however she felt about it—died with her. Because she was the most interesting of the six women, I focused on Eva Valdes. Her breast surgery happened eighteen months ago. A litany of happy posts followed. Then, she went quiet for a few months. A lone entry eleven months ago talked about how time eroded all things. Someone accused her of vaguebooking, but she never acknowledged it or followed up.

Eight months ago, Eva Valdes' relationship status changed from married to the ever-popular "it's complicated." I didn't want to make the uncharitable assumption that her surgery led to increased male interest, and either she strayed in the marriage, or her husband grew fed up and left her. He was also on Facebook, though the two were no longer connected, and his profile did not list a relationship status.

I wondered what he could tell me.

* * *

MARCO VALDES AGREED to talk to me over Google Meet. I would've been fine with a simple phone call, but he said he spent a lot of the day in video chat, anyway. This would be another tally mark in favor of a normal call for me, but to each his own. He popped up on my screen at the appointed time. Valdes looked to be a little older than me. He wore his short black hair neat, and the light pink shirt went well with his classic Latino complexion. His tie hanging askew, however, ruined the look. Maybe it was a sign of Zoom fatigue.

"What's going on with Eva?" he said after we finished with

the initial formalities. I heard resignation in his voice, like he'd become accustomed to a series of problems with his wife.

"I'm not sure," I said. "Her name came up in my investigation, along with a few other women. I'm working the murder case of Susan Sloan."

He frowned. "I think I saw something about it on the news. Didn't the police arrest a guy?"

"Yes. I think he's the wrong guy."

"All right," he said. "I'll tell you what I can."

"I appreciate it. Eva's surgery happened about eighteen months ago. As far as I can tell, it wasn't a medical necessity."

Valdes let out a dry, mirthless snort. "Definitely not."

"Why'd she do it?" I asked.

"She wanted to." He shrugged. "You've seen her pictures?" I bobbed my head. "Eva's always been a beautiful woman. I don't think she needed to do anything to look better, and I told her when she mentioned the idea of getting the surgery."

"I can't imagine you were happy about paying for something you didn't think she needed."

"We didn't pay for it," he said.

I paused. It's rare for me to be struck speechless, but an arrogant surgeon performing a multi-thousand-dollar procedure *pro bono* certainly did the job. When I recovered the ability to talk, I said, "Not a penny?"

"Nope."

I'd come back to this. "Mister Valdes, what happened after Eva got the surgery?"

"A lot," he said. "She told me she wanted it for some kind of self-confidence thing. Once she recovered, she definitely seemed more sure of herself. I guess going from a C to a double-D will do it." He snorted again. "Maybe she was a little *too* self-confident."

"She had an affair."

"More than one. I can't prove it, of course, but she started going out at night. Coming home late. There were probably men in the house when I was away. I smelled different colognes on her a few times. When I confronted her, she would tell me some guy was hugging on her at the bar. I didn't buy it."

"I know this will sound indelicate," I said, "but do you think one of these men paid for her operation?"

Valdes sipped from a metal water bottle. "I had the same thought a few times. She told me up front the doctor was doing it for free. I don't know why he would. There's no such thing as a free lunch, you know, but she swore it was all covered."

"Could you have paid for it?"

"Sure," he said. "We did well enough."

"All right," I said. "Changing gears . . . I guess the affairs killed your marriage?"

"Yeah. I knew what was going on. She had all this new self-confidence, and she used it to crawl into bed with a bunch of guys. I never knew any reason to suspect her before. It was like she became a different person just because she had bigger tits."

"This would've been about eight months ago?"

"Sounds about right," he said. "I suspected for a while. Finally, I felt I'd put up with enough. I kicked her out and filed for divorce. It's still in progress."

"Do you know the name Suzie Sloan?" I said.

He shook his head. "Other than being on the news, no." Nothing changed in his delivery, and he held my gaze across the virtual connection. I figured he was telling the truth.

"Online, Eva credited Suzie with referring her to the surgeon."

"Weird." He frowned. "She told me some cop's wife put her onto it."

For the second time in this conversation, I fell silent. A cop's wife? None of the names I saw jumped out at me. None were especially uncommon and certainly could've belonged to a police officer somewhere. "You know who she was?"

"I don't know her last name, no. I'm pretty sure her first name was Katrina."

Not a name one encountered every day. "I think I have a new avenue to pursue."

Valdes held up his phone and glanced at it. "I have to get on a call shortly. Do you need anything else?"

"We're good. You've been very helpful. Thanks for your time." We broke the call, and I went back to the assistant's PC to comb through the dreadful file system. A simple search showed two Katrinas out of the many patient records. One was a cancer patient originally from Estonia who needed reconstructive surgery.

The other was Katrina O'Malley, married to one Gannon O'Malley, a homicide lieutenant in the Baltimore Police Department.

What the hell did this mean?

CHAPTER 14

I dropped by Charles Stanton's house again. This time, I parked directly in front. No point in being cagey when he knew who I was and why I sat outside his home. He emerged a short while into my vigil, carrying a can of paint, a tray, and a roller on a long handle. When he saw me, he put his equipment down and walked up to the car. When he pointed to the passenger's door, I nodded, and he climbed in. "Just about to do some painting. You need to watch for your report?"

"Sure," I said. "I might even need to see the can. Mister Allen may want to know what color you're using."

"White. It's the lightest of the colors. Best to use with a bad back."

I nodded. "Sounds plausible. I'll put it in the report."

"You come here to watch me paint?" Stanton said. "Or is it something else?"

"You told me Doctor Fabian was an asshole."

"Sure did."

"Could he be worse?" I asked.

His brows knitted. "Worse how?"

"I'm not sure yet. Here's what I know. A few women went to him and got boob jobs done on the house."

"Really?" he said before I could continue. "Was it a charity thing?"

"I don't think so. I talked to one husband, and he said they could've paid. He also told me his wife used her newfound self-confidence to have a bunch of affairs."

"It's certainly shitty. I don't see what the doc would have to do with it, though. He can't control how someone behaves after a procedure."

"Why do surgery for free?" I said.

"Hell, I don't know." He shrugged. "It does seem out of character for someone like Fabian. I can't imagine he'd turn down a chance to toot his own horn. Maybe he wanted her to spread the word."

"I've heard of loss leaders, but he'd be sinking a lot of time and money into a few women and hoping they turned out to be good evangelists."

"He did this more than once?"

"I'm not sure yet," I said. "But if the pattern holds, I'm guessing he gave away breast surgery six times." I made a leap in presuming the other five encrypted files also belonged to women who got their enhancements on the house. It struck me as reasonable, however. Why hide the records otherwise?

"I don't know," Stanton said. "I'm a little out of my depth here."

"All right. I'll make sure to note how light the white paint is. Can doesn't look heavy, either. No strain on your back at all."

He grinned. "Mighty nice of you." Stanton got out of the car. I figured coming here was a long shot to learn more, and it turned out to be the case. I fired up the S4 and wondered what other rocks I could overturn.

* * *

THIS TIME, one of the rocks came to me. Or called me, at least. Liz Fleming from the public defender's office popped up on my caller ID. About two years passed since the last time we worked together. "What lost cause do you have for me today?" I asked when we'd exchanged hellos.

"Nothing too bad," she said. "You sound like you're in the car. Can you stop by my office?"

No other flash of insight came to me, so declining made little sense. I could always beg off any new work thanks to my current caseload—a claim I never could've made before. "Sure. Give me fifteen minutes."

Seventeen minutes later, I knocked on her door. "Come in." I entered. "You're late," she said as I closed the door behind me. Her face struggled to hide a grin.

"I've never been prompt for any of the times we've met when I worked pro bono. Why change things only because you can pay me now?"

Liz kicked her feet up onto her desk. She'd doffed her high heels, but I remembered how much I liked her legs. The navy miniskirt she wore helped my powers of recall. "A little birdie told me you're already involved in this case, so I know I'm not putting you out."

"Please tell me it's about a nurse who might not have a bad back," I said on the one-millionth of a percent chance I was right.

"What?" Liz frowned. "No. Some asshole might've beaten his girlfriend to death."

"I presume you're representing said asshole?"

"I am," she said, and then she paused. "I'm so rude. How are you after . . . everything?"

"A couple pounds lighter," I said. "Losing a lung lobe and spleen will do it."

She cringed. "Wow."

"Yeah. If your diet choice is getting shot or doing keto, go with keto."

"I'm so sorry," she said. "You're good to be back to work already?"

"It's been four months, Liz. I'm right as rain." She stared at me for a few seconds. On the whole, I would rate her unconvinced. It was only fair—I didn't convince myself, either. "Let's talk about Glenn Mathews. Two Ns, one T."

"Oh, my god, he said that to me, too!" She chuckled. "What do you think of him?"

"I don't like him very much, but I'm pretty sure he didn't beat Suzie Sloan to death."

"You have any proof yet?"

"Not even close," I said. "I'm looking into another suspect, but it's slow going."

Liz took her feet off the desk. I felt briefly disappointed. "Here's the deal." She leaned forward. Her white shirt was unbuttoned just enough to be interesting. "We're pretty thin on investigators. Have been for a while, really. Layoffs and all while courts only hear important cases. Mathews just got arraigned. I could use you on this, and since you're already looking into it, you wouldn't need to do any additional work."

"I'd need to document everything, though . . . right?"

"Eventually," she said. "I might need to go to court with whatever you give me, so it needs to be good. But I'm not going to hound you for updates all the time. You're a big boy. Do your job."

No extra toiling but I would snag an additional check? Maybe I could even fatten my rates with the city picking up the tab. "Sign me up."

"Great. Thanks." She paused and again fought in vain against an amused expression. "What are you still doing here? Get to work."

"Yes, taskmaster," I said. I stood and left the office. If I could figure everything out, I'd solve the case and collect two paychecks for my efforts. With a nascent business and spotty cash flow, I could use it. Now, I only needed to deliver.

* * *

From Liz's office, I drove home. The parking pad was empty. Gloria must have run out somewhere. I swung the S4 onto it and got out. When I did, I heard a pair of car doors slam a short distance away in the alley. Sure enough, two muscle-bound goons approached. One stood a little taller than me, and the other was short and squat. They crossed their beefy arms over their chests.

My pulse quickened, and I heard blood rushing in my ears. Prior to getting shot, my reactions had never been so visceral. Maybe I could get back to my old self in this respect. For now, I needed to not get my teeth kicked in by a couple guys who looked overqualified to do the kicking. "Guys, I only accept charity solicitations at the front door."

"We ain't here for charity," the short one said in a deep, rumbly voice belying his size. "You're stubborn."

"I have a few other character flaws, too," I said. "Let's all share. Maybe we'll each have a breakthrough."

"Look," the taller one said in a tone reminding me of one of my hippie professors in college, "cut the shit." He ran a hand through his brown hair. "You've been asked to back off once already. You gonna listen this time?"

Glenn Mathews sat in jail. Unless he possessed a great amount of reach, he didn't send them. A successful plastic surgeon would have the means to hire a brace of bullies who think with their fists, however. "While I think about it, why don't you tell me who sent you?"

"Enough," the shorter one said. He stepped forward. His left foot planted. His right fist went back. I turned my head to the side and closed my left eye. His fist thundered into my midsection an instant later. It folded me in half and caused me to back up a couple steps. "You gonna listen now?"

Had he pressed the advantage, I might have been in trouble. Instead, he allowed me a chance to get my wind back. I tapped my index finger to my ear. "Didn't hear you." He waded in again, but as before, my jumpiness disappeared after the first blow. It was a pattern I still needed to work on. For now, I turned aside two more punches, staggered him with a quick elbow to the face, and then bent him in half with a kick to the stomach. The larger goon advanced, so I only had time to shove the pint-sized one over before I found myself on the defensive again.

This guy looked big and dumb, but he was no amateur. He didn't give me an opening for any sort of counterattack. His max-effort punches stung as I blunted them. I could keep this up for a while, but he would tire, and after a few more blows, he did. The next few lacked the speed and power of his initial onslaught. Following a left jab, I stepped forward and elbowed him in the solar plexus. He backed off and sucked wind.

Before I could capitalize, though, the other one was back up. He lacked the skill of his larger friend, however. After turning away a couple haymakers, I hit him in the face with a left cross. He rocked back on his heels, and I kicked him hard in the jaw to put him down. The tall one still gasped as I turned my eyes to him.

He reached into his jacket and pulled out a revolver. Immediately, I flashed back to the fateful day at the harbor four months ago. Running past the pavilion. A gunshot. Pain blazing in my side, then again a couple seconds later. My desperate dive into the frigid Baltimore Harbor and its cold embrace. I couldn't go through it again.

I turned tail and sprinted down the alley as fast as I could. I heard a, "What the hell?" behind me, but I kept going. I made a left past another row of houses, then a right into another alley. After a couple hundred feet, my lungs burned, and I stopped. I sat against someone's rear fence and took shallow, quick breaths. My heart raced, and I'd never felt it beat so fast—not all from the exertion. I pushed past the memories of my dive into the water and focused on getting myself under control. The last time I felt like this, Gloria climbed into my hospital bed and brought me back down. I was on my own this time, and I'd never felt it more sharply.

After a minute, I got my breathing under control, and my pulse slowed. I heard voices nearby. The deep tone of the shorter one said, "Where the hell could he have gone?" I wasn't out of the woods yet. I hopped the fence behind me, stayed in a crouch, and moved across a stranger's yard.

CHAPTER 15

I crouched against the rear wall of the house. A light was on inside. So far, no one took note of me. If these people owned a dog and decided to let it out soon, I would be in trouble. I took care to breathe in through my nose and out through my mouth. With a moment to process everything, I drew my .45 from within my jacket.

Getting into a shootout while surrounded by rowhouses struck me as a terrible and reckless idea. My best hope was for the two goons to get tired of looking for me. Of course, they could go back and wait for me at my house, but I hoped they weren't smart enough to consider it. I crept closer to the rear of the small yard and peeked though the chain links as best I could.

The pair of enforcers made their way down the alley slowly. They stopped and looked in every yard. At their current pace, I had little more than a minute until they reached my location. Someone could notice them—or me—before then, and who knew what they would do if confronted by a homeowner? An innocent person didn't need to die over this. I looked around the yard for something I could use to distract them. Against the fence, I found a loose rock the size of a golf ball.

While braining one of the goons with it would be satisfying, I didn't want to escalate the situation. I simply wanted them gone.

Throwing it without standing and drawing attention to myself would sap some of the power I could put behind it. There's a saying about beggars and choosers, however. I inched closer to the goons' position and tossed the rock as hard as I could up the alley. No one would ever mistake me for a professional baseball player, but it was a good throw—probably boosted by adrenaline. The rock clattered against the concrete past their position. They both turned and jogged off to investigate.

With the enforcers distracted, I hopped the fence and trotted in the opposite direction. I picked up another alley to the right about a hundred feet later. I wasn't familiar with the network of backstreets running between rows of houses, but I knew where I lived, and I headed in the proper direction. A couple minutes later, I reached my street and walked into my house via the front door. I kept the lights off and padded into the kitchen. A quick look through the blinds showed me their car was still there. Gloria's remained absent, thank goodness.

I sat at the table with my pistol in my hand. A few minutes later, I heard an engine fire up and a car drive off. I got up and risked another peek through the blinds. Their car was gone. I let out a deep breath and leaned against the counter for support.

* * *

ONCE I'D CALMED myself down and guzzled a bottle of water, I retreated to my home office. After I got shot, I found a few different angles of security footage. My first couple attempts to watch it sent me spiraling into panic attacks. I felt similar back in the alley with the goons hunting me. One glimpse of the pistol brought it all back. I could hold my own gun with no ill effects. Seeing someone else brandishing one, however, was beyond the pale.

Even now, dwelling on it quickened my heart rate. I pushed those thoughts aside and called Doctor Parrish in Arizona. She sounded surprised to hear from me but promised we could Skype in about fifteen minutes. I spent the time alternating between reliving the past and chiding myself for doing it. At the appointed hour, my laptop trilled, and I answered her video call. "You don't sound so well, C.T."

"I'm not," I admitted. "I've been telling everyone I'll figure it out . . . I'll get past it." I shook my head. "Nothing's worked. I'm still jumpy any time there's a conflict."

"Tell me what happened." I heard the calm in her voice and hoped it transmitted with the ones and zeroes over the Internet.

"A couple guys accosted me behind my house." My throat felt dry, and I sated it with a sip of water. "A few months ago, I think I could've taken them pretty easily. Today, I flinched initially and got hit in the stomach by the first guy. Then, I was OK to fight them off." The image of the tall one pulling out his pistol played in my mind's eye. "One of them drew down on me."

She frowned in concern. "You mean like the Earps and Cowboys in Tombstone?"

Her Arizona roots showed, but I went along with it. "It was the OK Corral all over again, and I ran away like Billy Clanton. I don't think I've ever felt like such a coward. They came looking for me, but I was able to trick them and make it back home."

"Why would you call yourself a coward?" Parrish asked.

"Because I high-tailed it at the first sign of a gun."

"You're alive because of that. Have you stopped to consider that most people would do exactly what you did there?"

"I feel bad enough already, Doc," I said. "Let's not lump me in with most people."

Parrish showed a small smile. "Fine, but you get my point. It's a natural reaction. Fight or flight. Fighting someone with a gun is very foolish even if you have your own."

The intonation at the end of her sentence almost made me wonder if she asked whether I carried. "I do. I know everyone owns five guns in Arizona, but they're a little more rare out here. The guys who get paid to rough people up aren't usually carrying."

"It was still a wise decision," she insisted. "Even if you're some kind of quick-draw champion, it's likely he would shoot you before you got your gun pointed at him."

"I know." I fell silent. I must've done the math in my subconscious in the moment. If I reached, I was dead, and I ran. I'd survived to fight another day, but I still hoped I wouldn't need to get punched first. "I can't work like this, Doc. I can't *live* like this. People are counting on me, and I'm letting them down."

"You know who's counting on you most of all?"

"Gloria?"

"You." I should've seen the answer coming. No such thing as a straight question when posed by a shrink. "You ensured your own survival. Stop treating yourself like a coward. You suffered serious trauma, and yes, you still have some hurdles to overcome. I told you last time that I can't offer you a panacea. I still can't."

"I know," I said in a quiet voice.

"This is something you need to get past on your own," she said. "I can try to help you, but long-distance therapy isn't exactly a specialty of mine. The first part of this process, though, involves you being honest with yourself. You're not jumpy. You're not a coward. You're recovering from a serious injury. Despite the sage advice to get back on the horse that threw you, it takes time, and it takes patience."

"I've never had a ton of the latter," I said.

"Maybe you don't need it. Learn to be more forgiving of yourself. If you can do that, and you're working on something like sparring, I think you'll be able to make a good recovery."

"But not a complete one?"

"I hate to make sweeping predictions. At the end of this process, there may be a new normal for you, and you'll just have to incorporate it going forward."

"Can I still do my job?" I asked.

"I certainly hope so," she said. "It sounds like you're good at it, and I can tell it means a lot to you. Just promise me you'll go easier on yourself. When you did your physical recovery here, you didn't expect to run three miles the first time you were back on your feet."

In fact, the first time I tried to stand on my own, I sank right to the floor. "I see your point."

"I hope you do." Parrish jotted a note. "Be well, C.T. Call me again if you need to, but I honestly hope you don't."

"Me, too," I said. I thanked Parrish for her time and signed off. I could try to be kinder to myself. In the meantime, I still had a murder to solve, and whoever did it demonstrated a couple times he didn't care much about my feelings.

* * *

AFTER THE CALL WITH PARRISH, I took a walk to process what we discussed and what I might need to do to kick myself back into gear. Some part of me knew she couldn't offer a panacea. No one could. I remained vigilant for more muscleheads on my stroll around the neighborhood but encountered none. When I walked back in, I still enjoyed the run of the house.

I conducted some more research on Doctor Fabian. I'd looked into him as a potential suspect, but never much as a surgeon. With his free plastic surgeries potentially looming large, I wanted to know all I could. *Maryland Magazine* wrote a puff piece about him three months ago. I read it and tried not to feel sick at all the purple prose and fawning over a man who might be a killer. Hidden in all the saccharine text, however, were a few grains of true sugar.

Fabian routinely worked late—this being a relative term as the article author thought a doctor plying his trade until six o'clock constituted the first step to sainthood. The clock on my computer showed 4:45. Plenty of time remained to drive to his office. The piece went on to say he eschewed a special parking spot in the garage—another marker on the road to beatification, apparently. Because people care what others drive, the last useful nugget involved the doctor's car. He tooled around in a new Jaguar F Pace SUV with "an undisclosed vanity plate."

I headed for his office and pulled into the usual garage. While I didn't know his model of vehicle by sight, there would be few Jaguars sitting in parking spots, especially at this hour. It was past five o'clock, and other doctors in the building who weren't busy making their way to heaven would be gone for the day. Sure enough, on the second level, I found a black F Pace crossover backed into a spot. It sported a vanity plate.

BOTOX

I rolled my eyes as I parked nearby. Over the next several minutes, a few of the cars around me left. When the clock struck five-thirty, I exited the S4 and leaned on the driver's door of Doctor Fabian's British ride. Based on the location of his office and the nearest exit to street level, he would approach the car from this side. About fifteen minutes later, he walked from the stairwell. His expression soured when he noticed someone besmirching his luxury SUV, and I thought I saw a hint of surprise come over him once he recognized me. "What's up, Doc?"

"You're the detective, right. Ferguson?"

"The one and only."

Doctor Fabian set his shoulder bag down and fixed me with a bored expression. "I'm pretty sure I told you everything I could."

"You didn't," I said. "Among other things, what's with the alleged tough guys you've sent to take me out?"

"I have no idea what you're talking about." In the inconsistent fluorescent lighting, I couldn't get a good read on him.

"Let's discuss Suzie Sloan."

"We already did," he said. "I didn't want to fire her but felt I had to, and I certainly didn't kill her."

"Fine. How about Eva Valdes?"

He frowned. "I'm supposed to know who she is?"

"I should hope so," I said. "She was a patient of yours. Breast augmentation. Unlike a lot of women, though, she got hers done for free."

The doctor waved a hand. "I do charity work occasionally, Mister Ferguson. I believe men of my station need to give back."

I suppressed the urge to punch him and stayed on point. "Her husband says they could've paid for it."

"I don't know, then." He shrugged. "You're catching me at the end of a long work day."

"Something's going on with you," I said. "Maybe you didn't kill Suzie. I'll find out either way. But a few things don't add up around here, and a few muscleheads and a fancy SUV aren't going to save you. Whatever it is you're up to . . . I'll figure it out. How many puff pieces will they write about you then?"

"I'm not going to indulge your conspiracy theories," he said. "Too many of those in the world already." The surgeon picked up his bag again. "If you'll excuse me."

"Sure." I moved off the door and allowed him access to the Jag. "Oh, if you happen to talk to Katrina O'Malley, tell her I think her husband's a real prick."

For an instant, Doctor Fabian looked like someone walked over his grave, though he recovered right away. "Someone else I'm not familiar with." He scoffed. "Really, Mister Ferguson. Suzie's sister should have hired better help."

"See you around, Doc." I stared at Fabian as he pulled out of the spot and left the garage.

* * *

I stopped by my office on the way back home. The body shop was closed, though Manny still burned the evening oil in his office. We exchanged waves as I walked upstairs and unlocked my door. A minute later, I sat behind my desk. The keylogger showed results this time. I dumped the log and began parsing it.

The difficulty with utilities like this is they capture everything. People type a lot on their computers. They enter website URLs, write emails, fill out forms, and they make a bunch of mistakes along the way. My tool captured every stroke for good or for ill, and judging by the size of the text file, Doctor Fabian spent a fair bit of time at the keyboard today.

I wrote the script powering my keylogger in Python, and it understood inputs like the shift key, rendering the resulting letter as a capital. This made proper names and potential passwords easier to discern. The file still contained a lot of garbage to sift through. When accessing his encrypted folder, Doctor

Fabian would begin the process with a double-click of the mouse—an input my tool had no insight into. This meant his password wouldn't be prefaced by something like a URL or user name, so it would basically come out of the blue.

Passwords were usually a boon to someone like me. People rarely chose strong ones, and this made compromising an account easy. Some folks, however, understood best practices and chose either a very long or very strong password. These made knocking over an account harder, though it could still be done. I had no idea where Doctor Fabian fell on this spectrum, so I kept scanning the output. After a while, eye strain set in, and I needed to rub my forehead and look away.

A few minutes later, I found a promising string of characters. Despite letting his assistant read his emails, it appeared the good doctor understood at least some security practices. I copied the string, opened my remote access software, and tried to access the encrypted folder from the receptionist's PC. It prompted me for a key.

I pasted the pilfered string.

I was in.

CHAPTER 16

TARA MAYFIELD.

Shannon Getz.

Cecelia Henry.

Kate Watson.

Margaret (Peggy) Nichols.

Eva Valdes.

I found all their files. Because I knew their names already, unearthing the trove felt like a bit of a letdown. I downloaded the records to my computer and logged off my connection to the receptionist's PC. While I now possessed a plethora of information on each of these women, I wouldn't misuse it. I didn't care about their finances or their medical histories aside from whatever compelled them to visit Doctor Fabian.

A quick perusal of each file told me all of them underwent breast augmentations, which were cosmetic in all cases. Furthermore, none of the women received a bill for their procedures. The billing parts of their files contained entries corresponding to other visits, but none of them paid Doctor Fabian a cent starting a few months before they went under the knife.

None of the files made any record of who referred these ladies. Suzie Sloan supposedly put Eva Valdes onto the practice, though her husband claimed it had been Katrina O'Malley. Other than putting her name on entries and updates, Suzie was absent from all the records, and Lieutenant O'Malley's wife never appeared, either. The omissions didn't surprise me, but a fellow can hope for a smoking gun every now and then.

Once I finished going over the records, the principal result of all my reviewing turned out to be more eye strain. I put my head back and rested my eyes for a few minutes. Eva Valdes' surgery gave her a jolt of confidence which led to a string of affairs and the dissolution of her marriage. I wondered if any of the other women who got their surgeries *gratis* went through the same progression.

None did . . . at least not exactly. As far as I could tell from social media, Tara Mayfield had been the only other one of the six to be married at the time of her operation. About half a year later, she posted a cryptic update about how all things end, and her profile remained silent since. I took the liberty of presuming she was divorced or on her way. Kate Watson posted very little on any platform.

The other three were in relationships prior to their surgeries. Cecilia Henry and Peggy Nichols made a big deal of sharing their newfound single statuses with the world. Shannon Getz, on the other hand, stopped posting pictures with the man I presumed to be her boyfriend about four months post-op. Since then, her photos decreased in frequency but increased in raciness. She earned many likes and comments for her lingerie snapshots. Thirst traps are usually popular, and hers were no exception.

Six women. An equal number of free boob jobs. At least five relationships ended. Something lurked under the surface here. If I could find it, I just might crack this case.

* * *

WHEN I ARRIVED HOME, Gloria was back. She gave me a kiss and then studied my face. "You look like you've had a Eureka moment. Something in your eyes."

"Mostly strain from looking at a screen too much today," I said. "I'm at the point where I know more but still not enough. A few more pieces have to line up before I can really say I've found some piercing insight."

"I hope you get there soon," she said.

"Me, too." I didn't want to tell her about the goons with the gun. Not thinking of myself as a coward still proved challenging even after my chat with Doctor Parrish. Thankfully, the only solid blow either man landed connected with my gut, and other than a little lingering soreness, I felt fine. Physically, at least.

As if she were reading my mind, Gloria asked, "You want to invite Joey over to spar again?"

"Depends if his ego is recovered from the thrashing I gave him last time."

She grinned and shook her head. "If he's up for it, you guys can use the basement. I'll pick up food again."

"Have I told you I love you recently?" I said.

"No." Gloria kissed me again. "It's always nice to hear, though . . . especially when I'm picking up the check for you and your friend. You two eat a lot."

"I've bought him plenty a meal over the years," I said. "I empathize." I called Joey and asked if he were available again. He tried to protest by telling me about some new show on Netflix but dropped it when I told him he was full of shit.

"I might need to hit you at least once after this conversation," he told me. I assured him I understood. Gloria and I drove to her house in separate cars. She checked a couple of her favorite spots once we arrived, eventually settling on Japanese. Joey and I usually went for Italian. I figured he would eat whatever we put out, but I wanted to see his reaction to rice and chopsticks rather than mozzarella sticks and garlic bread—the latter of which Joey insisted made an excellent food delivery system as he dipped and topped it with abandon.

He arrived shortly after Gloria left to pick up dinner. As before, we used the large exercise room in the basement. Following our stretch routines and gearing up, Joey knocked his fists together. "Same as before?"

"I think so, yeah."

"Still flinching?"

I nodded. "So far, I'm two and oh in fights where it happens, but I can't count on the trend holding. Don't take it easy on me." Joey arched an eyebrow. "Try not to knock me out, either, but I need this to be a real test."

"All right," Joey said. He spread his feet and took an aggressive posture. I assumed my normal ready stance. I recalled my training, both here and in Hong Kong. Be calm. Stay in the moment. Let the adversary come. Use his force against him. I took a deep breath and focused. Joey's nostrils flared. His left fist raised as his right one went back. His weight moved toward the rear and then surged forward, rotating his hips.

As before, I turned my head away and cocked my left arm to the side. Joey's punch thundered over it, and he clobbered me in the side of the head. Moving my head may have spared me the worst of the blow, but it still rang my bell and drove me backward. I toppled to the carpeted floor.

Before I could get my bearings, Joey was on me again.

He crouched, putting his left hand on my chest and raising his right to deliver a knockout blow. I recovered in time to deflect the strike high and wide with my left forearm. With my free hand, I grabbed Joey's arm, brought my legs up and in, and rolled him onto the floor. He landed on his back with a thud, and I maintained the armbar. He tapped the floor three times. I released the hold.

"Nice recovery." He shook out his arm and rose to one knee.

"Nice right cross," I said, rubbing my jaw as I stood. I held out a hand and pulled Joey back to his feet. "It hurt, but I'm glad you didn't hold back."

We repeated the drill a few more times. With the initial recoil out of the way, I held my own and repelled Joey's attacks. We took a hydration break. Gloria, of course, installed a cold water dispenser in the room, and we each enjoyed a cup. "This is all well and good," Joey said. "I'm happy to help you get back on your feet, so to speak. What are you going to do if these assholes bring a gun?" When I looked down at the floor and didn't answer, he knew what it meant. "It happened already, didn't it?"

"I'm still here," I said.

"Fortunately. Tell me about it."

"Two assholes confronted me in the alley behind my house." I played the events of the encounter in my mind. "I caught a pretty good shot in the gut at the beginning, but they weren't skilled enough to take advantage. When things went against them, the bigger of the two pulled a pistol." A shudder ran up my spine.

"What did you do?" Joey asked.

"I ran as fast as I could. I think he was too stunned to shoot me in the back. They eventually gave chase. I managed to get away in the alleys and make it back to my house." I sighed. "I know I survived, and I shouldn't feel like a coward for running, but I do."

"Live to fight another day."

"Yeah, yeah," I said. I filled my cup from the five-gallon water jug again.

Joey remained silent for a minute before he spoke. "You been to the range after ... everything?"

I shook my head. "I pulled my gun when they were chasing me. It was the first time in months."

"You're probably out of practice."

"I'm a pretty good shot," I said more defensively than I wanted.

"It's not just about being a good shot," Joey said. "It's the feel of the gun in your hand. The movement of your arm when it kicks. The *sound*." He lapsed into silence again. "Remember hearing about my uncle?"

After searching my memory, I frowned. "I think so. Wasn't it a long time ago?"

"Almost twenty-five years. Shit, we're getting old. We were kids when he got shot. I didn't want anything to do with guns for a long time. Took me until I was seventeen to bring myself to hold one. I was eighteen before I fired one." He smirked. "By then, I realized I might not have the same nine-to-five job as everyone else." He turned out to be right. Joey made new identities for people who needed to get away and start anew. Like me, he saw them at their worst and tried to right the ship.

"Is this some inspiring tale of how you became a marksman?" I said.

"No," said Joey. "Like you, I'm pretty good. It took me a while to get there. The first time I went to the range, I was scared. Petrified. All I could think about was my uncle getting shot, and I barely knew him."

I saw where the story was going. "How did you get over it?"

"I stood there. Gun in my hand but not raised. I stood there, and I listened. Every shot. Pistol, rifle, whatever. I took it all in. I think it prepared me to finally take a stance and shoot. Maybe it'll help you, too."

"It certainly can't hurt."

"Food's here, boys," Gloria called down. "I hope you still have all your teeth. I didn't bring any soup."

Joey grinned. "You'd better marry that girl."

"Let me try not getting killed during this case first," I said.

* * *

JOEY DID NOT OBJECT to the Japanese dinner, in fact. He turned out to be a lost cause when it came to chopsticks, but he acquitted himself quite well with a knife and fork. Gloria picked up an assortment of spring rolls, four hibachi dinners, several sushi rolls, and too many sides of rice to count. Despite his long-standing love for Italian food, Joey demonstrated he could put away a starting lineup's worth of Asian cuisine, too. "I can't believe we don't have more left over," Gloria said at least once while we cleaned up and put the remaining food in her spacious fridge.

"Welcome to dinner with Joey," I said.

We called it a night a short while later. Gloria's king-sized bed was super comfortable, and I zonked out a few seconds after my head hit the pillow. In the morning, I woke before my girlfriend as I always did. I changed into some running clothes I kept in a drawer and hit the not-so-mean streets of Brooklandville. If anyone wanted to menace me up here, neighborhood regulations compelled them to wear a suit and tie and ask for things politely.

The view up here was so much different than in my neck of the woods. I'd grown used to packed houses, neighborhood bars and restaurants, the park, and the harbor. Here, my route took me past homes set far apart, winding roads, and plenty of trees. I could live up here if I needed to—being with Gloria would make the move worth it—but I would miss many aspects of city living. The quiet was hard to beat, however.

I walked back inside, showered, dressed, and investigated breakfast options in the kitchen. Reheating dinner tempted me as my stomach rumbled, but I toughed it out and scrambled some eggs to go along with toast, yogurt, and berries. As usual, Gloria joined me once the coffee brewed and the smells of breakfast reached the second floor. "What's on your docket for today?" she asked when we'd both finished eating and nursed our second mugs of java.

I realized we hadn't talked much about the case in the last few days. "I'm looking hard at the doctor for now," I said. "Something's funny about his practice. He gave away operations to women who could have paid for them."

"What kind of operations?"

"Boob jobs."

Gloria frowned. "Was he sleeping with them?"

"I don't think so. Most of them were in relationships at the time, but they all dissolved over the next few months. "

"What's his incentive?" she said. "It can't be a cheap procedure. I could see doing an occasional one as part of some charitable outreach, but this sounds a lot different."

"I'm still trying to figure it out," I said. "I'm going to try and talk to some of the women today."

"You really think they'll have anything to say to you?"

"I'll just have to turn on the charm."

Gloria rolled her eyes. "Try not to open the spigot all the way, stud."

"I promise I'll keep it under fifty percent," I said.

She smiled. "Good." We finished our coffee, I kissed her goodbye, and I headed back to Baltimore. While I did, I called the first woman on my list—Tara Mayfield. She picked up quickly.

"Miss Mayfield, I'm a private investigator. I'm looking into something involving Doctor Neal Fabian."

"Doctor Fabian? He's wonderful. What's going on?"

"I can't talk much about it," I said. "I'd like to ask you about a procedure he performed for you . . . one you didn't pay for."

"How do you know about that?" she said, and it sounded like she spoke through clenched teeth.

"I'm good at my job."

"Well, fuck you *and* your job." She broke the connection.

"Too bad there's no such thing as personality augmentation," I muttered to the empty car. Being a German make, it probably didn't understand me. While I waited at a light, I realized I could drop in on Shannon Getz en route to my office in Fells Point. She lived a few blocks away. A short while later, I pulled up in front of her end-unit rowhouse and killed the engine. After waiting a few uneventful minutes, I walked up to the door and knocked.

Footsteps approached. "You're early," a woman cooed as she opened the door. Shannon Getz wore jeans so tight they looked painted on and a taut sweater whose plunging neckline showcased Doctor Fabian's work—which was very good—to anyone who cared to look. The smile on her face turned to confusion when she realized I wasn't the party who'd arrived ahead of schedule. She crossed her arms over her chest . . . probably in a mix of annoyance and sudden modesty. "Who the hell are you?"

"Someone who's almost never early." I showed her my ID and badge. "I'm looking into a matter concerning Doctor Fabian."

"Who?"

I looked at her hands and inclined my head toward them. "You weren't exactly hiding his *pro bono* handiwork when you answered the door."

She narrowed her eyes and glared at me. "There's nothing wrong with what I did."

"Excellent," I said. "Would you mind talking about him?"

She slammed the door in my face.

One woman hung up on me, and now Shannon Getz couldn't get rid of me fast enough. I got back in my car, moved a couple houses up the street, and curbed it again. Sure enough, someone else took the spot I abandoned a few minutes later. A well-dressed man approached Shannon's house and knocked on the door. I didn't notice her open it, but the next thing I saw, she leapt into his arms and they kissed on her porch. He carried her inside.

What in the world was going on?

CHAPTER 17

FROM THE HOUSE, I DROVE TO RICH'S PRECINCT. MY cousin was not at his desk, but Paul King sat opposite at his. I dropped a coffee in front of him. "You remembered," he said. "I'm touched."

"I couldn't bear the sound of you complaining again." I set Rich's cup in front of his keyboard.

King jerked his head toward the empty desk. "He's in some sergeants' meeting." Jazz hands told me what King thought of the gathering.

"You!" called a voice from behind me. O'Malley again. "Get in here." He held his door open and glowered at me.

"Looks like I need to see the principal." King raised his cup to me as I walked away. Once I crossed the threshold, O'Malley slammed the door. "I'm not going to donate to the Police Athletic League at this rate."

"You can't keep your nose out of shit, can you?" He walked around and lopped into his chair. I remained standing. O'Malley was about my height but a little too heavy for his frame in middle age. His blond hair looked more unkempt than I could remember seeing it.

"What are you bellowing about?"

"Doctor Neal Fabian said he's thinking about filing a harassment charge against you," the lieutenant said. "Told me you won't leave him alone."

"So he called the complaint desk and just happened to be connected to a homicide shift commander? Mighty convenient."

O'Malley narrowed his eyes. "How he reached me isn't your concern. I think he's got a case. If he decides to press charges, I'll arrest you myself."

"I promise I'll resist," I said.

"You should leave him alone." O'Malley leaned back in the chair, a smug expression plastered on his face.

"What's your connection to him?"

"None," he said. "Just making sure a private citizen like you doesn't get too many ideas in his head."

"Too late," I said. "I have all sorts of ideas about the good doctor. One of which involves how certain women might have been referred to him."

He frowned but hid it in a scowl quickly. "I don't know what you're talking about."

"Fine. Play dumb. You're good at it. It's gotten you this far, after all."

"Go to hell," he said.

I thought about throwing the unmarked car following me in his face but refrained. The driver wouldn't fess up to getting made by an amateur like me. Let O'Malley stay in the dark. "Say hi to Katrina for me . . . Gannon." I snapped my fingers. "There's another reason people shouldn't trust you. You're named after a video game villain."

"Don't you come in here and talk about my wife." He leaned forward and jabbed his finger at me. "I'll haul you in myself."

"For what?" He didn't say anything. "Just what I thought.

Tell your doctor friend I'm coming for him. All the referrals and all the asshole lieutenants he knows won't save him." I opened the door and walked out while O'Malley seethed in his chair.

* * *

AFTER LEAVING THE PRECINCT, I recalled Joey's advice about the gun range. Other than taking out my .45 during the recent chase through the alleys, I'd barely looked at a pistol since being shot. Doctor Parrish would tell me this was a perfectly natural reaction to trauma. I felt certain she was right. The issue was perfectly natural reactions to trauma don't solve cases.

While I've long been a pretty good shot, no one would confuse me for a marksman. I figured I would start a little smaller and work my way back up to the hand cannon. I took the 9MM and a bunch of ammo in a case and drove to a range way up in Baltimore County I'd never been to before. No one would know me. I'd simply be a guy looking to shoot.

I checked in, paid for the time I expected to use, and received a pair of freshly-disinfected ear protectors. I made my way to the business part of the operation and slipped them on. Not many people came out today. I selected a stall a few spots away from the nearest person. A call came out over the speakers to bench all firearms with muzzles downrange and wait three minutes. Whoever made the announcement went on to inform us this was a regular security practice, and an employee would come around to check everyone's setup.

When a large bearded man arrived at my area, he saw I hadn't even taken my gun out of the case yet. He nodded and moved on. A couple minutes later, the audio system broadcasted a call to resume. I opened the hard case, checked the magazine, popped it into my 9MM, and racked the slide. It was ready to send seventeen rounds screaming downrange.

But was I?

The pistol felt heavy in my hand after all these months. Targets fifteen and twenty-five yards away beckoned. I knew I could pepper the closer one with center-mass shots and do almost as well on the more distant figure. My feet moved on their own accord, taking a proper shooting stance. I held the grip with two hands and sighted the nearer target. My finger slid inside the trigger guard.

I couldn't bring myself to fire.

Surrounded by muzzle blasts, I kept thinking about the man walking out from between the Harborplace pavilions and shooting me in the side. I ran, dodged, weaved. Another shot hit me in the back. I went down. People screamed. I scrabbled to my feet. The harbor . . . if I could just make it in time. I ran with what energy I could. A gun barked behind me. I dove into the frigid water. A moment later, I sank under its surface.

I placed the Smith & Wesson back on the table.

Throughout my recovery, I did a lot of things sooner than the medical professionals assigned to my case recommended. I pushed to walk in the rehab center's gym. My compatriot Rollins took me on a hike of a small mountain. I checked out before I should have. The gun stared back at me from the table.

I could do this, too.

I picked up the 9MM again and squeezed off seventeen rounds at the fifteen-yard target. A few center mass shots, plus several more which would seriously injure or incapacitate a person. Not bad. Not up to my normal standards, but we all needed to start again somewhere. I ejected the magazine and loaded a fresh one.

Again, I took aim at the nearer marker. This time, I focused harder on the front sight and shot a little better. My grouping looked tighter. More rounds to the chest of a theoretical human attacker. Like the man who shot me several months ago. Nicky Papers. I knew his name. For my mental health at the time—and at the advice of my cousin—I chose not to go after him. Now, I saw his face above the holes in the wood.

"Take that, you son of a bitch," I whispered.

The loudspeakers came to life again, and we all went on our enforced break. This time, Hagrid got to see my 9MM empty and pointed in the proper direction. He gave me a thumbs up and moved along. A few minutes later, we got the all clear. I popped another magazine in the nine as the rest of the range roared to life.

Rather than rack the slide, I set the gun down. No one used any of the stations to my left. I slipped the ear protectors off and immediately noticed how much louder all the reports sounded. Joey told me this helped him. Maybe it would be good for me, too. I closed my eyes, put my back to the noise, and listened. A pistol blasted nearby. Beyond it, an automatic rifle fired three-round bursts. Farther still, a bolt-action rifle thundered its larger bullets downrange and made its distinctive sound as the operator readied another.

If I played the memory in my head at the right time, Nicky Papers' shots matched the ones going on behind me. The barrage of sound hurt my ears, but I stuck with it. I went through the flashback two or three times and took a deep breath. Not wanting to run away counted as progress. I would take it. I still had a long way to go to get back to where I was. Might as well keep walking the path.

I put the ear protectors back on, popped in a new mag, and took aim at the twenty-five-yard target.

* * *

AFTER A QUICK STOP TO pick up lunch, I drove back to
Shannon Getz's house. I parked across the street and a few
houses down from hers. If she opened up for gentleman callers
again, I would see it through my windshield this time. If not, I
would enjoy a quiet place to eat. Win-win. I unwrapped my
burger and lifted it to take a bite when her front door opened.
"Shit," I muttered as I tossed it back into the bag.

A different man than the one I saw this morning walked
onto the porch. I slid down in my seat and raised my camera. I
snapped off a good shot of his face before he turned back
around. Shannon Getz stood just inside the doorway wearing
nothing but a skimpy robe she'd neglected to finish tying at the
waist. Her visitor put a hand on her breast, winked at her, and
left. I took another photo of him as Shannon disappeared back
inside. When the mystery man got into his Lincoln sedan, I
snagged a picture of his license plate.

No one came or went for a few minutes. I capitalized by
taking my burger from the bag again. It had shed much of its
lettuce—not to mention a good bit of its heat—when I tossed it
back in before. Still, it was lunch, so I ate it, lukewarm and
minimally garnished as it was. The fries fared little better. The
barbecue dipping sauce dragged them back to respectability. I
wiped my face and hands with flimsy white napkins, balled up
the brown paper bag, and tossed it onto the passenger's side
floor.

Between the food trash in my car and the pizza collection
in my office fridge, I felt like an official private detective. I only
needed a fedora and a drinking problem to level up.

About twenty minutes later, a Mercedes SUV parked in
the spot the Lincoln abandoned. A well-dressed man who
looked a few years older than me climbed out. I snapped his
picture and got another of his rear plate. His nice suit couldn't
hide his paunch. He walked up Shannon Getz's front steps and

knocked on the door. I readied my camera. She remained inside again, and a white teddy covered—to use the word loosely—the half of her body I could see. I took another couple photos as she grabbed the man's tie and pulled him across the threshold.

Forty-five minutes later, he opened the door and walked out. Shannon Getz stood in the doorway once more and blew a kiss to him as he looked back at her and smiled. Their business complete, he got back into his Benz and drove away. I waited about fifteen minutes, got out of my car, and knocked on the front door again.

Shannon Getz answered in a different teddy and a smile. The latter melted when she recognized me. "What the hell are you doing back here?"

"Expecting someone else? An investment banker this time, maybe."

"Fuck you." She pushed the door, but I blocked her from closing it with my foot. "I'll call the cops."

"Shannon," I said, "you might have just made the most ridiculous threat of the year."

She glared at me. "What do you want?"

"You in business for yourself? Or are you sending a cut to someone else?"

"Go to hell." This time, when she shoved the door, I let her close it.

CHAPTER 18

LATER, I DROPPED BY RICH'S HOUSE AFTER CALLING THE precinct and learning he'd left for the day. Sure enough, his blue Camaro sat in the driveway. I pulled alongside it, walked to the front door, and knocked. The smell of fresh paint greeted me before my cousin did. He popped the door open and struck his head through. "What's up?"

"You have a few minutes?"

Rich looked over his shoulder, then turned back to me and nodded. "Sure." I walked inside and found the living room in shambles. It lay empty for one, and much of the flooring was in various states of repair.

"Doing a little light renovation?" I asked.

"It was time. These floors were old."

The rest of the house could also be described the same way. Rich owned a vintage Victorian in the Hamilton area of Baltimore, its builders having poured the foundation at least a century ago. He'd done a few repairs and improvements over time, but this counted as the first time I saw something on this scale. "You could call me for help, you know."

"Riiiiight." Rich smirked. "I'm sure you're a regular Bob Vila."

"Is he the guy who painted the puffy clouds?"

Rich shook his head. "Bob Ross. Vila was a big home improvement guy. A little before your time, I think."

I shrugged. "I can lift things and hammer them into place. The rest is details."

"Fine." Rich walked through to the dining room, and I joined him. "Beer?" I gave him a thumbs up as I sat at the table even though our tastes in the brew department diverged. He returned with two longneck lagers. "What's on your mind?"

"You know I'm looking into the Suzie Sloan murder." Rich bobbed his head. "I wondered why O'Malley made some entries in the file early on."

"I told you it was no big deal," Rich said.

"I've done a little more digging," I said. "It turns out six women got free boob jobs from Doctor Fabian, and they weren't charity cases. They could pay. Their relationships and marriages fell apart after. I'm pretty sure one of them is prostituting herself out of her house."

Rich took a long pull of his beer. He frowned at me like he expected me to drop the hammer any minute now. "So?"

"At least one of the women was referred by Katrina O'Malley."

"As in . . .?"

"Yeah," I said. "Your lieutenant's wife. Something's going on here, Rich. I don't know what yet, but this whole situation is weird. Who performs surgery for free when people can pay for it? And why did all the women's relationships dissolve in the months following?"

"Maybe their new breasts drew a little too much attention," he said, answering the second question first.

"Maybe it was the plan all along." Rich wanted to interject, but I held up my hand and kept going. "Like I said, none of these were charity cases. They also weren't for middle-aged cougars looking to troll the bars for younger studs. All these women are in their twenties or early thirties. They're all pretty."

"You don't think pretty women can have confidence issues?"

"I spent six years in college," I said. "I know they can. This is something else . . . something sinister."

"And you think a lieutenant in the Baltimore police is involved?" Rich said as he stared at me.

"His wife certainly seems to be. Have you met her?"

"A couple times. O'Malley's not big on socializing."

"Probably because he's an asshole."

Rich rolled his eyes, though I knew he agreed on some level. "What's your point?"

"Did her appearance change between the times you saw her?" I said.

I could visualize the wheels turning in Rich's head as he paused and frowned. "She did seem a little . . . bustier the last time I ran into her."

"Something's. Going. On."

"I know you don't like O'Malley, but it doesn't make him dirty. What evidence do you have tying him to . . . whatever this is?"

"None yet," I admitted.

"So you're playing fast and loose as usual, and you expect me to believe my lieutenant is shady because you have a flimsy connection between a couple data points involving his wife."

"Well, when you put it in such uncharitable terms, it doesn't sound very good."

"You don't have anything," Rich said.

"Would you listen if I did?"

Rich narrowed his eyes. "Of course I would. Don't give me

some thin blue line bullshit. I don't want dirty cops on the force."

I drained about a quarter of my lager in a long pull. "You going to help me figure it out?"

"No." Rich shook his head. "I can't get involved at this point. You've got a bunch of speculation, and it all centers on the man's wife. Even if she's involved in something bad, it doesn't mean he is."

I expected Rich to take this position, but it still felt a little disappointing. "Fine. I'll keep digging. If I uncover something telling me your boss is dirty, I'm going to bring it to you and expect you to do something about it."

"If it's good evidence, I will," Rich said.

"All right." I slammed the rest of my beer and stood.

"You're leaving?"

"I have work to do."

"What about all your charitable lifting and hammering?" said Rich.

"I can help you with the floor, or I can go dig up dirt on your boss, but I can't do both."

"Convenient."

"It is," I said.

Rich pondered it for a minute and then jerked his head toward the front door. "Go."

I went.

* * *

I HEADED BACK HOME when my phone buzzed on the passenger's seat. Gabriella Rizzo's name popped up on the display between my speedometer and tach. I blew out a deep breath as I pondered answering. The vibration continued unimpressed with my deliberation. I pushed the answer button on the wheel.

"Hi, Gabriella."

"You've been a stranger," she said.

Her accusation carried a ring of truth. I'd indeed been a stranger, and it was entirely by design. "I'm a little busy."

"You?" Her voice brightened with mirth.

"Me. I'm on my own now, Gabriella. I guess both our circumstances changed."

"All right," she said. "I was just wondering if you wanted to drop by the restaurant. I've . . . had a little work done."

Little Italy wasn't really on my way home, but it wouldn't be too bad a detour. "Fine," I said. "Give me about fifteen minutes." I hung up. From Rich's house, I'd taken I-95 because it brought me close to Federal Hill. If planning to go to Little Italy, I would have taken Route 1 into the city instead. I exited at O'Donnell Street and worked my way back to *Il Buon Cibo*.

When I arrived, I saw a large sign for Rizzo's.

I parked in the closest spot I could get—two blocks away— and hoofed it to the rebranded restaurant. The interior underwent a remodel, too. The maitre d' station remained in the same spot, and the guy whose name I didn't know offered a familiar nod. The main dining room looked a lot different. The fake brick murals, dark colors, and round tables were gone, replaced by lighter tones and square tables. The former *Il Buon Cibo* belonged to a prior generation of Little Italy, and the new name and look solidified the fact for anyone who walked in.

Rizzo's was entirely Gabriella's, and she put a more modern stamp on it.

I looked toward the table by the fireplace where the late Tony Rizzo and I enjoyed many a chat. It was gone. "Miss Rizzo is waiting upstairs," the maitre d' said, gesturing to the short hallway. A set of steps went to the second floor, and I realized I'd never been up there in my many trips to this restaurant.

"Of course she is," I said with a confident nod as I headed

toward the next level. The narrow staircase emptied onto more hardwood floors. Another fireplace roared in the corner. The tables—square up here, as well—were partitioned off into separate banquet areas. Gabriella sat at a lone setting near the flame. She'd always been pretty, but the firelight dancing on her classic Mediterranean skin proved a nice effect. Her wavy dark hair was pulled back in a ponytail held together with a silver clasp. It lent her jeans and sweater a more professional look. She smiled as I approached.

"What do you think?"

"You might have the most modern restaurant on the block." I pulled out a chair and sat down. Little Italy had changed over the last several years, starting even before I went to Hong Kong. The classic heavy Italian dishes started sharing menu space with newer, healthier fare. As the neighborhood grew younger, the food in its famous restaurants changed to match the tastes of its younger clientele and their CrossFit lifestyles.

Gabriella smiled again, and it was her usual good one. "Thanks. I know my dad resisted change for a while. I felt it was time for an update."

"Starting with the sign on the outside," I said.

"Yeah." She wrinkled her nose. "It never fit in with names like Sabatino's and Chiaparelli's. I mean . . . 'The Good Food'? Let people come in and decide for themselves how good it is."

"Makes sense." A waiter strode up to the table.

"My father always treated you to a free meal," Gabriella said with a grin. "I guess some traditions never die."

"I guess not." I glanced at my watch. "A bit early for dinner, but . . . sure." I thought of my last time eating with Tony. A frost had grown over our once-friendly relationship. Lunches which used to feature camaraderie and laughter instead starred animosity. I hoped the same wouldn't happen with Gabriella.

"I'll keep it classic," I said to the waiter. "Chicken parm, whole wheat pasta, side Caesar."

"Very good, sir," he said, and I fought an urge to refer to him as Jeeves. He turned and walked downstairs.

"It's good to see you," Gabriella said. "I heard you're working again. You mentioned you're on your own?"

"My parents ended our arrangement," I said, "after the shoo . . . what happened."

"And you stayed on the job." She nodded. "Impressive. The city could use you."

"It can use a lot more than me."

"You're a start," she said.

"I guess I am." Our waiter returned to fill our water glasses. Not to let his effort go to waste, I took a sip.

"I miss him, you know." Gabriella looked toward the window. The last rays of sunlight bathed the skyline in bright orange. It made me think of the Orioles. When she turned back to me, her eyes glistened. "Every day."

"I'm sure you do," I said.

"I know what he did for a living, but he was a great father." I felt I needed to contribute something, so I bobbed my head. Tony had been friends with my parents for ages, and I'd known him most of my life. When our friendship soured, I never imagined he'd put a hit out on me. But he did, and it tainted my memory of him. Gabriella couldn't know any of my thoughts on the matter, of course. "You all right? You're fidgeting."

"I'm good." I forced a smile. I wondered—not for the first time—if my table companion knew her dad hired Nicky Papers to kill me. What if she did? What if she approved? Hell, what if it were her idea? Gabriella and I had been friends since we were middle school age, but she was her father's daughter, and his empire now belonged to her. I couldn't put any of it past her. These thoughts were deleterious to my mental health, so I tried to force them aside. Giving back whatever progress I'd made wouldn't benefit anyone . . . least of all me.

"All right," Gabriella said. "I just wanted to see how you were. We haven't been in the same room since Dad's funeral."

"I always hate to sound like a cliché, but I'm taking it one day at a time." I searched Gabriella's face for a sign she knew something more about what happened to me—or her father, who shot himself in front of me—than she let on. I found nothing. She'd make a heck of a poker player.

"Me, too." The waiter brought my food. Steam wafted up and the familiar smells of the restaurant's excellent food filled my nostrils. "Go ahead." Gabriella gestured toward my salad and entree. "I'll eat later."

While it might be customary to begin with the salad, I took advantage of my chicken parm being hot and cut into it. After a few minutes, I pushed half to the side to take home to Gloria. As I added pepper to my Caesar, I said, "I haven't seen Bruno here today."

"I let him go." Gabriella shrugged. "He was my dad's guy. Old school like him. I wanted some new blood."

"Good. I hated the prick. Did he go quietly?"

"He did," she said. "No animosity. I think he knew it was coming. There are plenty of other cities where he can ply his trade. He worked for my father for years. That'll give him some cachet."

"The thought of Bruno working on a résumé is funnier than I expected," I said.

Gabriella grinned. "It is."

When I finished, the waiter boxed up the rest of my food and left it on the table for me. "Thanks for the invite," I said to my hostess. "It's been good to catch up."

"It has. Don't be a stranger, C.T." We both stood, and

Gabriella wrapped me in a hug. "It's always good to have friends."

"It is," I said. As I walked away, I pondered how it was very much not good to wonder if your friends played a role in your attempted murder. Gabriella was a complication I didn't need right now, and while I enjoyed sitting and chatting with her, I hoped she wouldn't call me again until I'd put these dual cases behind me.

CHAPTER 19

AT HOME, I GAVE GLORIA A HELLO KISS, TOLD HER I LEFT her dinner in the fridge, and sat behind the desk in my home office. Having a separate place was nice, but I wanted to be in familiar confines after my impromptu dinner with the city's new organized crime queen. The Shannon Getz situation nagged at me. Either she received a lot of right swipes on Tinder or she slept with men for money. If it were the latter, a boob job would attract more suitors. But she hadn't paid for it. Hard to call it an investment in her future.

Maybe it had been a gift. My experience, however, told me men in power didn't bestow multi-thousand-dollar surgeries on younger, pretty women out of the kindness of their hearts. Shannon's current occupation wasn't the only issue, either. All of the women in relationships saw them dissolve. Marco Valdes told me Eva enjoyed a string of affairs.

What if they were something shorter-term and more trans-actional?

None of this painted Doctor Fabian in a good light, so I returned to the keylogger to see if it could provide me any additional gifts. If I were lucky, he checked his bank accounts from his work PC. As usual with a keylogger, I combed through a lot of crap I didn't care about. The tool provided a timestamp to blocks of text, and the doctor answered email at his desk at the end of the day. I skimmed them but found nothing.

A few minutes later, I got lucky.

Doctor Fabian visited a bank website and then entered a string of characters composing a decent password. I fired up an anonymous browser and entered the credentials. The surgeon maintained a primary account which saw regular payroll deposits, bills, car payments, and the usual expenses incurred by a working adult. He also kept a separate account with a much more irregular history.

Occasional deposits came in. The most recent happened to be from Shannon Getz for $215. Going down the incoming history, the names corresponded to the six women who received the good doctor's free handiwork. This clinched it: Fabian was dirty. I recalled what Charles Stanton told me, and he'd been vindicated.

Next, I checked outgoing funds. The transactions in this column didn't fit a regular pattern, either, but they all went to one person—Gannon O'Malley. "Shit," I muttered even though this counted as good news. Rich's lieutenant rolled in the mud with a shady surgeon. I took screenshots to help make the case to my cousin, whom I knew would be skeptical without something concrete. He would probably complain about how I obtained the evidence, but I knew someone in the BPD could make it work.

I wondered how O'Malley fit into this scheme. His wife referred at least one of the women, and she'd been a paying patient of the practice herself. Did the lieutenant keep the police from sniffing around? He inserted himself into Suzie Sloan's case, but to what end? Was he covering for the doctor and his wife? If so, he didn't extract any extra money for his efforts. I totaled up the payments made over the last year or so, and it came to a little shy of a hundred thousand. A tidy sum, to be sure, but not enough for a lifestyle change in a modern major city.

I couldn't prove it, but I felt confident O'Malley ordered me followed before. Now, I would get to return the favor.

* * *

First, I wanted to know more about the man whose sour demeanor and general churlishness might have inspired Nintendo to name the villain of *The Legend of Zelda* franchise after him. While I didn't have a magical sword, I could do pretty well with a laptop. Gannon and Katrina O'Malley—he a police lieutenant, she a "marketing consultant"—lived in a condo overlooking the harbor. Nice flat on an honest cop's salary, though I suspected Mrs. O'Malley plied her nebulous trade to earn more than her husband. Still, units in their building listed for a tidy sum today, and this was before one paid the parking fee to keep a car or two in the garage.

I scoured social media profiles, background checks, credit reports, and plenty of data repositories to compile as much information on the O'Malleys as I could. They'd recently refinanced their place and trimmed seven hundred a month off the mortgage. Only one car payment—a late-model Acura MDX—showed on their credit. No way O'Malley would tool around in a grocery hauler. The couple had a small circle of friends, and as far as I can tell, Katrina did the heavy lifting there. Her husband was a huge asshole, so this made sense. Mrs. O'Malley enjoyed a large professional network of people whose job descriptions were vague and their rates high. Nice work if you can get it.

Their building sat less than a mile from my house, so I bade Gloria farewell and watched it from across the street. The

MDX probably belonged to O'Malley's wife. The lieutenant would need a loud American car to help maintain his brand of boorish masculinity. I sat in just such a car, using the Caprice to better blend in with other vehicles on the road should I need to follow someone.

Despite the sun being down, lights lining the street and the exit from the O'Malleys' building provided plenty of illumination. About an hour into my vigil, a dark orange BMW coupe emerged from the garage. I used the zoom lens on my camera to help me get a good look at the driver. It was O'Malley. I pulled out behind him and immediately noted he drove a recent 8-series. The couple's credit report showed only the one car payment. Unless the lieutenant tooled around in a car confiscated from a drug dealer, he paid cash for it.

I hoped the BPD kept an eye on the finances of people who achieved certain ranks. O'Malley could probably hide some of his largesse by putting it on his wife. She ran a successful business, after all, and he couldn't be held responsible for her income. The secret account receiving dirty money from Doctor Fabian must have slipped through the cracks, and paying cash for an expensive ride wouldn't create a paper trail.

O'Malley drove his cushy coupe to Captain's Landing. I parked in the lot while he ran in, picked up takeout, and got back into his Bimmer. I snapped photos of him every step of the way. From the restaurant, O'Malley headed back home. Sure enough, he returned to the safety of his underground garage, and I got a couple more pictures of the car before it vanished down the ramp.

As I parked behind my house, I reviewed the snapshots. One showed O'Malley's rear plate clearly. It was surrounded by a plastic holder promoting a local BMW dealership. I called them on the chance they might still be open, and they were. The fellow I got transferred to in finance sounded very surprised to hear from the IRS at this hour, but he confirmed Gannon O'Malley paid cash for the car four months ago. He also hoped the lieutenant would suffer no ill effects from the government. I told him audits were fickle beasts before hanging up.

Rich would need all the evidence I gathered to listen to me. It grew late, however, and I'd already intruded on him once. It would keep until tomorrow.

* * *

After dinner and dessert, Gloria fell asleep on the couch around ten. I should've been tired, but I wasn't. Mostly, I felt annoyed. O'Malley's involvement introduced as many question as it answered, and taking him down through proper channels would require a glacial investigation from the BPD. I didn't want to wait months to get justice for Suzie and Amy Sloan. I flipped through stations looking for something to watch. In the sports range, I stopped on a boxing match. I remembered Doctor Parrish asking me about boxing specifically. She used it to segue into sparring, which I'd only done with Joey. While he'd been helpful, I really need to drag myself to the dojo and get some proper work in.

A new match began. Two men with absurd nicknames and wearing garish trunks squared off. I'd watched some MMA in my day but never got much into boxing. I was about to flip the channel when the fighter in the black shorts leaned away from his opponent's opening salvo. No one I tangled with counted as a trained fighter, and I stood there and got clobbered a few times.

I rewound the match. The opponent in green bobbed his hands, then shifted his weight and loaded up a powerful left. It was a punch he'd thrown a few thousand times. He delivered it quickly and with a lot of power behind it. The fellow in black moved his rear foot, threw his head back, and arched away from the blow. He kept his hands up the whole time.

I replayed the footage five more times. Then, I got up from the sofa and stood in the center of the living room. I took my usual stance and played the clip again. When the green-clad gladiator unleashed his left cross, I shifted my foot and leaned away. My hands dropped. No good. Even if I avoided the first attack, I left myself wide open for a follow-up punch. Getting flattened by the second strike instead of the first didn't matter much at the end of the day—I'd be on my back and in a bad spot either way.

Using the fight footage to guide me, I worked on the move. It took until the third try to get my hands to stay up. After a few more attempts, I streamlined the move with my foot, barely needing to pick it up. It also meant I transferred less weight, so I wouldn't be susceptible to someone pushing me over. The quick lean away required flexibility. I figured I would need to add some stretches to my routine. I worked on my refined version of the dodge some more.

"What are you doing?" a sleepy Gloria asked from behind me as I tangled with an imaginary opponent.

I turned and smiled down at her. "Working on solving my big problem."

"That's good," she said as her eyes drifted shut again.

I hoped it would be.

* * *

When I woke up in the morning, I called Rich as soon as I walked downstairs. "You're awake before nine," he said. "I'm impressed."

"We can't all shoot out of bed at dawn."

"You have something?"

"I do," I said, "but I'm not sure if you're going to like it."

Rich's sigh hissed in my ear. "I don't even want to guess."

"It's best if I show you. Are you working today?"

"I'm not supposed to be," Rich said. "These floors won't install themselves."

"You can do them anytime. Come see what I have."

"Is it good?"

"Yes," I said, "so bring breakfast with you for us non-early risers." I hung up and brewed a pot of coffee. Gloria wandered downstairs a few minutes later, yawned, and gave me a minty-fresh kiss. "Rich is coming soon." I grinned at her small shorts and skimpy top. "You don't need to change on my account, so I'll leave it up to you."

"I see you're not cooking." Gloria fixed her java and took a long sip. "Is Rich bringing breakfast?"

"He is."

She set her mug down. "I'll get dressed. Maybe you'll see me in this outfit later." She sashayed to the stairs, and I watched the sway of her hips with significant interest.

"I certainly hope so," I said.

Fifteen minutes later, Gloria came back down. She threw on jeans and a Brown hoodie, giving her alma mater free advertising it didn't need. Her chestnut hair which always ended up splayed on her pillow was now tamed and held in a ponytail by a decorative hair tie. The only makeup she applied was a little eyeliner. As usual, she looked terrific, and my heart quickened with joy as she walked into the living room.

I threw on a similar getup—sans ponytail and makeup, of course—and rejoined her in time for Rich to knock on the door. My cousin and Gloria shared a quick embrace before he set a bag from Panera on the kitchen counter. "I took the liberty of presuming what breakfast sandwiches you'd want," he said. "There are also a few bagels in here in case I got it wrong."

"I'm sure it's fine," I said. I let Gloria choose something first, and I grabbed something appearing dark and greasy even through the tan wax paper wrapper. Sure enough, it turned out to be a bacon, egg, and cheese sandwich on a whole grain bagel. Rich poured himself a mug of coffee, and the three of us sat at my small kitchen table.

"Give me the summary," Rich said.

"All right. Doctor Fabian is dirty, some women who got free boob jobs from him are prostituting themselves, and your boss is getting a cut." Gloria's eyes widened, and she picked up her coffee and sandwich.

"This sounds like a serious conversation," she said. "I'll leave you to it." I realized I hadn't told her about the recent developments in my case. Early in our relationship, Gloria never wanted to know what went on. Over time, she took more of an interest in my work, and began doing her own as a fundraiser. Ever since, she knew about my investigations before most other people did, and she'd proven a very useful sounding board on more than one occasion.

"Did you hear me?" Rich asked.

"No." I pulled my gaze from Gloria—who now sat in the living room—and looked at Rich. "Sorry, what?"

"I said . . . how do you know O'Malley is getting a cut?"

"My usual methods." Rich rolled his eyes. "I know what you're thinking. You almost never approve of the things I do. I have printouts, though. Let me get them." I fetched them from the office and dropped the small stack onto the tabletop. "The first few are from the doctor's hidden account. You can see incoming payments from six women. They're the ones who went under the knife for free."

Rich sipped his coffee and stared at the paper. "Should I ask how you happened to gain access to a surgeon's financials?"

"No," I said. "You'd be better off wondering how he set up this little operation. Six women got free breast surgery, saw their relationships end, and now make regular payments to the man who operated on them. I watched one of them for a while. She's either the most popular woman in the history of Tinder or she's turning tricks out of her house."

"Maybe it's a payment plan for the surgeries," Rich said.

I shook my head. "Two strikes against it. One, the payments are rarely for the same amount. The schedule is a little loose, but even if we ignore it, why is the money random? Two, this is an account I'm pretty sure Fabian doesn't advertise. He doesn't use it for anything else."

"All right." Rich pointed to the papers. "I presume the rest of what you have goes toward implicating my boss."

"Pretty much," I said, flipping the page. "Remember when I told you his wife referred one of the women?" My cousin nodded. "Maybe she knew she had a good thing going. Gannon O'Malley has been getting discreet payments from Doctor Fabian for over a year and a half. It roughly coincides with the second woman's surgery."

"How much are we talking?" I tapped the total at the bottom of the sheet. Rich frowned. "Fuck."

"Yeah, it's a lot. I followed him from his condo last night. What kind of car does he drive to work?"

"A Mustang, I think."

A loud American car. I had the man pegged. "He wasn't in a Mustang last night," I said. "He drove a BMW Eight-series coupe. A car which doesn't appear on his credit report, by the way, so I was thinking he paid cash for it." I pointed to the sum again. "Exactly how much it costs depends on options and all, but you can expect to pay at least ninety grand, and it could top a hundred. The dealership confirmed the transaction, by the way."

"Cash?"

"Four months ago."

Rich blew out a deep breath. "I can't sit on this. I need to take it to internal affairs, but I don't think I can use a lot of what you have considering how you probably got it."

"Uncover it yourself, then." I put a hand over my face and tried my best Elvis impression. "This is an anonymous tip."

"Flimsy," Rich said with a smirk, "but I'll see what I can do. There's a lot of scrutiny on the police now. We don't need a corruption scandal. Handling this in-house and getting O'Malley out quietly would be best."

"I told you he was an asshole," I said.

Rich nodded. "Yeah, you did."

CHAPTER 20

A SHORT WHILE AFTER RICH LEFT, MY PHONE RANG. THE
number looked familiar, but I couldn't place it. The halting,
"Mister Ferguson?" I heard when I answered also didn't shine
any light on the caller's identity. After a moment, she added,
"It's Tara Mayfield."

"Good morning, Miss Mayfield," I said. "I admit I'm
surprised to hear from you. You sounded very much like you
didn't want to talk to me the last time I got you on the phone."

"I know." She paused. "I wasn't expecting a detective to call
me and ask about Doctor Fabian. I guess I was surprised to hear
from you, too."

"What can I do for you?" I asked.

"You said you're looking into something the doctor's
involved in?"

"I am."

"Can I ask what it is?" she said in a quiet tone.

"Is someone there with you?"

"No. No, I'm alone."

I wasn't sure I believed her, but calling Tara Mayfield a liar
at the moment would only ensure she would curse me out and
hang up on me again. "All right. Someone beat his former

assistant to death. I have some questions about the work she did for him and his patients."

"That poor woman," she said. "I couldn't believe it when I heard. You don't think Doctor Fabian is involved, do you?"

"I'm not sure what to think at this point," I said. Something seemed fishy about this whole conversation, but I would play along. "The police arrested a suspect, but I don't think he did it."

Tara Mayfield sighed. "I'd like to talk to you. The surgery you mentioned? I was the first woman to get it for free." I already knew this, but I didn't interject. "I don't know if what I can tell you will help your case, but I'd like to try."

"All right. Where would you like me to meet you?"

"There's a small coffee shop in Lutherville . . . Rise and Grind. You know it?"

"I'll find it," I said. "When?"

She paused again. "Can you do a half-hour?"

I wondered if I would meet anyone besides her. "I think so. See you there."

We hung up. I made sure to strap a holstered 9MM around my waist before I put my jacket on and left.

* * *

RISE AND GRIND occupied what must've been a house decades ago. It sat along York Road next to yet another strip mall with at least one store or eatery closed. Windows on the upper floors had the curtains drawn, and it made me wonder if the proprietor lived above the business. From the outside, the first floor appeared spacious enough to seat a fair number of guests. A narrow road ran alongside the shop, leading to a lot in the rear. I parked the S4 and got out.

An attractive blonde woman stepped out of a Honda SUV

about twenty feet away. She tucked a lock of hair behind her ear and flashed me a smile which didn't make it to her eyes. "Mister Ferguson?"

"The one and only."

"Thanks for meeting me on such short notice." She started toward the cafe, and I fell in line beside her. No windows faced the parking area, and only a single door led here. As I pondered her reasons for choosing such a secluded location, a car zipped into the lot and parked behind Tara Mayfield's vehicle. Two men who looked like they could toss her SUV to the side if they wanted the space got out. "I'm sorry," she whispered as she scampered back to her ride.

"Guys, I need to try the coffee before I can leave a Yelp review," I said. "You'll be able to see it when it goes live, though."

"You been told to give it a rest," the one on the left said. They both stood a little shorter than me, though their muscle-bound frames meant they outweighed me by about eighty pounds each. Both men wore their hair very short, and their similar features led me to wonder if they were related. The mouthpiece of the pair braved the elements in a light windbreaker. His partner wore a heavier coat and a scarf.

"You two cousins or something?" No answer. "Brothers? Maybe your family tree is just a straight line?"

"We ain't related," the other one said, and his frown told me I'd offended him. Too bad.

As they drew closer, my pulse picked up. The back of my throat felt dry. I fell into a ready stance out of habit. They both eyed me up, and the oaf in the light jacket stepped up. "This is your last warning," he said as he drew his fist back. His hips twisted, and his hand surged forward.

My back foot shifted a little, and I fought the urge to flinch, instead leaning away from his right hook. My living room practice in front of the TV worked. The two goons afforded me no time to celebrate my achievement, however, as Scarf Guy joined the fray. They were big and strong, and both knew how to get power behind their punches, but whoever hired this pair paid them for brawn over skill. After blocking a few volleys, Scarf Guy's neckwear came loose and hung out of his coat. I grabbed the ends and pulled him toward me just in time for his friend to clobber him in the face. He looked stunned as his partner dropped like a stone.

I capitalized by kicking him squarely in the midsection. He folded in half at the waist. I elbowed him in the face, then twice more in the side of the head. To his credit, he wobbled but didn't capsize. A hard kick to the mouth bounced his head off the car and put him on the ground. The other guy stirred. His scarf finally came off in the fray. He rubbed his jaw and sat up, which gave me an opening to drive my knee into his face. He joined his partner in dreamland.

For the first time in a while, I made it through a physical altercation without flinching. Even so, I wondered if the opening dodge I learned watching boxing would be part of my new routine. Maybe Doctor Parrish could illuminate it all for me. Focusing on the here and now, I rummaged through each man's pockets, snapping a picture of their licenses and finding the car keys in the jeans of Windbreaker Guy. I heaved them as far as I could toward the nearby strip mall, and they clattered to a stop somewhere behind the building. The goon's car boxed Tara Mayfield in. She couldn't get out without attempting about a thirty-point turn.

It seemed like a good time to have our overdue conversation.

* * *

Tara Mayfield's passenger door was locked. She stared at me as I tried to open it. Undaunted, I returned to the unconscious pair of alleged enforcers, snatched the discarded scarf, and wrapped it around my elbow. When I reached her SUV again, I rapped on the glass. "We need to chat, Tara. Open up." She shook her head.

I drove my enveloped elbow into the window. It still hurt, but the glass shattered. I reached inside, opened the door, and used the scarf to sweep shards from the seat. I got in and shut the door behind me. Tara Mayfield regarded me with wide eyes. "I have mace," she said.

"Good for you." I patted the left side of my jacket. "I have a pistol. Who do you think would win the exchange?"

"I'll call the cops." Defeat edged into her voice.

"You're the second person to make the threat while in a completely untenable position." I cracked my knuckles and crossed my feet as much as the vehicle's legroom allowed. "Go ahead. I'm sure they'll be very interested to talk to you."

Tara stared out the windshield for several seconds. She probably figured this would go differently. Tweedledee and Tweedledum would beat me down, and she'd be able to go on living her life. Now, I sat a foot away from her, and reality sank in. "What do you want?" she said in a voice barely above a whisper.

"The truth. Tell me what's going on with Doctor Fabian and the women who got free boob jobs . . . including you."

"I didn't go there for surgery," she said. "I wanted to get a couple of moles removed."

"And he offered breast augmentation as a free upgrade?"

"He told me I was beautiful." A wistful smile played on Tara's lips. "My boyfriend at the time almost never paid me a compliment." She paused, and I stayed silent in the hopes she'd keep talking. "I know it sounds silly." I again didn't say anything, though I would've agreed. "Doctor Fabian told me I could get a lot more attention with larger breasts. I was a B at the time . . . I'm a D now."

"How did the offer of doing it for free come about?" I asked.

"He told me I could pay him back in other ways." Tara shot me a sidelong glance. "I knew what he meant. I just didn't care. I couldn't have afforded it otherwise, I was unhappy in my relationship, and I looked at the surgery as an investment in a new me going forward." A tear slid down her cheek, and she shook her head. "I was a damn fool."

She kept a pack of tissues in the console. I offered her one, and she accepted it with a small smile of acknowledgment. "What happened next?"

"I spent a few weeks recovering. At my last checkup, Fabian gave me a clean bill of health and told me it was time to start paying off my debt."

"You had sex with him," I said.

Tara bobbed her head slightly. "Yeah." She trailed off again. I was going to follow up, but she pre-empted me. "At first, it was just him."

I hadn't expected this turn in the conversation. "Are you saying other people joined you?"

She grimaced. "God, no. Nothing like that. I mean . . . Fabian had friends. They wanted to sleep with me, too."

"What did you want, Tara?" She stifled a cry and dabbed at her eyes again. "I thought so."

"None of them were violent," she said. "It . . . wasn't bad. I know I'm rationalizing. They weren't old perverts or anything. They all had nice houses or apartments. He even paid me a little."

"Only a little?" I said.

"Yeah. This went on for a couple months. It's taken me a while to realize he was pimping me out, but I know now. He probably put me with six or seven guys. Then, he said I could strike out on my own so long as I gave him a cut."

I checked the side mirror. No one had come into the lot or emerged from the cafe, but I didn't know how long these twin strokes of good fortune would continue. The two idiots behind us still lay on the asphalt. "Did you?"

Tara closed her eyes. "For a while." She took a deep breath, one I figured served to buck her up for the rest of the story. "The money was OK, and I needed it. Made it hard to leave. I kept giving him his cut, but I felt dirty. I stopped a few months in. He tried to lean on me a couple times, but I think he knows I have dirt on him."

"Let me guess," I said. "You went to him after I contacted you, and today's setup was his idea."

"Yeah."

This established the dirt on Doctor Fabian, but I already knew him to be a slimeball. "You ever hear the name O'Malley?"

"A woman," Tara said after a moment of thought. "I think she had a boob job, too. She paid for it, though. I saw her in the office a couple times."

"Not her husband?"

She shook her head. "She was alone. Why?"

"Just hoping I could take down two slimy birds with one stone." I looked over at Tara Mayfield. In a different context—when she hadn't conspired to have two goons try and beat me down—I would've called her pretty. Despite a lapse in judgment, she probably wasn't an idiot. She could do a lot better than this sordid situation. "You said you kept it up because you needed the money. Was the same true for the other women?"

"I don't know. We didn't exactly have a club. If I had to guess . . . I think it's likely. Fabian would have chosen us wisely."

He picked or stumbled upon one woman of means, but it didn't seem to shake him. "Don't take the doctor's calls anymore. I'm going to bring him down." I opened the door and stepped out of the SUV.

"What do I do about the two guys behind me?" She gestured out her rear window. "And their car?"

"You brought them here." I shrugged and shut the window-less door. "You solve the problem." I walked back to my S4, got in, and drove away.

CHAPTER 21

I DROVE BACK TO MY OFFICE. DOCTOR FABIAN WAS DIRTY. I'd suspected it for a while but getting the confirmation was nice. Being an asshole who took advantage of women didn't make him a killer, however. I still needed to connect a few dots. It had been a while since I talked to Amy Sloan, so I called her. "I was hoping you'd be able to tell me something," she said.

"I can. I know it's been a while, and you probably thought I worked as slowly as the police. Some questions have come up, though, and I'm wondering if you can help me."

"I'll try."

"Did Suzie ever talk bad about her boss?" I asked.

"I don't think so." Amy sighed. "Maybe here and there. I mean . . . no one gets along with their boss all the time, right?"

"I'm self-employed, and sometimes even I think my boss is a jerk."

She chuckled. "She probably complained here and there, but I don't think I remember a specific time." Amy paused, and I guessed the reason I posed the question sank in. "Why?"

"Doctor Fabian is . . . involved with some bad things," I said. "I know he claims he had to let Suzie go over some insurance mistake. My current theory is he realized she was on to him, and he canned her before she figured it all out."

"I guess he could have," Amy said. "Suzie never mentioned anything about Doctor Fabian being into something shady. What's he wrapped up in?"

"I'd rather not say," I told her. "The less you know about his activities, the better. I didn't see anything on Suzie's social media about this. Did she have a blog or somewhere she might've written about it?"

"No, I don't think so. It took me months to convince her she should be on Facebook. You know . . . Suzie used to say she kept notes at work."

"Like in a notebook?"

"No," Amy said. "I think she meant on her computer. Suzie's handwriting was terrible. If she could avoid using pen and paper, she would."

Of course. I hadn't considered files Suzie herself might've created and maintained. I only focused on the ones belonging to the six women because they were encrypted. Suzie may have left behind a trove for me to explore, and I still maintained an illicit connection to the PC she used. "All right. Thanks, Amy. I'm probably close to wrapping this up. I'll let you know when I do."

"Oh, thank you!" she said. "It'll be the best news I've gotten in a long time."

I broke the connection. Amy Sloan definitely needed some good news in her life, and I was determined to deliver it to her.

* * *

WHEN I INSTALLED the keylogger onto Doctor Fabian's PC, I used the account name and hashed password used by Digital Sales, the company which maintained all the office equipment.

They created an administrative credential to do the typical tasks requiring privileged access. All told, their setup was good. I couldn't fault them for a Windows vulnerability, but I could exploit it to find what I needed.

My remote access program let me enter credentials over the wire, and it understood how to pass hashes for authentication. I used the digitalsalestech account name and the one-way hash value from before. A DOS prompt awaited my commands. First, I changed directories into the Users folder and looked for the handles. I navigated into the ssloan directory. The typical files and folders in a standard Windows user account stared back at me. I poked around.

Suzie was smart. She created a hidden folder, and I found a notes.txt file inside it. Even if Doctor Fabian used an administrative account, he would still need to know the directory existed and be able to unhide it. I transferred the file to my computer and opened it in a text editor. It didn't take long to stumble upon something interesting.

Doc is bad at closing his door all the way. He's really easy to overhear. He also doesn't know about the intercom on the phone.

I heard Doc tell a woman she could get a free boob job. WTF? If I want any surgery, I only get a small discount.

A second woman got her boobs done for free. They're both really pretty. Don't see why they need any work done. This is weird.

Doc might be in over his head. Some woman named Katrina said her husband is a cop, and they would need to have a conversation.

A third woman now. I wonder what's going on. These aren't charity cases. I hate to think things like this, but I wonder why Doc is really doing these surgeries. He charges a lot of money for them normally. Can't just be for sex???

This is a shit economy to go looking for a job, but I may need to.

I think I met the cop today. He's kind of an asshole. I thought he might know the intercom trick, so I just listened to them in the office. Sounded like he and Doc made some kind of arrangement.

I should quit, but I'm too curious.

Two more women this week. Five all together. Doc and the cop talk here and there, too. I think Doc is paying him off, but I don't want to get too curious about it. He doesn't seem to know I suspect anything.

Had my annual review today. Doc spent a lot of time talking about HIPAA, discretion, etc. I wonder if he suspects I've overheard some of his weird conversations.

I wonder if Doc would give me a good reference after all this.

A sixth woman just got a free boob job. This is really strange. Doc does some occasional charity work. I wish he'd do more. It's always small stuff. These are major operations.

The cop gave me the side-eye when he came in with his wife today. Maybe it's really time to look for a new job. I wonder what's going on, but I don't want to get in trouble if Doc is dirty.

Doc is complaining about insurance. Something about the practice not being listed correctly. I wonder if he's looking for a reason to get rid of me.

THE FILE ENDED THERE. Suzie definitely suspected something. I could only speculate, but it sounded like Doctor Fabian made up or exaggerated the insurance angle to find a reason to get rid of his assistant. O'Malley giving her the side-eye was ominous, too. It helped explain why his wife recruited other women. More people involved would bring in additional money, some of which Fabian funneled to the lieutenant.

Between this and the transactions in O'Malley's private account, we could take him down. I wondered what kind of progress Rich made on it from his end.

* * *

I TEXTED Rich but didn't get a reply. He must have been busy on the streets. I knew he wanted to take down O'Malley, and even though I kept my message cryptic, I figured he'd get back to me when he could. As I pondered this, my phone buzzed. I thought it might be Rich calling, but a 602 number showed on the caller ID.

"Doctor Parrish, I presume?" Once I answered, her video feed appeared. I hoped this would be quick in case Rich got back to me. I appreciated Parrish's time but didn't want to spare a lot of my own at the moment.

"I have a few minutes between appointments," she said. "I wanted to see how you're doing."

"Right as rain," I said. One of these times, I would believe it. I came closest today.

"We don't get a lot of precipitation in the desert. Explain it to me."

"I've been working on my struggles, and I might've found a way to overcome them."

She eyed me skeptically, and I could feel the stare even from two thousand miles away. "I want to correct you on two things. First, if you're talking about flinching, you've been treating the symptom. Second, overcoming shouldn't be your goal here. You've been through a lot. Things may never completely get back to the way they were before. You're probably looking at a new normal. I don't like the term much, but it applies."

"Wow, Doc,"I said. "I didn't know they handed out advanced degrees in wet blanket."

"Call me what you want," she said, "but it's true. There's nothing wrong with focusing on the symptom for now. I know it's holding you back in your job. You'll need to move past it at some point, though. Your life has changed."

"Do you even want to hear what I did?"

She leaned back in her chair. "Sure."

"I guess my 'new normal' is the instinct to flinch when a fight starts. It's cost me a couple of hits I shouldn't have taken. Recently, I watched boxing, and one of the fighters leaned away from the first punch."

"And you were able to do this?" she asked.

I nodded. "I'd practiced a bunch of times. Getting the move down wasn't too bad. I wanted to practice it doing some sparring, but I didn't get the chance. The first test came in the field."

"It sounds like you passed."

"I did," I said. "Considering where I've been, I'm going to call it a victory."

"I want you to," she said. "Despite you thinking me a wet blanket, I want you to recover. A big part of that is realizing it's a process, not a single hurdle to overcome. Be proud of your progress, but I'm going to guess you still have more work to do. What about guns?"

"I went to the range recently. It was the first time since I got shot." I thought about my trip there and how weird the whole thing felt. Joey's advice had been golden, however. "I'm still pretty good with a nine, though I was a little rusty at first."

"What about everyone else around you? All their rounds going off?"

"I took it all in," I said. "I slipped off the ear protection, turned my back to the rest of the range, and just listened."

Parrish pursed her lips and nodded slowly. "Not a therapeutic method I would endorse, but it sounds like it worked for you."

"A friend suggested it."

"Maybe your friend should charge by the hour," Parrish said.

"I have to feed him. He makes out better as much as he eats."

"Do you want something to work on next?"

"I was hoping to bask in my most recent triumph," I said, "at least for a couple days."

"Far be it from me to stop you," she said, "but I'm going to give something to work toward when you're finished gloating."

"Fine," I said with a theatrical sigh. "What is it?"

"Learn to be patient with yourself." I frowned at the platitude. Parrish filled the conversational gap when I didn't reply. "I think I mentioned it before. Maybe you'll take it to heart this time. When you were here in Arizona, you were basically at zero. A full stop. You want to get back up to a hundred miles an hour right away. Recovery doesn't work like that no matter how much you want it to."

"Maybe I'm not at a hundred yet. I feel I should be doing at least eighty-five in third gear."

"It takes time," Parrish reiterated. She held up her hands and slowly moved them up and down. "If you're in second near the redline, be all right with it."

I grinned. "I didn't know you liked cars, Doc."

"You didn't see my Corvette in the parking lot when you were here? It's bright red and has a seven-speed manual."

"If I ever make it back out there, I hope you'll let me take her for a spin."

"All right," Parrish said, "so long as you learn to take this at its own pace. Recovery from trauma doesn't have an accelerator. You need to be patient and forgive yourself if there's a setback."

"All right," I said, "I'll do it. If it gets me behind the wheel of a 'Vette."

"I hoped your motivation would be closer to home," Parrish said, "but I'll take it."

So would I.

* * *

* * *

I sent another text to Rich but still got no reply. Again, I got a call a few minutes later. This time, it came from Liz Fleming. Considering I worked for her as a paid investigator—for a case already on my docket—she probably wanted an update. "Of course I want to know what's going on," she said when I asked.

"I'm still finding the right forms to fill out in triplicate. And I probably need a dot matrix printer to help."

"C.T., this is no joke."

"I know," I said. "Have you tried finding a dot matrix these days?"

She sighed in my ear, and I pictured her rubbing the bridge of her nose. "Do you still think the boyfriend is innocent?"

"As much as I don't like him, he didn't kill Suzie."

"I'm going to need more than your word on it," Liz said.

"Working on it," I said. "Right now, the leader in the clubhouse is her boss."

"The doctor?" Enough skepticism dripped over the connection I checked my phone for moisture.

"There's something very sordid going on there. I'm still unraveling it all, and it reaches beyond Suzie's murder."

"For Christ's sake," she said, "I hoped this one would be easy."

"Telling you Glenn is innocent is pretty simple. The rest of it . . . not so much. The police are going to get involved. I'm not sure how much more I should say."

"You're working for me. I want it all."

"All right," I said. "Fabian gave six women free boob jobs and pimped them out. Along the way, he got on the radar of a police lieutenant and paid him off to keep the scheme going. The lieutenant's wife recruited at least one of the women."

Liz fell silent for a few seconds. Her exasperated breathing served as the only sign she remained on the line. "You're gonna need to type all that up. I need as much proof as you can get it . . . especially if you got it legally." She paused. "Yes, I know who I'm asking. I can't go in front of a judge with some convoluted story about a respected surgeon running a little prostitution business on the side. I need to be able to prove it."

"Good thing I'm fast on the keyboard, then," I said. "If I can get this over to you, do you think you can spring Glenn tonight?"

"I don't know," Liz said. "Maybe. Tomorrow morning at worst."

"All right. I'll get to work. I'm billing you for these hours."

"Good thing you're fast on the keyboard," Liz said and hung up.

"Touché," I said to the empty line, and I got to work.

CHAPTER 22

AFTER A FURIOUS ROUND OF TYPING AND EMAILING, I WAS about to pack it up for the day when I heard someone coming up the stairs. While they were a noisy eyesore, they also provided a lot more notice than my old setup. I opened the top drawer of my desk, took out the .45, and held it as the door swung open to reveal Elliot Allen.

He probably wanted an update, too. I kept the gun on him a second longer than I needed to before setting it atop the desk. Let him see it while he came in here and tried to play tough middle manager. Allen frowned at me a moment, looked at the gun, and eventually moved to a guest chair. "Expecting someone else?" he said as he plopped down.

"I'm trying to be more welcoming when someone comes in," I said. "Guess I still have some work to do."

"Yes," Allen said with a pointed stare. "You certainly do. My client is not used to being ignored, Mister Ferguson."

I leaned back in my chair. "Let me tell you exactly how much I care about your client's feelings."

"Regardless, we're paying you for a job, and you're not doing it. You didn't present me with a contract, so we can probably cancel our payment. The hospital keeps good lawyers on retainer, by the way, so good luck challenging it in court."

"I've got a pretty damn good attorney, myself," I said. A couple months ago, James Snyder supervised my resurrection under the law after I got declared dead to protect my family. If he managed legal Lazarus legerdemain, he could wipe the courtroom floor with whatever stuffed shirt the hospital would trot out. "I don't think it'll be necessary, though. I've observed Mister Stanton several times."

"Are you waiting to file the report?" Allen said.

"You know I'm also investigating a murder."

"Your time management is your problem."

"The stairs are going to be your problem," I said, "when I toss you down them. Murder comes first. It's a complicated case, and let's just say a few people have tried to dissuade me from continuing to work it."

Allen rolled his eyes as if he were some feudal lord indulging a peasant with a wild story. "Very well. When can we expect your report?"

"You'll have it by tomorrow," I said.

"What, if I may ask, will it tell us?"

"I don't do spoilers."

"I'll look forward to reading it." Allen regarded me with an inscrutable look as he stood. "By close of business tomorrow, then, or we look into revoking your pay."

"How are your company's firewalls?" I said.

"Excuse me?"

"Have a nice day, Mister Allen." I imbued a smile with as much fake sincerity as I could—this was a lot in my current mood. "Be careful on the stairs. Wouldn't want you to fall."

He left without another word. I didn't care if Charles Stanton lied about workman's comp and robbed the place blind at night. I would never side with an empty suit like Elliot Allen.

Once he got my report, I wondered if he would try to withhold the other half of my pay.

He was a prick. He probably would.

* * *

BECAUSE THE UNIVERSE wanted to make my day even longer, Rich finally got back to me once I sat behind the wheel. He asked if I could drop by the station. I said I would. When I walked inside a short while later, my cousin was not at his desk. Paul King sat at his, however, and he jerked his thumb in the air. "Upstairs . . . Captain Sharpe's office."

"Must be serious," I said.

"Must be," he said. "They don't tell me shit until it's all figured out."

I took the elevator up and exited onto the floor where BPD bigwigs like Captain Leon Sharpe hung their hats. Despite numerous shakeups and an ass-kicking from the federal Department of Justice over the last several years, Sharpe survived as an old-school cop in a city constantly embracing the new thing. He headed up violent crimes enforcement, and his preferred methods of kicking in doors and cracking skulls should have earned him a pink slip two commissioners ago. He remained, however, which probably meant he knew where a lot of bodies were buried. I hoped the corpses were metaphorical.

Sharpe was a massive man, and opening his office door reminded me. He stood about six-six, weighed at least 270 pounds, and his physique suggested he bench pressed old cars for fun. His bald black head reflected the overhead light. Rich sat in one of the captain's guest chairs, so I took the other. "Nice of you to join us," Sharpe said in a voice matching his overall size.

"I hope I'm not here only to find out O'Malley's getting kicked to internal affairs."

"No. They'll be involved because they have to be. We'll be involved because a woman is dead."

"We're running point," Rich added.

"I admit I'm kind of surprised," I said.

Sharpe grinned. "I can be very persuasive."

I pictured some scrawny IA lieutenant folded in half and stuffed into a trash can. "I don't doubt it, Leon. What's the game plan?"

"We have a warrant," he said, tapping a paper on his desk with a meaty finger. "I want to keep looking into O'Malley and this Doctor Fabian both. Whatever shit they're involved in, they're doing it together."

"I'm a little surprised you don't want to grab O'Malley in the middle of the night and make him sweat."

"We're doing it right," Sharpe said. "O'Malley's no dummy. He's been a cop a long time. He'd lawyer up and try to poke holes in everything. I want bad cops off the street as much as anyone, but we have to dot every I and cross each T."

"Agents of the system know how to circumvent it," I said.

Sharpe frowned. "A little Orwellian for me, but . . . well, you're not wrong. How's your case coming?"

I shrugged. "Fabian's slimy. As far as I can tell, he gave six women free boob jobs and then basically whored them out. I don't know how long the arrangement lasted. At least one of them is still doing it."

"Do you know how O'Malley fits into it?" asked Rich.

"Not entirely," I said. "My suspicion is he caught wind of it and threatened to shut the doc down unless he got a cut. His wife got a boob job there, but as far as I know, she paid for it. O'Malley's cashed quite a few of Fabian's checks, though . . . enough to drive a nice new eight-series coupe."

Sharpe frowned. "He didn't list it on his disclosure forms."

"Don't make a big deal of it, Leon. IA might jump us if they know he lied on his paperwork."

"I'll see about getting a warrant for Fabian, too," Rich said.

"We probably won't be able to do much until tomorrow," the captain said. "Why don't you both go home? Rich, I'll see you in the morning. C.T., stay by your phone in case we need you to do something."

"You will," I said.

Sharpe rolled his eyes. "We solved plenty of crimes before you came along."

"But you didn't look as good doing it. Style points count, too, Leon."

He waved his hand and dismissed Rich and me from his office. "Want to get a beer?" Rich asked as we rode the elevator down.

"Not tonight. It's been a long day."

"I was gonna offer to pay." Rich grinned. "With you being a working stiff like the rest of us now."

"Rain check," I said as we exited into the short hallway which would take us to the parking lot. I got into my car, headed toward home, and hoped this would be the last job-related intrusion of the day.

* * *

GLORIA HAD RETURNED at some point, and she and I enjoyed a quiet night. I cooked a simple chicken curry for dinner and yawned my way through something Gloria wanted to watch. On the third occasion she told me I looked tired, I called it a night. She remained downstairs, and I fell asleep before she joined me. Before I got shot, I didn't remember tiring so easily. Maybe it was a combination of being over thirty and still in some stage of recovery. At this rate, I'd need an elevator in my house before I turned forty.

I ran from Federal Hill Park across Light Street. The carousel and Maryland Science Center were on my left. Despite a lingering fall briskness to the air, I felt plenty warm as I pounded the red pavement near the harbor. The pavilions loomed ahead. I remembered thinking they were cool in my youth. Since then, shops and restaurants came and went, and the buildings entered receivership, which was very much not cool.

Someone stepped out from between the pavilions. I saw the gun, but it was far too late to do anything about it. A shot broke the quiet and tore into my left side. People ran around in a panic. I figured I couldn't elude the shooter inside a building, so I turned toward the water. Pain now flooded my senses. More reports barked out behind me.

Another hit me. Left side of the back. Down I went.

I scrabbled to my feet as chaos ensued. The harbor managed to be close and far away at the same time. Somehow, I made it without taking a third bullet. The cold water shocked my system. I stayed under as long as I could, but it wasn't very long. I swam out as far as I could, but it wasn't very far. My strength deserted me by the second. I waved to a water taxi a few times before going under.

Instead of sinking to the bottom, I plopped down in an alley. The two goons who chased me a few days ago rounded a turn behind me and shouted, giving me no time to evaluate the weirdness of my situation. I took off, uninjured and hauling ass at full speed. Before I could pull away, they opened fire. Two shots hit me in the left side of the back. I went down hard on the concrete. From the rear, they strolled toward me like they had all the time in the world.

Somehow, I made it back to my feet. They didn't appear

interested in giving chase, which was a good thing as I hobbled along at far less than full speed. At some point, my limbs grew heavy, and my head became light. A thought about duality fluttered in and out of my head as I staggered into someone's yard and collapsed.

Instead of hitting the ground, I landed on an operating table. Machines beeped and booped all around me. An IV tube ran into my arm. A nurse stood with her back to me. I tried to ask her a question, but my voice didn't work. My wrists and ankles were bound to the rails. The nurse turned around.

I stared into the brutalized face of Suzie Sloan.

A door whipped open, and a doctor I couldn't see scrubbed up for surgery. He whistled a song whose name escaped me. A moment later, he dried his hands and arms and approached the table. Neal Fabian smiled like a devil down at me. "Don't worry . . . we'll get you all fixed up."

I found myself sitting in bed, breathing heavily. Sweat covered my forehead and neck. Beside me, Gloria stirred but didn't wake up. I let her be as I situated myself under the covers again. In my mind's eye, I saw Doctor Parrish telling me to treat this as a warning sign. I'd never been a big fan of attaching meaning to dreams, especially not one so absurd in many parts. A quick look at my phone showed me the time was 3:40. I nestled into the pillow and tried to get back to sleep.

I woke at eight forty-five and felt like I'd barely slept. Gloria, of course, snored quietly. I sat on the edge of the bed, rubbed my bleary eyes, and stood. I felt like a zombie as I walked downstairs and put a pot of coffee on, and even the wonderful aroma of brewing caffeine didn't make a difference. I poured a cup and drank some. Not much better. Maybe cooking would help.

Gloria made her way to the first floor while sausage sizzled in the skillet. By the time she'd kissed me a few times, fixed herself a cup of coffee, and sat at the table, the toast was ready, too. I set out a few hardboiled eggs I'd prepared a few nights ago, and we enjoyed a simple breakfast. Gloria broke the silence quickly. "You have a rough night?"

I nodded around a mouthful of egg. "Bad dream," I said when my manners told me it was OK to talk.

"About the shooting?"

"More or less. Probably tied to my recovery, too." I went into the details with her.

"Wow," she said. "You weren't kidding. That's a weird one. What do you think it means?"

"Probably to avoid jumping in the harbor," I said. Gloria stared at me. "I don't know. I've never put a lot of stock into what dreams mean. Once you get past a few obvious explanations, it all sounds like poppycock. I'm sure it's my brain processing everything . . . including being back to work." I added the last bit before she could.

"You already know how I feel." Gloria sipped some coffee. "Maybe you could at least take it easy after this?"

"I'll try." I would, but Gloria and I both knew I couldn't refuse someone who really needed my help.

After breakfast, I eschewed driving for a stroll down the hall to the home office. I went through the pictures of Charles Stanton on my phone and camera. It was time to put his case behind me and get Elliot Allen off my back. The Sloan case was going critical mass soon, and I didn't need to divide my attention. In the end, I really didn't care if a nurse who needed a break cheated a stingy hospital and the stooge their insurance company sent to guarantee the desired outcome.

I selected several pictures. A couple showed Stanton trimming his bushes with a small pair of shears. I cropped the power trimmer out. A few others showed him with paint cans and brushes. Nothing too heavy. Nothing too physically taxing. Allen and his fellow bean counters could run this before whatever medical advisory board they employed, and they'd get told these were light-duty activities.

Once I'd chosen all the photos, I attached them to an email.

DEAR MISTER ALLEN,

I've attached several photos of Charles Stanton. I'm no doctor and neither are you, but I think you'll agree the light effort he's exerting is in bounds for someone with a back injury.

At no point did I observe Mister Stanton perform demanding physical labor which would make me question his injury.

What I question is your sincerity. I found out I'm the third private investigator your company has hired to try and punch a hole in Mister Stanton's claims. The third time will not be the charm. I'm not here to satisfy your company's apparent vendetta against a nurse whom I'm sure worked hard at his very difficult job.

Please remit payment to the address in my signature block or use the email for electronic payments. I probably didn't give you the results you were seeking. I don't care. The other two detectives didn't, either, and I hope you didn't stiff them.

Should a dispute over payment arise, my attorney is James Snyder. If your lawyers are local, ask them about him and his firm. If they want to take him on, I'll be happy to see you in court and eat your proverbial lunch.

I trust you and your company will leave Mister Stanton alone now. I plan to check in on him and be sure.

. . .

SINCERELY,

C.T. Ferguson

PART of me hoped he played tough and tried to withhold the rest of my money. James' fees were usurious, and I knew he would enjoy taking on the shysters a company like Countrywide would hire. In the end, though, I expected Elliot Allen to pay me. He was a tough guy behind a desk but nowhere else.

I sent the message and got on with the rest of my day. Now, I could keep a singular focus on Suzie Sloan's murder.

CHAPTER 23

About an hour later, Rich called me. "Name Cecilia Henry mean anything to you?" he barked into the phone.

"Sure. She's one of the women Fabian operated on for free. I'm pretty sure I put you onto her, in fact."

"Yeah, we'd be lost without you." Enough sarcasm dripped from Rich's voice to dampen the ground around a cell tower.

"I do what I can," I said. "You get a line on this woman?"

"She's in one of our interview rooms."

"I'll be right there." I hung up, grabbed my keys, and drove into downtown. Traffic lights cooperated, and I made the jaunt in record time. Rich looked at his watch when I stepped off the elevator and offered an appreciative nod.

"King just went in with her," he said. "You ready?"

"Sure." We walked into the small room. A drab table occupied the center. Cecilia Henry sat on the far side of it. I placed her in her early thirties, and I wondered if the bits of gray in her roots were normal or induced by the stress of the last year-plus. Unlike in many of her photos after getting her *gratis* surgery, she wore a modest sweater. Two metal chairs were set on the other side of the table, and Paul King had parked himself in one of them. Rich quickly moved into the room and snagged the other. As usual, I got to stand, so I took up a spot beside the entrance.

"It takes three of you to talk to me?" Cecilia Henry asked.

"We're simple city cops," King said. "You should see us change the lightbulbs in here."

Rich handled the introductions. A long window ran down the wall closest to the door. I wondered if anyone watched the interview. I also wondered if anyone didn't know this was a one-way mirror by now. "You're not under arrest," my cousin said in conclusion. "We're hoping you can help us learn some more about what's turned into a murder investigation."

"I didn't kill anyone," Cecilia said.

"If you did, this would be a different conversation." Rich paused. Cecilia Henry frowned and crossed her arms under her chest. "We'd like to know more about Doctor Neal Fabian." Cecilia remained quiet. Rich, a seasoned interrogator, kept going. "We know he has a good reputation, and we know you were one of his patients."

"I'm not getting into my personal health information," she said.

"What about the free plastic surgery?" Cecilia again offered no response. "It's not a cheap procedure, but I'm pretty sure you could've afforded it. Why let him do it for free?"

"If someone offered you something for free, wouldn't you take it?"

"There ain't no such thing as a free lunch," I said. "I'm guessing the same applies to cosmetic surgery. Once you recovered, what did the good doctor expect you to do to start earning your keep?"

"I don't know what you mean." Cecilia looked away from us. A small window split the far wall, though the bars on the outside ruined the aesthetic. She kept looking this direction, anyway.

"We're not here to harass you over turning tricks," King said.

"Turning tricks?" Cecilia said, scowling at King. "I wasn't some common street walker!"

Rich put up his hands, though the venomous glare from across the table remained. "Forgive my colleague for his crude phrasing. The question remains, though . . . was sex involved in your arrangement with Doctor Fabian?"

It took her a moment to come down from Mount Indignation, but Cecilia soon nodded. "It started as just him. I'm no fool. I wondered what strings might be attached when he made the offer, even though he told me there would be none."

"Why not tell him you weren't going to do it?" King said.

"Easy for you to say, Detective. When you're a woman on an examination table, and a man with a bunch of surgical tools is telling you the bill is due, you're going to pay it." I could buy this. Fabian wasn't a small man, but Cecilia Henry might have been five-three and a hundred pounds. Add in her being prone on a table, and the power dynamic tilted heavily toward the surgeon.

"Excuse me for saying so," Rich said, "but you don't strike me as someone who needed plastic surgery."

A ghost of a smile played on Cecilia's lips. "Thank you, Sergeant. You said Fabian was a good surgeon, and he is. He might be a better salesman, though. I complained about my boyfriend at the time, so he knew I wasn't happy. So he made his offer. I'd look even better, he told me, and be able to attract the kind of men who deserved me. It was a good pitch, and I bought it. Even when I asked what I'd have to do, he told me nothing. He wanted to help a few women here and there, and this was the way he knew how."

"Did you know the other women?" I said.

"Not at first. Eventually, I met a couple of them by accident. Shannon and . . . Kate."

"How did you meet them by accident?" Rich asked.

Cecilia shrugged. "Fabian had rich friends. Nice houses, boats, all that shit. They wanted some girls to come by. One night, a few of them got together, so a few of us went over there. I got the impression it was an impromptu thing."

Rich and King looked at each other. "When was this?" King asked.

"I don't know," Cecilia said. "Maybe eight months ago? Early summer, I think. It started out nice. We had a day on the boat. Great weather. Paying it off that night made me feel dirty for the first time. I told Fabian I wanted out."

"Did he let you go?" I said.

"Eventually. He told me my surgery wasn't cheap . . . it took time to pay it off . . . all that. I told you he was a good sales-man, and he roped me into another month. Then, I was done."

"Have you talked to him since?"

She shook her head. "I don't want to see him again. It was kind of liberating at first. A new body, new lovers. I guess the shine wore off quickly. I've found a new doctor. I might even get rid of these implants. Turns out they cost too much after all."

I found it hard to argue with her conclusion. Rich and King dismissed Cecilia Henry. Once she left, my cousin said, "There's confirmation from another woman."

I leaned against the one-way window. "Did we really need it?"

"It all helps when you're building a case and taking it before a judge. You got us part of the way. We need to color inside the lines now."

"Enjoy your crayons," I said.

* * *

I DROVE BACK HOME from the station. Gloria sat at the kitchen table working on her laptop and sipping from what must have been her second or third cup of coffee. She smiled when I walked in, and the day got a little bit lighter and brighter. "How did it go?"

"The investigation continues," I said. "I got them to a certain point, and now they have to go and build a case the proper way." I waved a hand. "It's all very boring and official. They'll probably need me later once all the boxes have been checked."

"Sounds like they don't need you for it." Gloria closed her laptop. She stood and sidled up to me. "I was hoping we could go to lunch." Her left hand rubbed my chest. "But I don't have any plans until then. How about you?"

"My calendar is clear." I kissed her, wrapped my arms around her, and picked her up. Navigating the stairs with Gloria wrapped around me proved a challenge, but I'd grown adept at overcoming challenges these last few months. My bedroom being a straight shot from the steps helped.

Later, we put our clothes back on. "I worked up an appetite," Gloria said, swatting me on the butt as she walked past.

"Good thing we're about to get lunch." I slipped my sweater back on over my head. "Where are we going?"

She grabbed a handful of her chestnut hair and worked on tying it into a ponytail. "How about the Rusty Scupper?"

The mere mention of the eatery made me flash back to the morning I got shot. The Rusty Scupper was on my route to the harbor. I ran right past it. Since then, I'd driven by it a few times but never been in. I'd never even given it a long look.

Gloria frowned at my silence, so I put my silver tongue to good use and said, "Sure."

"It's turned into a nice afternoon." She finished arranging her hair. It looked like someone did it in a salon. "We could walk."

And follow the route I took on the fateful morning, no doubt. I wondered if this were just version two of hitting tennis balls at my head. Again, my girlfriend expected me to pull my weight in the conversation, and being a loquacious devil, I said, "OK."

A couple minutes later, we walked outside via the front door. Gloria walked down the three steps. I remained rooted to the porch. She must have realized I didn't walk with her, so she stopped. I stared in the direction of the harbor and our restaurant destination. One foot in front of the other. I could do it. I'd run around the park, looked across Key Highway, and glimpsed the scene of my near-demise before.

"You all right?" Gloria stood at the base of the concrete stairs and grabbed my hand. "It's just a restaurant."

"I know." I did—and it was. One I'd been to quite a few times over the years, in fact. I could probably rattle off sections of the menu from memory. I focused on moving my foot. Take a step. Then another. I took three and joined Gloria on the walkway leading from the sidewalk. She squeezed my hand, and we set off for the Rusty Scupper.

I breathed deeply as we waited to cross Key Highway. Once we did, I stared at our destination. I couldn't shake the memory of running past it. Doctor Parrish would tell me this was an important progress marker in my recovery. If I wanted to go all-out, I could sprint from the pavilions and dive into the frigid water. Maybe in the summer.

As we reached the eatery, I stopped outside the door. Gloria offered a gentle smile. She'd been smart to choose this place. Not for the first time, I wondered what I did to deserve her. "Let's eat," I said and pulled the door open. She went in first, and I followed. The hostess led us to a table where Rich already sat.

"Surprise," he said.

"At least it's not my parents again." Gloria walked around the table. The only seat left for me would face the pier where I took my header into the harbor. "You guys have planned this to an alarming degree."

"Some things are happy coincidences," Rich said. "I didn't ask for this table. Once they sat me here, I figured we could lead you to a specific chair." He shrugged. "It worked."

"I'll be asking the kitchen for some tin foil to mold into a hat." I took my seat, glanced at the water, and then focused on the menu. "I figured you'd be busy signing forms and getting a warrant."

"King and Sharpe can do a lot of the paperwork." He drank a soda, so he was still on the clock. "Besides, I haven't been here in a while."

"Good," I said. "You can pick up the check."

"Fine."

A waiter with a thin, serious face approached. "He's paying." I pointed to my cousin. "I'll take one of everything." The waiter did not raise his pen to record my order. "Fine. Ladies first."

Gloria ordered shrimp cocktail as an appetizer for everyone, and we all chose different seafood dishes. Once we all had drinks in front of us, Rich started the conversation. "You seem to be doing better."

"A combination of therapy, boxing, and having tennis balls blasted at my head. Plus some good old-fashioned moxie."

"I was wondering when you'd give yourself credit," Rich said.

"Notice I gave props to others first." I patted Gloria's knee. "Including this lovely lady and her own attempts."

Rich leaned in and lowered his voice despite the lack of crowd. "The reason I'm asking is this is all going to be coming to a head soon. We're going to get warrants for Fabian and O'Malley. Sharpe has let you play ball on this stuff before, so he probably will again."

"Do you think I should?"

"I don't know," Rich said. "It depends how recovered you are."

"What if I tell you I think I'm good?" I asked.

"Then, I'd probably take you at your word. We don't know what's going to happen when we go to arrest these guys. Fabian's a private citizen. He's got money. He'll be mouthy, but he'll come quietly. O'Malley is the wild card."

"He's never done anything quietly."

"Exactly. Even if we catch him at home, he might make us shoot him."

"Should be no lack of volunteers," I said. "Maybe you guys can even make a police fundraiser out of it."

Rich rolled his eyes, but the smirk on his face belied his amusement. "Even so, I want you to be ready for what might happen."

"Bring it."

As if on cue, the waiter returned with our lunches. Gloria patted my knee under the table. I looked over at her. She tried to smile, but her lips were pursed, and she held my gaze. I knew how she felt.

* * *

I HATED MOVING at official BPD speed, but this is where we were. After lunch and a leisurely walk back home, I texted Paul

King to see where things stood. No response. I called Leon
Sharpe's office and reached his secretary. How could people
work like this? Justice demanded swift action, and instead,
criminals got the drop on the police because the process moved
at a glacial pace.

A couple hours later, King called back. "We got two other
women to confirm the story," he said.

"Why did you need them to?" They had two accounts
already. More were superfluous.

"When you're going after someone like O'Malley, more
evidence is better."

"Sure," I said. "And when he's halfway to goddamn Belize
while you're running down some facts, what happens then?"

"We can't all be private."

"More's the pity. What's the next move?"

"We're going to pick up the doctor first," King said. "Then,
go after everyone's favorite lieutenant. The warrant will be
ready in a few minutes."

If everything went correctly. If the judge had a couple extra
questions, or someone stopped for a coffee, or one of a hundred
other reasons, it could take longer. "Great. I guess I'll sit tight."

"You probably should. We'll be in touch." King hung up.

"Are you really going to sit tight?" Gloria asked from
behind me, causing me to jump.

"Not a chance," I said. I kissed her goodbye, grabbed my
keys, and took the Caprice toward Hopkins. I turned into the
garage, drove to the top, and then came back toward ground
level. I didn't see any sign of Doctor Fabian's fancy Jaguar SUV.
Maybe O'Malley told him things were getting hot, and he hit
the road. Rich and King would probably include a BOLO with
the warrant. If Fabian were in the wind, someone would pick
him up.

I walked into the office on the small chance he was actually there. When I entered the suite, the waiting room sat empty. Even the TV was off. "Haven't seen him since first thing this morning," Nancy the receptionist said. "He left all of a sudden and told me to postpone his appointments." She blew out a deep breath. "A few people have been pissed, but—"

"He might be in trouble," I broke in, showing off my powers of understatement. "Are you sure you haven't heard from him since?"

"I haven't." She held my gaze the whole time. "What's going on?"

"You might want to update your résumé, Nancy. I doubt the good doctor can ply his trade from a prison cell. Do you have his home address?"

She crossed her arms. "You're not a cop. I'm not giving it to you."

"Fine," I said. "When the real cops show up, I'll make sure they have a chat with you about obstructing justice." She kept staring at me, so I left. On the walk back to the garage, I found Fabian's address. He lived in a high rise a short walk from Camden Yards. I parked in a visitor's spot and entered the lobby. A thin man behind the reception desk scrutinized me as I approached. I flashed my badge. "I'm here to see Neal Fabian."

"I'm not sure the doctor is in, sir," he said, emphasizing the man's profession.

"I'll surprise him," I said as I walked toward the elevator.

"Sir! You can't just go up uninvited."

A car arrived, the doors opened, and I walked in. "Then, you'd better hurry up and stop me." The doors slid shut. I pushed the 10 button for Fabian's condo. A minute later, I walked down the hallway, found his front door, and crouched in front of it. One of the items I picked up from my hacker friends in Hong Kong was a key ring of burglar's tools. I'd gotten pretty decent at picking locks over the years, but it took time. A few months ago, I bought a snap gun to speed the process along, and I used it to bypass the front door quickly.

For the price tag this place probably commanded, I wasn't impressed. The carpet looked like apartment grade. If I bought this condo, I'd replace it right away. A small foyer emptied into a living room. The surgeon owned modern furniture. I couldn't imagine he shopped for himself. Maybe he bartered a tummy tuck for some interior design advice. A wooden dining table sat empty. The kitchen needed an appliance refresh. Both bedrooms were finished in the same style as the rest of the house but were unoccupied. I poked around in closets and saw no evidence of the doctor.

In the coat cubby, the middle suitcase in a set of three was missing. He probably packed it and went on the run. No clues announced themselves in Doctor Fabian's pile of unopened mail. Footsteps drew closer in the hallway outside. I drew the 9MM holstered at my hip and held it at my side. A pudgy security guard in a white shirt, black pants, and cheap tin badge walked through the entrance. His eyes went from me to my pistol and widened. "Who the hell are you?" His hand moved toward a taser on his overworked belt.

"Private investigator." He'd already seen my gun, so I used my other hand to fetch my wallet and flash my badge.

"You need to go."

"You first," I said.

"This is private property," he said.

I kept an eye on his hand. "The police are going to be all over this place soon. You know anything about the guy who lives here?"

"You need to go," he repeated.

"Did the shitty guard factory only program you with three phrases?" I moved to my left, putting a tacky chair between me and the rent-a-cop. If he went for the taser, I would enjoy some cover. "The guy who owns this place is a murderer. Anything you want to tell me besides something you've already said?"

"I don't know most of the residents."

"How about this one?" He shook his head. "Fine. I'll go. Nothing to see here, anyway." The guard insisted I get on the elevator with him. I told him to stuff his insistence and took the stairs. In the lobby, he and the guy at the desk eyed me as I left. I considered flipping them off, but I realized it would make me seem like I was twelve. I prided myself on acting at least thirteen.

As I pulled out of the lot, I saw a phalanx of police vehicles zooming down the street. They'd tear Fabian's condo apart but probably come up empty—at least in the near term. I wondered where I could go to try and stay ahead of them.

CHAPTER 24

BEFORE I GOT TOO FAR AWAY, RICH CALLED. "COME TO headquarters," he said.

"Are we starting up a posse?"

"Remember what I said about coloring inside the lines? We're going to give you your own set of crayons."

"I've always been more of a colored pencil guy," I said.

Rich sighed. "Did you just leave Fabian's condo?"

I looked around to see if he made the call from a nearby car. "Yeah . . . how do you know?"

"Because his assistant said you left Beleza a few minutes before we rolled up. Where else would you go next?"

"He's not there," I said. "Looks like he packed a roller bag and left."

"We'll process the scene," Rich said.

"Great. And while we wait for all the lab work, he'll be sipping a mai tai on a beach somewhere with no extradition."

"Dammit, just get down here," Rich said and hung up. I headed toward police headquarters and parked in the lot a few minutes later. Rich and Paul King were both at their desks when I stepped off the elevator into the homicide squad room— or "bullpen" as Rich liked to call it.

"You could've brought coffee," King said when I walked up empty-handed.

"Talk to your partner." I jerked my head at Rich, who rolled his eyes. "He told me I needed to get down here. So . . . here I am. What's going on?"

"What's going on," Rich said, "is we have a full team at Fabian's now. They're going over everything." He lowered his voice. "We know he's not the only target here, though. Sharpe wants us to get O'Malley."

"No sign of him today, I guess?" I asked.

Rich shook his head. "Not even a phone call pretending to be sick. It's like he knows we're onto him, and he's already in hiding."

"We figure he's with Fabian," King added. "They had some sort of arrangement . . . probably based on O'Malley being a bully. The lieutenant might have roped him into something here."

"You think they're still local?" I said.

"Getting out of town takes coordination," Rich said. "It's not a simple matter of getting in a car and picking a direction. You need to know where you're headed, get cash, find a place to stay . . . we don't see any signs of it yet."

I thought he vastly overestimated the difficulty involved. Getting cash exposed your debit card—and thus, location—but doing it right away wouldn't leave a trail. From there, it was exactly as simple as getting in a car and picking a direction. Rich should have understood this. He was in the army. How could he not consider a go bag and a quick getaway? This seemed like a poor time for an argument with Rich, however. "You're on their phones?"

"Sure, but they're quiet. Probably using burners."

"What about GPSes in their cars?"

"We thought of those, too," Rich said a little defensively. "Nothing."

"They're in another vehicle, then."

"Already on it," King said. "The doc has some fancy Jag in his name. O'Malley has a Mustang, plus an Acura and some ritzy BMW in his wife's. They're all where they're supposed to be."

Stashing the Bimmer in Katrina's name made sense. O'Malley was a lout but not a fool. "Sounds like you're covering all the bases," I said. "Where do you want to look?"

Rich ran a hand through his short hair. "You've researched Fabian a lot. Does he have some hidden apartment somewhere? A boat in Annapolis?"

I shook my head. "If he does, he's concealed it better than anyone I know. Some of the women mentioned rich friends, though. The kind who might also live in expensive high-rises."

"We don't have names."

"But you have his phone," I said. "Before it went dark, did he reach out to anyone?"

"No," King said as he flipped through some printouts.

"What about his contacts?"

"What about them?"

"You should be able to get them. See where they live. Anyone who's nearby and pays a lot in property taxes might be harboring the doc. O'Malley, too, if he bullied Fabian to take him into hiding."

"I'll get on it," King said. "The tech guys should be able to send me his contacts." He picked up his desk phone.

Rich threw a coat on and jerked his thumb over his shoulder. "You're with me."

"Where are we going?" I asked.

"To find a couple murderers . . . once we figure out where they are."

"Good thing I brought my sleuthing cap," I said.

* * *

In a giant middle finger to the police regulations, Rich let me drive the unmarked Charger. He commandeered the BPD-issued laptop affixed near the passenger's seat. "I'd rather keep your fingers off the keyboard," he said when I inquired about the arrangement. "You'll probably get me in less trouble behind the wheel."

"I'm really good at *Grand Theft Auto*," I offered.

Rich shot me a quick glare. "Don't hit anything. Or anyone."

"If O'Malley walks in front of us, all bets are off. I'm flooring it if I see the prick."

Rich looked at something on the screen. The laptop was one of those rugged models which could take a beating and keep working. The display looked small and lacked great resolution, but compromises needed to be made for all the protective layers. "Speaking of O'Malley, let's head to their place. His wife's SUV hasn't moved all day."

"She could have taken an Uber out of the state by now," I said.

"Her phone is showing as in the building, too." Before I could say it, Rich added, "I'm aware she might also have a burner. This isn't my first rodeo."

I headed toward their building. It offered a great view of the harbor, especially for anyone who lived on a higher floor and whose unit faced the right direction. Those probably commanded a premium. When we arrived, I swung the boaty Charger into the garage. With no pass or windshield fob to open the gate, I pressed the intercom. "Yes?" a man's voice said a moment later.

"Police," Rich said. "Can we park down here?"

"Can you hold your badge up?" Rich obliged. "All right. There should be some visitor spots. Come in if you need to see a resident." The gate rose, and I parked in the closest space.

"This is going to be tough," Rich said when I'd killed the engine. The lack of its V8 growl in the enclosed space made things a lot quieter.

"Why?"

"She's a cop's wife."

I shrugged. "So?"

"You don't get it." Rich waved his hand. "She's made a lot of sacrifices over the years."

"She's also complicit in the murder of a young woman," I said, "not to mention the effort to pin the whole thing on Glenn Mathews."

"I just think we need to tread lightly."

"No." I shook my head. "The hell with treading lightly. Let me go talk to her."

"No way."

"I can probably get more out of her," I said.

Rich scoffed. "Why would she talk to you?"

"Because I'm not the one weeping over her status as a cop's wife. I don't give a shit who she married. It doesn't make her special, and it certainly doesn't entitle her to some protection now."

Rich crossed his arms and stared straight ahead. "I don't know."

"I do. You'd talk to her for a minute, she'd bawl about poor Gannon, and you'd cut down a tree to make her fresh tissues. Let me try first. Give me fifteen minutes or so to take a run at her. Then, you can come up."

"Goddammit." Rich rubbed his forehead and blew out a deep breath. "I might be a little close to it." He offered a small nod. "Fine. You go first." When I went to leave, he grabbed my arm. "Don't browbeat her too much. You may not care she married a cop, but I do."

"Rich, please. I'm much nicer than you."

He let go of my arm. "No, you're not."

"Ask anyone." My cousin frowned and spread his hands, but I left him to stew on it in the car.

* * *

I ENTERED THE LOBBY. Unlike Fabian's building, this ritzy high-rise employed a security guard who looked the part. He had a ruddy Irish complexion, red hair and beard to match, and large arm muscles threatened to shred his sleeve if he flexed. He eyed me up as I fished my wallet out of my pocket and flashed my badge. "We just pulled into the garage. Need to see Missus O'Malley."

He keyed something in on the computer and then said, "Unit seven-thirteen. Should I call ahead for you?"

"Not this time," I said. I tried to keep my voice somber and hoped he would pick up on it.

"All right." He nodded. I mentally pumped a fist and headed for the elevators. I rode a car up to the seventh floor, stepped off, and found the door for 713. It hurt me I had no idea if the O'Malleys owned a dog. Gannon was a prick, and even man's best friend would struggle to love him. Still, I rapped lightly on the door. A pooch would hear it, while a person would need to be sitting nearby. No response came.

The snap gun remained in my trunk, so I scanned the hallway for nosy residents, saw none, and got to work with my special key ring. Many similar places cheap out on the locks because they have controlled entry and want to recoup a few bucks. Not this place. It was a good lock, and it took me almost two minutes to massage the tumblers properly and get it open.

I opened the door just enough to stick my head in and look around. All clear. I tiptoed in, closed the door behind me as quietly as I could, and sat on the couch. The O'Malleys decorated the place well, and I figured it all came from Katrina. Gloria occasionally roped me into watching home design shows, and I recognized some of the items and styles from them. I thought better of telling her, though. "A dirty cop and his wife watch the same shows as you!" is not a great line to include in a conversation.

Rich told me Katrina O'Malley's SUV GPS put it in the garage, and her cell phone still beaconed from this condo. None of this meant she was home. If her husband employed a burner phone, she could as well, and the couple didn't lack for resources to get away. I texted Rich while I waited.

I'm in. No sign of the wife yet.

His reply came quickly.

Rgr

I rolled my eyes at the abbreviation as I shoved my phone back into my pocket. Past the living room, a hallway led to the kitchen—part of which I could see via a pass-through in the wall—and then the rest of the condo. If Katrina O'Malley were here, she could be at the other end of the residence taking a nap. I waited and tried not to let my attention wander.

Thankfully, I wouldn't need to wait long. A door closed, and footsteps started toward me. I fired off a quick text to Rich and then called him, slipping my phone back into my pocket. We'd done this before; he would be smart enough to answer and mute his end of the line.

Katrina O'Malley paused and did a double take when she saw me sitting on the sofa. For a loud, unattractive boor,

Gannon O'Malley certainly married up. Katrina was pretty in the classical sense of the word. Shoulder-length dark hair framed her face. Her Fabian-enhanced figure stood out even through a fleece top and jeans. "Missus O'Malley." I offered her a smile and a nod. "Sorry to drop in like this, but we need to talk."

She put her hands on her hips. "Do you know who I am?"

"Considering I just called you by your last name, yes. Would you prefer Katrina?"

"Do you know who my husband is?"

"Very much," I said. "It's why I'm here." I gestured to the rest of the living room furniture. "Please."

"Inviting me to sit in my own home?" She recovered from the indignity and stomped toward a comfortable chair, which she plopped onto. "How nice of you. Who are you and what the hell are you doing here?"

"I'm a private investigator looking into the murder of Suzie Sloan. My name is C.T. Ferguson."

"I don't know who she is." Katrina crossed her arms under her chest. It produced a nice effect, which it should have for the price tag.

"Was," I said, "and I find it hard to believe. She referred to you by name at least once."

"Maybe you should enlighten me."

"Maybe you should drop the bullshit. You're not in a position to make requests."

"I could get a gun, you know."

I patted my side. "I already have one. I came prepared. My goal was for this to be a nice conversation, all things considered."

She stared at me, but some of the fire went out of her eyes. "If you're looking for Gannon, he's not here."

"I didn't think he would be," I said. "He left you holding the bag."

She waved a dismissive hand. "He's important in the police department. He's often away. Should I call the cops?"

"Oh, go ahead." I pointed toward a landline phone sitting on an end table. "I'm sure they'd love to hear from you."

She didn't make a move for the handset. I knew she wouldn't. Katrina looked from the table to me a few times. She probably wanted to project the illusion she had a choice in the matter. Finally, she said, "All right . . . I know who Suzie is. Was."

"Good," I said. "Do you know how she died?" When Katrina remained silent, I answered my own question. "Someone beat her to death with a baseball bat. Pulped her face." She winced. "Bashed in her skull." A grimace. "She was barely recognizable to her family." Katrina covered her mouth with a fist and turned away. "Want to know why she died?"

She didn't look at me for a while. Eventually, she faced me again and dropped her fist to reveal pursed lips. "Why?"

"Because she was smart," I said. "Smarter than her boss and your husband both. She caught wind of something she shouldn't have."

"If you're here for my husband," Katrina said, "why did you break into our condo and browbeat me?"

"Because you were involved, too. Suzie mentioned you by name in her file. You referred at least one woman to Doctor Fabian."

"So? Happy patients and their word of mouth are good for any practice."

"Do you think I don't know what happened?" I said. "There's no upside to playing dumb here. The cops have Suzie's hard drive. She kept a running file of everything she heard and saw. All her suspicions are in there . . . the six special patients . . . you and your husband . . . the money Fabian paid you . . . it's all there."

Katrina sneered. "Suspicions? Do you know what those are worth?"

"Not much by themselves," I admitted. "Good thing they've been matched up to real events and bank transactions." I probably overstated the work the BPD had done so far, but Katrina wouldn't know this. As a bonus, if she thought her darling lieutenant husband kept her in the dark about the investigation, it gave her more incentive to turn on him.

"I'm a cop's wife," she said with as much defiance as she could muster. "Do you know what I've sacrificed?"

"From where I'm sitting, you sacrificed a young woman's life and your husband's career for money and a nice pair of tits. I hope it was worth it."

Katrina shook her head and looked away. Without turning back to face me, she said, "Gannon never gave me any of the money. He bought himself a fucking *sports car*. Like we didn't already have one. We even had to pay extra for a third parking spot."

This was a promising new development. O'Malley, being an asshole, already poured the foundation on his wife ratting him out. I only needed to add some structure. "He's left you holding the bag. No money. No cover from the investigation. Now, he's holed up with Fabian somewhere, and the only person we can find is you." I paused for effect. "You're a cop's wife. You know how these things go. How do you think this is going to shake out?"

When Katrina O'Malley turned back to face me, tears rimmed her dark eyes. "What did you say your last name was?"

"Ferguson."

She smirked. "Gannon has a sergeant working under him named Ferguson."

"My cousin," I said.

"Your cousin wants my husband's job," she said.

I shook my head. "No. He just wanted him to do it better."

With no tissues visible in the room, Katrina used the sleeve of her fleece to wipe her eyes. "Gannon told me he needed to calm Fabian down. Said the doctor was getting restless. They were supposed to go somewhere."

A dark thought came to me. "Missus O'Malley, do you think your husband would kill Doctor Fabian?"

"I don't know." She snorted. "I don't know anything about him anymore, apparently. He's never been the cleanest cop around. I was kind of surprised he got hired here a few years ago. But strong-arming a surgeon into bribing him for silence . . ." She trailed off, and her head wagged from side to side. "I went along with it. What else was I going to do in the moment? I played the loyal cop's wife."

"He hasn't exactly rewarded you for it," I said.

Katrina O'Malley fell silent. She stared off toward a curtain closed over a door to the outside. Their condo didn't face the harbor, but it might have been visible from one end of the balcony. "Gannon's uncle owned a bar," she said in a quiet voice. "It closed a few months ago, but it's still his building. It's somewhere in the county . . . up Route 40, I think. I've only been to it once. It was a dive. He's probably there. It's the only place I think he'd go where he figures no one will be able to find him."

I retrieved my phone from my pocket. "Rich, you got all this?"

"Every word," he said after a moment. "We have some uniforms down here waiting to come up and bring Missus O'Malley to the station."

"I'll be down in a moment." I hung up, slipped my mobile back into my pocket, and stood. Katrina still stared toward the balcony door, and I figured I would leave her to her reverie.

"It wasn't worth it," she said as I walked toward the entryway. She glanced down at her chest and snorted. "None of it. It wasn't worth someone's life."

"It never is," I said. Then, I left.

CHAPTER 25

Rich and I drove back to headquarters, my cousin insisting on manning the wheel this time. When I tried to use the laptop, he glared at me, but I saw him fight a grin when he turned back to the road. "You did well up there," he said.

"You probably could've gotten it out of her, too."

"I don't think so. You heard what she said toward the end—O'Malley thought I was gunning for his job."

"Have you been?" I asked.

"You defended me to her."

"Of course I did. I would've said the same thing if you'd been out raising campaign funds for the position. I needed her to see me without looking through a lens colored by you."

"Fair enough," Rich said. He paused before adding, "I don't like O'Malley. Never really have. I've always tried to minimize saying it because I want the detectives and officers to respect and work for their commander. For what it's worth, I don't think he's ever much cared for me, either. I've never sought his job, though. If I get a promotion one day, so be it, but I don't want it to be on the back of someone else."

"Should I get my suit dry-cleaned for your ceremony, Lieutenant?" I said.

"It's pretty obvious O'Malley is done, but I'm sure there are plenty of good candidates."

"Spoken like someone who's already getting used to department politics."

"Don't remind me," Rich said as we parked at BPD headquarters.

Once inside, we stopped in Leon Sharpe's office to update the captain on what happened. "Rich, I want you to be acting lieutenant for now in homicide," Sharpe said.

"Yes, Captain." Rich betrayed no emotion, though I knew he must feel proud. He'd been a fast riser in the department, and while I loved to needle him by taking credit for his accolades, he earned them all.

"You sticking around?" Sharpe asked me.

"Nothing better to do," I said.

"Good. I'll talk to the county brass and get everything squared away. You two and King, get ready to roll out."

"We will, sir," Rich said. He and I left and went down a couple floors to the homicide squad room. King already sat at his desk. Rich took his seat at the one butting against it. I dropped into a nearby guest chair.

"I'm looking into the place in the county now," King said. "Property records are slow, but I should have it soon. Based on where O'Malley's wife said it was, I don't think we'll have many choices."

"Sharpe is going to clear everything with their brass."

"Joint operation?"

Rich shrugged. "They might tag along. Otherwise, someone out there will get a burr up his ass. We'll be the ones making the collar, though."

King sat forward and looked at his screen. "I got a hit. Patty O'Malley's Irish Pub. Operated by a Patrick O'Malley for the last thirteen years. Closed for business six months ago, but he owns the deed outright. Hang on . . ." King typed a few keystrokes. "There's still power, too. Someone could be there."

"Good work," Rich said. "As soon as we get the OK from the captain, we'll go."

A few minutes later, Sharpe called down. Rich, King, and I rolled out.

* * *

THE FORMER PATTY O'MALLEY's Irish Pub took up space in Rosedale, which indeed fell across the city-county line. Katrina had been mostly right—it was located about a block from Route 40 at the intersection of Route 7 and Chesaco Avenue. This put it across the street from Dick's Halfway Inn, a name I found very funny in my teens and much less so as time wore on. Rich, King, and I sat in the lot at Dick's near a few other cars. We'd seen no vehicles or people at the pub.

A few minutes prior, King ran in and got coffees. We had caffeine in hand, and a source of both food and restrooms close by. Rather than take an obvious Charger, we classed up the lot with one of the BPD's undercover pickups. As the non-member of the department, I defaulted to the backseat but didn't lack for head or legroom.

"We don't know they're in there," King said after another several minutes of nothing happening.

"True," Rich said.

"You don't think O'Malley's wife would try to misdirect the men coming to arrest him?"

"Not this time," I said. "He left her in a bad way. I think she's pissed. She probably doesn't know if he's here, but it's a place he could go. Personally, I wouldn't be surprised if he and Fabian have already split town."

"We have BOLOs out everywhere," Rich said, "plus people at the airport, Penn Station, and the bus terminals."

"They had a head start of several hours. O'Malley could have pushed Fabian over Niagara Falls by now. Maybe he's sitting in a truck drinking coffee, too . . . except he's in Canada."

King shook his head. "I doubt it. This shit came crashing down all of a sudden. We don't know if either of these pricks made a contingency plan. If O'Malley did, coming here ain't bad. Not in the city. Not in his name. There are worse places to hide out."

Another fifteen minutes passed without incident. We'd all finished our coffees. Once they grew lukewarm, keeping them around was pointless. Rich switched the engine off so as not to give away the fact three men sat in a truck watching another building. I thought the window tint would hide us pretty well. As the day wore on and the sun went down, it grew colder, and I found myself sitting on my hands to keep them warm.

"This is bullshit," King said. "I'm going to check the place out."

"Not yet," Rich said.

"We've been here almost an hour and seen nothing."

"Patience."

"I'll be careful. O'Malley and the doc are probably avoiding the front, so I figured I'd scope out the back."

Rich frowned and stared at his partner. After a few seconds, he inclined his head toward the door. "Go. Get on the radio if you think you've been spotted. O'Malley probably won't hesitate to shoot anyone who comes looking for him at this point."

"Aye-aye, Sergeant," King said. He opened the door quietly, dropped to the asphalt, and shut it without making much of a noise. He moved along the passenger's side toward the bed, went around the rear, and then to the far side of Dick's. It was a circuitous route, but it decreased the odds of someone in the pub spotting him. If anyone actually occupied the place. He'd be visible crossing Chesaco Avenue, but King often looked like a mashup of a homeless man and a rocker who fled rehab, so he'd only draw scrutiny from O'Malley.

"How many guys do you think he has?" Rich asked as we watched King shuffle across the intersection with his hands in his pockets. His shabby coat and unkempt hair would help defray suspicion he was a cop.

"I'm not sure. If Fabian's in there, he's probably not going to get involved in a shootout. I've seen four goons so far, two of whom came armed." I paused and thought how to best phrase my next query as King vanished behind the old pub. "I . . . have a question you may not like."

"You're wondering if O'Malley has any dirty cops in there with him." Rich glanced at me, and I nodded. "It's a shitty thought, I know, but I've been wondering, too." Rich's head moved fractionally from side to side. "I have no idea. With increased scrutiny on the police, we've used IA to weed out some bad apples. For all I know, some of them could be in there, too. We can't do this alone."

"Sure, we can," I said.

"No, we can't." Rich looked at me again. "If we breach the door, and it's guns blazing in there, I don't know how you're going to react." He held up a hand to cut me off. "Don't tell me you're right as rain or whatever. You haven't fooled anybody with it yet, but we've been giving you space to sort everything out." He pointed to the building we might need to enter. "There's no time or space to sort things out in there. You need to have your head screwed on straight, and I need to believe it."

"Or what?"

"Or I'll handcuff you to the goddamn steering wheel," Rich said. "And don't think I can't."

I figured he enjoyed fifty-fifty odds, but Rich didn't need my opinion of his close-quarters combat prowess. He needed me to tell him I was OK to walk into a potential gunfight. My usual carping about how the BPD wouldn't have much of a case without my legwork—while true—wouldn't play here. I'd done better in a fight recently, but a wide chasm separated brawling with a pair of enforcers and wading into flying bullets.

I thought back to my day at the range. The gun felt odd in my hand at first, but I came around. My accuracy came back. The sounds of other gunshots didn't make me want to run away. I was probably as recovered as I was going to get, but I didn't know if it would be enough. The only way to find out would be to kick in a door and go in with my pistol leading the way. "I'm all right," I said.

"If you die in there," Rich said, "your parents are going to disown me."

I shrugged. "You get over it."

Outside, King walked back across the street. He reversed his course before, going behind Dick's before returning to the pickup. He opened the door and climbed in the passenger's side. "I checked out the back. One door, two windows. I could look into the kitchen, but nothing was there. The other window was closed. I didn't see or hear anyone. No fresh footprints or cigarette butts." He spread his hands. "I can't say for sure anyone's inside or not."

"No worries," Rich said. "We'll presume they are because we know this is a place O'Malley might go. His wife isn't interested in protecting him right now. I'm going to call Sharpe. He said he'd be waiting to come down here." Rich picked up his phone and made the call.

* * *

About a half-hour later, Leon Sharpe rolled up in a BPD Tahoe. His driver, a uniformed officer, waited in the car. Two other cruisers joined them a moment later. At least some of the vehicles would be visible from the windows of O'Malley's if anyone were inside to look. The captain climbed out carrying a bullet-resistant vest and got into the pickup next to me. He tossed me the protective garment. "Sorry it says POLICE on it." His booming voice filled the car. "I know how important your image is to you."

"I need to be alive to enjoy it." I shrugged out of my jacket and slipped the vest on over my thin sweater. At home, I owned at least two such garments given to me by the BPD. This one completed the set. Once I'd zipped my jacket up, Sharpe handed me an earpiece and the corresponding radio unit for my belt.

"Any visuals on O'Malley?" Sharpe asked.

"No," King said. "I checked out the back of the place. No sign anyone's in there."

"So this could all be for nothing."

"If he hasn't left the state," Rich said, "we think he's here. The place has been closed for a few months, but someone's still paying the electric bill."

Sharpe's brown eyes narrowed as he regarded the darkened erstwhile pub. "Doesn't look like they're incurring any charges at the moment."

Rich inclined his head toward the nearby cruisers. "Who's in the cars, Captain?"

"Three uniforms. They're all good. I requested them personally. The guy in the suit is from IA. He's here to make sure we take O'Malley down the right way."

"Does on a slab count?" I asked.

"If he doesn't give us a choice," Sharpe said, "sure. We all know O'Malley. He doesn't have much of a play at this point, but he's a proud man. He may want to cash in his chips by making one of us shoot him."

"Suicide by cop," King said. He snorted and shook his head. "It would be just like O'Malley to do it, too."

"Enough chatter." Sharpe opened the truck's rear door. "Let's go in there and see what's going on. We'll break it down properly. I'll be in the SUV. Rich, you put the plan together and carry it out."

"I will, Captain."

We climbed out of the truck. The three officers and guy from IA joined us. He was a lanky Latino man with short hair and an inscrutable expression. I figured he hadn't raided too many Irish pubs recently. "We got two entrances," Rich said. "The rear door probably leads into the kitchen. Plenty of places for someone to hide in there if it hasn't been gutted."

"Two windows bracket the rear entrance," King added. "None on the sides."

"You all have battering rams in your trunks?" The uniforms nodded. "Good." Rich pointed at King. "You take two uniforms and go in the back. The rest of us will take the front. We're not sure of the level of opposition we'll see inside. Probably at least four men plus O'Malley, and you can expect them all to be armed. Any questions?"

"No, Sergeant," one of the officers said.

While two of them ran to their cars to get battering rams, the IA man introduced himself. "Detective Sanchez." He nodded toward me. "Who's he?"

"Private investigator," Rich said. "Helped us make the case against O'Malley."

"You're going to take a citizen in there?"

"I'll vouch for him. If you'd like to ask Captain Sharpe, we'll all wait, but I can tell you what he'll say."

Sanchez frowned at me but offered a small nod. "Fine. I hope you're not a liability."

"You must be fun at parties," I said.

The uniformed officers returned with the rams. One also brandished a shotgun. Our assault squad was complete. We walked out of the parking lot and across Chesaco Avenue to breach the doors at O'Malley's.

CHAPTER 26

Rich, Sanchez, Officer Thaler, and I stood two apiece on either side of the front door. Thaler held the battering ram, and I wondered if he really needed it. He was a little portly, but he stood at least six-five, weighed a good 270, and clearly did some serious working out when he wasn't eating. He probably could have lowered his shoulder, taken a running start, and blasted the door from its hinges. We waited for confirmation from Paul King and his retinue. It came a moment later. "We're in position," I heard in my police-issued earpiece.

"Good," Rich said in a quiet voice. Thaler took a step closer to the entrance. His body stayed mostly to the side of the door, but he could swing the ram into it near the lock. "We'll go through in three . . . two . . . one." Thaler drove the large blunt instrument into the wood. To its credit, the door remained on the hinges, but it splintered under the force of the powerful blow and swung into the pub's interior.

Rich and Thaler went first and headed to the left once inside. Sanchez and I moved to the right. I held my .45 in both hands. The interior was dark. No lights were on anywhere. The fading late afternoon sun provided a little illumination through the windows, but we entered in twilight conditions at best. Large round tables were set in their places on the floor. Someone had moved the chairs and arranged them in a couple of stacks along the wall to the left.

The bar bisected the interior. A corridor ran past it, leading to two restrooms whose illuminated signs no longer worked, plus the kitchen and however many offices and storage rooms a place like this required. Behind the long mahogany counter, racks of alcohol stood empty. I wondered if O'Malley's put on a blowout event before closing or if the owner drank the booze while lamenting what became of his pub.

A long-haired man rose from behind the bar and opened fire.

I ducked behind a table. The beefy center leg held it up nicely but provided poor cover against bullets. Detective Sanchez joined me, and together, we pushed it over, leaving the thick round top to soak up the flying lead. From somewhere else in the restaurant, I heard more muzzle blasts. My pulse raced. I flashed back to the day at the range. My ear protection off. Listening to each report as they thundered behind me. It didn't feel like adequate preparation for today.

Voices barked in my ear, but I couldn't make out what they said. As a bullet blasted into our upturned table, my heart rate spiked more, and my breathing matched it. My brain chose this moment to replay the images of Nicky Papers stepping out from between the Harborplace pavilions, gun in hand, ready to fire at me.

I couldn't shake it, and I also couldn't let everyone else here down. We could have been outnumbered for all I knew. Rich vouched for me, and everyone I walked in with counted on me. I focused on my breathing. In. Out. Slower. In for four beats. Hold. Out for eight. Repeat. I did this until I felt the panic ease. My pulse remained elevated but manageable under the circumstances. "One man down back here," King said in my ear. "Another shooter headed your way."

More slugs slammed into our heavy wooden shield. Sanchez stood to return fire, but he dropped back to the floor quickly as bullets whizzed past him. One shattered the window behind us.

The assailant's gun clicked empty. I exhaled and stood.

* * *

THE GUY WITH LONG, greasy hair ejected his magazine as I sighted him over the housing. He looked up at me and popped in a new one. I fired, hitting him in the right side of the chest, and he collapsed behind the bar. "One shooter down out here," I said as I crouched behind the table again.

Another man replaced him soon enough, and this one carried an automatic weapon. I didn't get a good look at it before I covered up against the barrage. The table held, though a few pieces broke off its outer edges. We probably couldn't count on it much longer. Sanchez glared at it and looked at me. His hand trembled slightly as he held his department-issued 9MM at the ready.

When the bullets stopped, we all stood and opened fire on the shooter, who ducked behind the bar. Rich kept low and moved parallel to it. He reached the open end when the guy came up with his weapon ready again. Rich blasted him with three shots to the chest, and he crumpled to the floor. His gun clattered off the linoleum. "Another down," Rich said. "Clear of shooters."

"There's a locked door back here," King's voice announced in the earpiece. "We're clear otherwise."

"Total of two down out here," Rich said. The fellow he shot was clearly dead. Thaler, Sanchez, and I moved closer, while my cousin checked the vitals on the one I hit. "The other one's alive but not by much. Captain, we'll need an ambulance."

"Roger," Sharpe said, and he barked an order to his driver to make the call.

The four of us moved down the hall and joined King and one uniformed officer. "How's Herzog?" Rich asked, and I realized I must have missed what happened while panic gripped me a few minutes ago.

"He should be fine. Got winged in the leg. I had him sit by the back door and make sure no one other than us got in or out."

"Good call. Take us to the room." We walked through the kitchen. Appliances remained, though a layer of dirt and dust meant they would need thorough cleanings before being used again. Pots, pans, and knives were gone. The room felt a little cramped considering the size of the dining area, and I wondered how many workers toiled back here while the place operated at its peak.

In the rear of the kitchen, a door labeled *Office* remained shut. In addition to the knob, it featured a pair of deadbolts. "Lot of security for a simple Irish pub," I said.

"It's O'Malley's family," King said. "Who the hell knows what they were really up to?"

"We still have a ram?"

"Sure do," Thaler said. He and Sanchez retrieved it from the dining area and returned a moment later.

"All right." Rich pointed at the entrance we needed to batter down. "It looks pretty secure. Thaler, I want you to make sure you're standing as far to the side as you can. If it takes an extra whack or two to open it, so be it. These assholes might be shooting while you're doing it. King and I will take the right side of the door. The rest of you are on the left. If someone raises a gun, you shoot. I don't care who it is. We'd like to take O'Malley alive, but if he doesn't give us the choice, it's on him."

Everyone nodded their concurrence, including Sanchez, who probably wanted to bring O'Malley in alive more than anyone. I occupied the extreme opposite end of the spectrum. If O'Malley so much as sniffled, I hoped everyone lit him up.

Thaler took up his position with the large bludgeon. The rest of us fell in line on either side. Rich gave the large officer a thumbs up. Thaler drew the ram back and crashed it into the door. It rocked and buckled but didn't give. We all stood ready for a barrage of gunfire, but none came. Thaler repeated the process, and the door gave way to the second blow. The six of us spilled into the room.

Despite the sign—which now lay in two pieces on the floor —promising we'd enter an office, this looked like an empty room. Four shopworn stools composed the whole of the furniture. A case of bottled water and a bag of snacks lay off to the side. O'Malley, Doctor Fabian, and the two pricks who chased me in the alley each sat on a perch. My two prior assailants narrowed their eyes when they saw me walk in.

"Hi, boys," I said. "Miss me?"

"Screw you," the shorter one said. "You're lucky you got away from us."

"Which one of these two assholes do you work for?"

"I knew it would be you." O'Malley stared at Rich as he spoke. "If they sent anyone, they'd send you. Did Sharpe volunteer you, or were you chomping at the bit?"

"It's 'champing at the bit,'" I broke in.

"Fuck you," O'Malley said. "You always were a dick."

"Thanks . . .but I prefer 'sleuth' or 'legendary private investigator.'"

"Sharpe did recruit me for this, yes," Rich said. "We brought IA along."

"Odd of Leon to want to make sure the paperwork is done

right." He jutted his chin toward Sanchez. "Figures a Spic would be the rat."

Sanchez showed no response to the barb. "We could've found a long line of people who wanted to take you down, O'Malley," Rich said.

"Maybe." He shrugged. "I knew they'd send you, though. You wanted my job from the start."

"No." Rich shook his head. "I just wanted you to do it better."

"Gun!" King shouted as the shorter goon raised his pistol. O'Malley followed suit. I dropped to one knee and took aim on the guy who'd menaced me before. Gun smoke filled the air as bullets flew back and forth. I thought I hit my mark, though I wasn't the only one. Red wounds littered his chest, and he sagged from stool to the floor.

The exchange only lasted a few seconds even though it felt much longer. Doctor Fabian and the other enforcer cowered on the floor. O'Malley bled from two gunshot wounds—one to his upper right arm and the other on the side of his head. Neither looked serious, though the latter leaked a lot of blood "Captain, we'll probably need another ambulance or two," Rich said.

"You should have three arriving momentarily," Sharpe answered a moment later. "What about O'Malley?"

"He's alive. Fabian, too. Some hired gun didn't make it."

"Good job. Lock everything down. The county's going to send a crime scene team in to process everything."

Rich cuffed O'Malley, who protested about the pain in his arm the whole time. King slapped the wrist warmers on Doctor Fabian, and Thaler hauled the remaining goon to his feet and did the same. All got read their Miranda rights.

"Gannon O'Malley," Rich said, "you're under arrest."

CHAPTER 27

AS WE WALKED BACK TO THE PICKUP, RICH CLAPPED ME on the shoulder. "Good job in there."

"Thanks." I accepted the compliment even though I found it a little patronizing. Would he have offered the same praise if I'd never been shot and bumped over a few potholes on my road to recovery?

"You looked like you were struggling for a moment," he said. "I didn't get to see a lot, considering everything happening. But you pulled it together."

"Never a doubt," I said despite harboring several uncertainties throughout.

"You ladies ready to go?" King said as he paused on his way to the front of the truck. "Or are we still getting in touch with our feelings?"

"We were talking about knitting if you must know," I said.

Rich grinned and rolled his eyes. He walked around to the driver's side. King and I waited by the passengers' doors. "You did good in there," the detective said. "I know you had a lotta shit going on. Looks like you're all better from where I stand."

"Thanks," I said. "I'm getting there."

"Hurry up, will you?" King climbed in as Rich unlocked

the doors. "I need someone in my corner if this guy makes lieutenant."

"Why would he be in your corner?" Rich asked. The truck's V8 rumbled to life. "He's my cousin."

"Lieutenants are tools of the system," I said. "I might have to side with a simple detective."

"Who you calling simple?" King said as we drove away.

Rich parked the truck in the lot, and we walked into headquarters. I sat in a guest chair as my cousin and King plopped behind their desks. Rich checked his phone. "Fabian should be here soon. O'Malley's in the hospital. He's not critical, so we can get in to talk to him."

"Fabian first," I said.

"I think IA would rather go after O'Malley," Rich said.

"We're not IA, and he wasn't the mastermind. This started as a murder case. It was Fabian's scheme. O'Malley just attached himself to it when he realized he could exploit the doctor for money."

"He's right," King chimed in.

"Another reason I'll be siding with him over your reign of tyranny," I said to Rich. "He agrees with me more."

"I haven't even taken the damn exam yet." Rich gripped a pencil like it could be someone's neck. "Fabian's going to lawyer up. I don't know how much we'll get out of him, but we can take a run at him first."

We waited. Rich and King did paperwork. I read emails on my phone. Elliot Allen hadn't sent a reply yet. I wondered if he stewed over my final report and the requirement to pay the rest of my fee. He hired three private investigators in his quest for a specific answer, and none delivered it. I doubt my two compatriots reached the conclusion for the same reasons. Maybe they simply liked Charles Stanton better than Elliot Allen, and I didn't have a good argument there.

A few minutes later, Rich picked up a file folder and said, "Fabian's ready. His lawyer's here. They're in interrogation room two."

The three of us walked down the hall and around the corner. The glitz and luster of the new homicide bullpen faded here. Old paint showed its stains and yearned for a fresh coat. The metal door sported a few dents, probably from cops or suspects kicking it in frustration. We walked in to find Neal Fabian sitting in an uncomfortable chair handcuffed to the metal table. Sitting beside him was a man I would've pegged as a lawyer even if I didn't know his profession. The cheap suit, slicked-back hair, new briefcase—I wondered how often he cycled through them to keep up appearances—and smug expression gave him away.

"Gentlemen," he said as King and Rich sat in the other two chairs. I leaned against the nearest wall. "My client is a respected plastic surgeon. He's helped countless people. I'm sure this is all a misunderstanding." Rich remained quiet, leafing through his papers. He pointed a couple things out to King which I couldn't see, and they shared a few conspiratorial whispers. The attorney frowned at the lack of response. He couldn't help himself but to talk some more. "We can resolve this quickly, right?"

Again, no response came. The lawyer's brows knitted further. "Look, I'm sure we can make a deal here, right?"

"A deal?" Rich said right away like he'd been anticipating the offer. With his experience, maybe he had. "Doing one means you have something to offer me. What do you have?"

"My client has plenty of information he'd be willing to part with."

"How generous." Rich eyed them both. "We know all about the dead woman, the six women who received free breast augmentation, what they did to pay it back, and . . . yes, the police lieutenant who attached himself to the scheme. What the hell can you offer me I don't already know?"

"The lieutenant's involvement!" The lawyer sat up and pointed his finger in the air like he'd just made a major discovery in the courtroom. "We can tell you all about it. I'm sure you'll want to make sure he's off the force and in prison."

"We're already working on it," King said. "He'll bring his union lawyer and probably be a dick about everything, but the writing's on the wall. He knows he's going away."

"Still no deal," Rich added.

"You're not the state's attorney," the lawyer said, crossing his arms.

"If you'd like to take your chances with her, feel free. In the meantime, I think your client should answer our questions and make sure he tells us everything. Starting with why he killed his assistant."

Before the lawyer could say anything, Fabian answered. "I didn't kill Suzie. I could never."

"Was the insurance line a bunch of bullshit?" I said.

"It was partially true. I got omitted from one network's list of covered providers, but it's a pretty easy solution these days. They're all maintained online. It gave me a convenient reason to fire her, though. I thought she suspected a little too much." A ghost of a smile played on the surgeon's sad face. "She was a smart one."

Fabian's attorney shook his head and put his hand between his client and the police. "Neal, stop talking. This is my official advice."

"What's it matter?" Fabian shrugged as much as he could with one wrist bound to a post on the table. "They have it all, anyway. What do you want to know?"

"Start at the beginning," Rich said.

"I do all right for myself . . . at least, I did. Baltimore's a bit of a . . . limited market for cosmetic surgery, however. I spent some time here as a kid, so it seemed like a good place to get started. I always thought I'd move to LA or New York and do tummy tucks for celebrities."

"Why didn't you?" King asked.

"What do you call the guy who graduated last in his class at medical school?" When no one piped up, Fabian answered his own question. "Doctor. That guy was me. Hopkins took a chance when they hired me, and it worked out. I wanted to leave after a while. Big outfits in places like LA didn't want me because of my medical school record." He shook his head and snorted. "It's not like the clients would ever find out."

"Some doctors actually call them patients," I pointed out.

Fabian waved his free hand. "You know what I meant. I started my own practice here because I couldn't catch on in a bigger market. I did well until things slowed down a little more than a year ago. Right after I'd expanded my office. I got a little jealous of my friends. They were doing better than me. They'd needle me and suggest I should give a woman new tits for free just so I could screw her on the side."

"And you thought it was a good business plan?" Rich said.

"Like I said, my friends were rich, and I'd become overcapitalized. I figured some of them would pay for . . . well, you know. Pretty young woman with large breasts attract wealthy middle-aged fools, which they did."

"But Suzie caught on," I said.

"For certain." Fabian nodded. "I always knew she was smart. I guess she figured it out somehow . . . probably by the lack of bills for the women. Your lieutenant heard about it from his wife. He promised he could keep the cops away for a fee. I was worried, so I paid him."

"Who killed Suzie?" Rich said.

"Karl. Karl Blair. He beat her to death."

Rich looked at a paper in his folder. "What about Glenn Mathews?"

"He's the real killer," Fabian's lawyer said, but everyone ignored him.

"O'Malley told us the cops were sniffing around him." Fabian shrugged. "He said he'd take care of planting the bat. You'll have to talk to him about it."

The attorney smiled at hearing this development. "Sounds like something you didn't know before. Can we make a deal now?"

"Fuck off, counselor," King said, speaking for all of us.

I WAITED AROUND on the hope O'Malley would be cleared for questioning, but it was slow to develop. Instead, I headed home. Rich promised he would call me when something came up. O'Malley's union lawyer would probably object to me being there, but the hell with him. Or her. I parked next to Gloria's red coupe and walked into my house via the back door. My girlfriend rushed into the kitchen to greet me. "I was so worried." She wrapped me in a tight hug.

I squeezed her for all I was worth. The Fabians and O'Malleys and Elliot Allens everywhere on the planet were manageable so long as I could come home to Gloria. For a moment, the problems of the world and my role in fixing them stopped, and our embrace was all that mattered. When we finally pulled apart, she said, "Tell me everything."

So I did. We sat on the couch, and I recounted the afternoon, leaving nothing out. Gloria listened intently, wringing her hands during the shootouts in the bar and enjoying a hearty laugh at our treatment of Fabian's jackass lawyer. When I finished, she kissed me and then rested her head on my chest. "This is going to be a rough segue, but what's for dinner?"

"Whatever we're carrying in. I'm not going to miss the chance to stick it to O'Malley one more time."

To my surprise, Gloria ordered subs from a local deli. Her app promised a delivery time of forty minutes, so she grabbed me by the shirt and dragged me upstairs for thirty-five of them. A moment or two after we walked back downstairs, our dinner arrived. I'd managed to eat a few bites when Rich called. "Come to headquarters," he said. "We'll leave from here."

"Where's O'Malley?"

"Franklin Square. It's in the county."

"I know where it is," I said. "I grew up around here, too. We just got some dinner delivered, so I'll eat it in the car and meet you there."

"We'll be at the emergency room entrance," Rich said and hung up. I kissed Gloria goodbye, took my sub and chips to go, and headed back to the Rosedale area. The trip gave me plenty of time to finish dinner. I'm good enough with a manual to steer, eat, and shift with no loss in any performance area. The hospital sat pretty near the erstwhile O'Malley's Pub, making it a convenient place to get injured in a gunfight. I parked in the garage and walked in via the emergency entrance. Rich, King, and Sanchez from IA sat in chairs in the waiting room. Leon Sharpe squeezed into one and looked sour for the experience. I thought him being in a lousy mood before seeing O'Malley was a terrific idea.

They all stood when I joined them, and we got visitor passes from a security guard who looked bored the whole time. A nurse working the desk told us O'Malley left the ER and had a private room on the fourth floor with a county cop at the door. We rode the nearest elevator and found the room in question. The officer checked our badges and IDs, frowned at mine, and relented when Sharpe glowered at him. There were perks to traveling with the captain.

O'Malley lay in a hospital bed. An IV ran into his right arm, and his left wrist was cuffed to the rail. He sported a bandage on his head and another wrapping around his upper arm. The only other person in the room was a tall, lanky man with a mane of silver hair who occupied one of the two guest chairs. Sharpe inclined his head to the man. "Patzwall."

"Captain."

"He's a union rep," Rich explained to me. I noted he didn't call the man a lawyer.

While everyone else stood around, I snagged the other seat. Rich frowned at me, King smirked, and Sharpe bored holes into O'Malley with his stare. "How's the arm?"

"You're not gonna ask about my head?"

"Nothing important up there."

O'Malley scowled but could muster no response. It's hard to refute the truth, after all.

"Lieutenant O'Malley has waived his right to counsel," Patzwall said. Sanchez jotted a note in a small leather-bound book. "He's prepared to answer your questions." This surprised me, but O'Malley must have seen the writing on the wall. His former brothers in arms hauled Fabian off to Central Booking. Our presence at the pub meant Katrina gave him up. O'Malley was alone in the ocean, and even driftwood proved hard to come by at this point. His face lacked its usual fire and bluster. Now, he merely looked ruddy and tired.

"You know how this goes," Rich said. "Tell us what happened."

"How'd you find the pub?" O'Malley asked instead.

"Katrina gave you up."

O'Malley's head wagged from side to side. "We were gonna

hole up there a couple days. Good spot . . . kitchen, water, room for sleeping."

"You were about to tell us what happened," Rich said, refocusing the conversation away from the disgraced O'Malley's laments.

"The doc had the bright idea to give some girls free tit jobs. Something about needing money and having his rich friends looking down on him . . . you'd need to ask him the specifics."

"We did. How did you hear about his scheme?"

"My wife did," O'Malley said. He snorted and shook his head. "I guess she's turned on me, too." No one offered any sympathy when he paused. O'Malley cleared his throat to cover it and continued. "She's a patient there. Got her cans done, too, but we paid for it all. Too much, I thought, but she wanted them. Anyway, she was in an exam room one day. Arrived early and got taken back before her appointment. Fabian probably didn't know she was there. He had one of the girls he worked on for free in the next room. They weren't loud, but Katrina put herself up to the wall and heard the whole conversation."

"And she told you?" Sharpe asked.

"Yep."

"Did she think you would investigate what was going on?"

I scoffed, and everyone turned to look at me. "Come on. Katrina doesn't seem like a dummy. She knew who she married."

"You're a real prick, you know?" O'Malley said.

"I'm right, aren't I?"

O'Malley tried to glare at me, but he was a wounded man in a hospital bed. Not exactly prime conditions to be intimidating. "Yeah," he said after a moment, "you are. She knew I wouldn't do anything about it, but she figured we could get a piece of it."

Rich shook his head. "Were you ever an honest cop?"

"Maybe." He paused. "Been a while. It's too easy to take a little here and there."

"You took enough to buy a ninety-thousand-dollar car," I said. "Your wife probably figured she'd get a little piece of the action, too. Instead, you spent all the ill-gotten gains on yourself. It's one of the reasons she was willing to give you up. You put her in a bad spot with no cover, and then you left when we caused a hail storm."

"Let's get back to your arrangement," Rich said. "You heard about what Fabian was doing. How'd you get yourself involved?"

"I went to see him. Waited for him in the garage . . . figured the fancy Jag was his. He knew who my wife was, of course. I told him he was doing some very illegal shit, and I couldn't let it go. I could either turn him in, or he could compensate me for the hit to my conscience." I doubted I was alone in finding the idea of O'Malley possessing a conscience extremely dubious, but no one offered a spoken objection. "We worked out the terms. He said he'd need to get a couple more girls involved. I told him he could work out the numbers he needed so long as I got my cut."

"Incredible." Sharpe glowered at the prone O'Malley, who couldn't meet the captain's baleful gaze. "You could have stopped all this near the beginning. Suzie Sloan would still be alive."

"She knew too much," O'Malley added. "The doc told me she was smart. She was . . . too smart for him."

"Who's Karl Blair?" I said. O'Malley frowned. "Yeah, we know. I met him a while ago, actually. He's not as tough as he thinks he is."

"Katrina's cousin on her mother's side. Once we knew the

receptionist needed to go, he seemed like the best choice. He didn't have a problem cuffing people around for money."

"Or killing them?" Sanchez said. "He didn't just 'cuff her around.' He murdered her with a baseball bat."

"We paid him extra for it," O'Malley said as if it justified beating a woman to death.

"You disgust me," Sharpe said. He looked at Patzwall. "If you weren't here, I think I'd throw him out the window." The union rep's expression remained neutral. If Sharpe hoisted O'Malley overhead, I didn't think Patzwall would stop him from completing the toss.

Sanchez closed his notebook and slipped it into his jacket pocket. "I think I have everything I need at this point. It's nice to get a pretty black-and-white investigation every now and then."

"You're welcome," I said. Sanchez shot me a funny look, but I ignored it. Sharpe spared a final glare for the disgraced lieutenant, and then we left O'Malley to sulk in his bed.

* * *

IT WAS WELL into the evening when I arrived home, but I needed to make a phone call. Amy Sloan picked up quickly. "Do you have some news?" she asked after we'd exchanged brief pleasantries.

"You'll be happy to know the police have made a couple arrests thanks to my legwork."

"Oh, my gosh." She fell silent. "You really did it," she added after a moment. Quiet sobs replaced her voice.

"Take your time," I said. "I'm sure it's an emotional moment." I knew how she felt. When I found my sister's killer after being lied to for thirteen years, it hit me like a train. It still packed a wallop if I dwelled on it.

"Yeah," she said after collecting herself. "I don't think the police would have gotten me here."

"If they did, it would've taken them a long time. It was . . . complicated for them." I told her about Doctor Fabian, the six beneficiaries of his free handiwork, and O'Malley inserting himself into the whole mess. "He could've stifled the investigation. Detectives are unlikely to look around if a lieutenant says nothing's there."

"I can't believe her boss was involved." Amy sighed into the line. "He always seemed like a little bit of a jerk. I figured it was just arrogance from being a doctor. Some of them are like that, you know? Wow."

"The good ones aren't," I said, "but he wasn't one of those."

"What do we do now?"

"I'm not sure what you mean."

"We never talked about your rates," she said. "I'm sure you're not running a charity."

Not anymore, at least. Amy never asked, and I didn't bring them up. In an ideal world, a future bill wouldn't discourage anyone from seeking justice for a murdered relative. The world we lived in was far from ideal, but I still didn't want Amy to mortgage her future for justice today. Considering the time I put in and the danger I encountered, I could have justified a fee in the thousands. "Just pay whatever you think my time was worth," I told her.

"Seriously?"

"Seriously." Presuming Elliot Allen sent his check, it would be a nice payday. Then there was the matter of Liz Fleming putting me on the books for the investigation I'd already been doing. While my nascent business could use the money, I didn't feel right double-dipping on this case at Amy's expense.

"I don't know if I can do it all this month," she said. "I might need to pay you over time."

"Amy," I said, "I don't think you're getting it. One payment. This month. Whatever you think my time was worth. Put any remainder toward living your life and remembering your sister."

"I will," she said, and I could hear the tears in her voice.

CHAPTER 28

I DROVE BACK HOME. OUT OF HABIT, I SCANNED THE ALLEY for goons and miscreants before getting out of the car. All quiet on the concrete front. I walked into my house and grabbed a beer from the fridge. "I'll take one, too," Gloria said. I plucked a second longneck for her, and we walked together to the living room.

Sinking into the sofa felt good. This had been a grueling case—technically two if I counted Charles Stanton, though I'd shifted focus away from him days ago—and it wore on me. I took a long pull of the IPA, closed my eyes, and leaned my head back. "Another one in the books," I said.

"Just in time, too," Gloria said. "You look tired."

"I am."

"Is there anything left to do?"

I shrugged. "Nothing major. I need to make sure the insurance weasel pays me. Glenn Mathews should get out of jail with the actual killer caught, but I don't need to be there for it."

"Good." Gloria rubbed my shoulder. "You can sleep in. Skip the run."

"How else will I build my stamina back up?"

She flashed a lascivious smile. "I can think of a couple ways."

After finishing my beer in record time, I adjourned upstairs with Gloria. Her methods for recovering my endurance proved to be much better than running on a cold morning. Afterward, I slept the sleep of a conquering hero. When I woke up a little after nine, I felt refreshed for the first time in days. I got out of bed, put some coffee on, and drank a fresh cup. I didn't feel especially creative in the kitchen, and I needed a trip to the grocery store, so I made a pot of oatmeal.

Gloria joined me, and we ate breakfast together at the table. My phone buzzed. I ignored it. It had the audacity to do it again. This time, I picked it up. Charles Stanton texted me.

Hey . . . I just heard from the insurance company. They're going to process my claim. I guess the third time was the charm. I know I put you in a bit of a bad spot. Thanks for doing me a solid. I just need a break. Maybe I'll go back in a couple months. Anyway, hope your other case turned out well. Thanks.

I would reply later. If Countrywide stopped their investigation and decided to pay his workman's comp claim, maybe they'd be paying me soon, too. I would need to check my bank account later. Maybe I ought to set up invoicing. It would be a lot easier than telling someone to submit a balance and hoping I remembered to follow up. All these things I never needed to do before were suddenly important.

The joys of being fully self-employed.

* * *

AFTER BREAKFAST, Liz Fleming called. Someone else to hound for money. If she wore miniskirts and kept putting her legs on her desk, I'd be tempted to give her a break on the rate. It may be better if I farmed out the collections end of the business. "I thought you might want to be here when Glenn Mathews gets released," she said.

"Not really. I don't much like him."

"So? Take a victory lap with me."

"So I'm happy he's going to be released," I said, "but I don't need to be there. For what it's worth, I doubt I'm one of the people he wants to see first."

"All right," Liz said. "At least come by the office. I have a check for you."

"I'll see you soon." I put a sweater and jeans on and came back downstairs. "This'll be the first payment I collect," I told Gloria as I put my coat on.

She smiled. "Exciting."

"I guess. I was hoping I'd get to break someone's fingers . . . at least threaten the poor sap a few times."

Gloria rolled her eyes, kissed me goodbye, and shoved me out the door. I knocked on Liz Fleming's office door a few minutes later. She didn't have a miniskirt on, but she made up for it by wearing a pair of jeans which looked like they'd been molded just for her. She capped it with a red turtleneck. The usual near-mess in Liz's office was under much better control, and I soon saw the reason: much of her stuff sat in two boxes.

She followed my eyes and said, "I'm leaving soon."

I took a seat in one of her guest chairs. "Why?"

Liz sighed and leaned back in her seat. "I think it's time. This was my first gig out of law school. I knew being a public defender wouldn't make me rich, but I also wanted to help the kind of people who don't have an attorney on speed dial. I think I've been able to do that."

"You have," I said.

"Now, it's time for something else. The state's attorney wants me to be a prosecutor, but I turned her down. I couldn't bring the power of the state to bear against someone. I want to strike out on my own."

"You're still going to be a defense lawyer?"

"Yeah." She nodded. "I've been saving up for a while. It might be lean at first, but I want my own practice. The deck is stacked against a lot of people, and even this office can't equalize some things. We're part of the system, too."

"All lawyers are," I said. "Besides, you're sounding a little cynical about everything. Don't move in on my turf, Fleming."

Liz grinned. "I know that's more your territory than mine. This job kind of did it to me, however. It wasn't just the Mathews thing, though he was the latest example. Who better than a lieutenant to frame someone and maneuver the investigation so the truth never comes out."

"But it did."

"Thanks to you," she said. "It could have gone badly."

"You think you can do more in private practice?"

"I think I want to try." She sat up. "You didn't come here to talk about my future plans, though." Liz slid a check across her desk, which bore the least clutter I'd ever seen on it.

I picked it up. The logo of the city of Baltimore dominated the top left. As my eyes scanned down, I frowned. "The amount looks right, but why does it say 'Void?'"

"I just wanted you to see it," she said. "We don't actually write people checks anymore." Liz chuckled. "What do you think this is? The early aughts?" She typed on her keyboard and clicked the mouse a few times. "There. I just emailed you the direct deposit forms. Send them back, and the PD office will make sure you get paid."

"Thanks," I said. Even though the check was worthless, I folded it in half and slipped it inside my pocket. It meant something to me besides its nonexistent monetary value. "It's been nice working with you."

"Now that you're out on your own, you might get to again."
Liz smiled. "I doubt I'll have a full investigative staff right away.
Want a job?"

"I have one," I said, "but thanks."

* * *

AFTER DRIVING TO MY OFFICE, filling out the forms, and
emailing them to Liz, I texted Rich to see what he was up to.

*Let me know when if there's a ceremony for yet another
commendation you've earned thanks to me.*

He replied a few moments later.

*I'm home, actually. Studying for the lieutenant's exam.
Sharpe wants me to take it.*

Do you want to make the move if you pass?

Yes.

Good luck, then, future tool of the establishment.

His replies stopped there. Maybe I hit a nerve. I checked
my inbox to find a new message from Elliot Allen.

DEAR MR. FERGUSON,

A CHECK IS *on its way to you for the full remaining balance.*

*There is no need to threaten me or the company with legal
action. While we didn't get the result we were after, perhaps we
pursued it too hard. We will seek no further action against Mr.
Stanton. Despite the unprofessional tone of your last message,
you generally did a good job.*

*This said, please don't be offended when I say we won't be
reaching out to you again for any future work.*

. . .

Regards,
    Elliot Allen

I fired off a quick reply.

Mr. Allen,

I would only be offended *if you came back. Your company served as a shining example of why I didn't accept corporate clients before. Institutions rot from the top, and you should check yourself for gangrene.*

I hope the twenty-dollar bills your pillow is stuffed with make a comfortable spot to rest your head.

C.T. Ferguson

After I sent the message, two sets of footfalls came up the stairs to my door. My parents walked in a moment later. What the hell were they doing here? I did my best not to look surprised. My father strode directly to a chair while my mother made a show of looking around before eventually dropping into a seat. "There's no family discount," I said.

"We're not here to hire you, son," my father said.

"Coningsby, are you going to decorate?" My mother waved her hand in basically every direction. "The walls are mostly bare. I don't know why you didn't put another poster or two up. How can you work with the racket from downstairs? What about new carpet? This looks like . . . like—"

"Like a place I could afford? There's a good reason, you know. Sure, I don't have a suite in a managed building in Canton Square anymore." I shrugged. "Maybe this is more my speed. It's a bit of a work in progress, but people can easily find me here."

"It's a good fit," my father said. My mother sniffed and folded her hands in her lap. "We heard about the case you just worked. It made the papers and online."

"I guess I can expect some new potential clients, then." Before, when I operated under the auspices of my parents' foundation, I sought coverage in the press as a way to keep clients rolling in. Now, it occurred to me I would still need to do the same thing. If I got mentioned in the Fabian and O'Malley story, then reporters would start calling. I didn't like whoring myself out to the media, but if it brought in revenue, I would do it.

"Another shootout, Coningsby?" my mother said. "We didn't want to cut you and your work off before, but we thought it had gotten too dangerous. It was like you went out and sought conflict. Don't roll your eyes at me. We felt you were being too reckless, and we hoped what we did would teach you a lesson."

"It did," I said. "It taught me I can't count on you."

"Now, wait a minute, son, we—"

"No, Dad, *you* wait. We made a bargain three years ago. You didn't specify a certain threshold of danger would void it. I can't help the fact your friend Tony turned into a vengeful old bastard. If you want to put it on me . . . fine. Whatever. I'm going to keep doing my job with or without your support. If you make me keep having this conversation with you, I'm not going to feel so great about the *detente* we agreed to. Give it a rest. You want to come by and talk? Great. Talk about the Orioles. The weather. Not whether someone pulled a gun on me. It's going to happen, and I'm going to deal with it when it does."

My mother started to reply, but my father held up his hand. "Fine. You're probably right. We don't need to keep going over this again." He glanced sidelong at my mother as he said the last few words. "You're an adult, and you're doing good work. Right, June?"

"Yes." My mother nodded. "You know we worry about you."

"How could I not?" I asked.

"You and Gloria come for dinner tonight," she said.

"We will."

They stood and left. Texts came in from reporters who wanted to talk to me about O'Malley, Fabian, and the whole mess at the pub. I reminded myself how this part of the job was necessary as I combed through their messages.

* * *

A COUPLE HOURS LATER, after I'd answered a bunch of messages, conducted a few brief phone interviews, and gone over the details more times than I cared to, I finally sat down to lunch. A chicken salad wrap and curly fries awaited me. I'd need to get back to hitting the pavement tomorrow morning, especially considering whatever fancy dinner my parents were planning on having. They usually brought in a cook and served way too much food.

After I took one bite, two more sets of footsteps came toward my door. A moment later, Melinda walked in with another girl trailing behind her. It took me a moment to recognize T.J. She'd cut her long blonde hair to shoulder length, added about ten pounds she probably needed to gain, and wore a sharp pantsuit. Melinda looked stunning in dark jeans and a heavy sweater. T.J. dashed around her, and I stood barely in time for her to wrap me in a hug. "It's good to see you."

"You, too." T.J. stole one of my fries before walking back around to the front of the desk. She and Melinda both sat in the provided chairs. "What can I do for you?"

"You don't know why we're here?" Melinda said.

I shook my head. "Should I?"

"You remember me telling you T.J. recently finished a program to work as an administrative assistant?"

"I said I would think about it."

"And?"

"I haven't given it much thought," I admitted. "Between having two cases, getting into fistfights, a shootout in the county, and now answering a raft of reporters' questions, I haven't gotten around to considering my office staff." I pointed at the door. "Not exactly fending potential clients off with a stick."

T.J. frowned, but Melinda continued undaunted. "I asked a few other people. The consensus is that it's not a great economy to place someone with no work history."

"Is it ever? How did you think a new business would make a good destination?"

"I know you're out on your own," she said, crossing her legs. "I also know how it feels to start a business that helps people, wonder if you're doing enough, think you don't need help when you do . . ." She trailed off. I sympathized. "I understand your concerns. Your business is different than a lot of others. You're sometimes in danger. Anyone who works for you might also face the same problem."

"I'm ready," T.J. said. "I didn't have any qualms about helping you go after some creepy old pedo." She shrugged. "Same here. Melinda helps people. You help people . . . just like you did for Libby and her family." Libby Parsons died—as both T.J. and Melinda knew—but interjecting this fact didn't seem like it would help me. Even though her death happened before I got involved, the level of aid I provided to her family could be debated.

"I can see you thinking about it," Melinda said as a grin turned up the corners of her mouth. I was, and not only to help out a friend. Even today, I came up with a few times when an assistant would've been a boon. As I picked up more clients— and I hoped I did—this need would only intensify. If I got busier with the investigation side of things, the administrative side would atrophy, and I couldn't shrug and pass it off as a charity anymore.

"Fine," I said. "We can try it out."

T.J. squealed, shot to her feet, ran around the desk, and hugged me again. "Thankyouthankyouthankyou. You don't know what this means to me."

I probably didn't. For her part, Melinda beamed. "The Nightlight Foundation will pay half her salary during the probationary period," she said in her best businesslike voice. "We just need to figure out how long it'll be."

"You pay half?" She nodded. "Forty years, then."

"Very funny. I was thinking more like ninety days."

"Six months," I said.

Melinda nodded. "Deal."

"When do I start?" T.J. asked, bouncing beside me.

"Monday morning," I said.

"Thanks, C.T.," Melinda said. "T.J. is the first placement from our program. This is a big day for the foundation. I'll email you some paperwork."

"Great. I'll let T.J. deal with it Monday morning."

T.J. hugged me again, as did Melinda this time. They left, and I blew out a long breath after the door clicked shut. It had been an interesting few weeks. A new business on my own, a different office, learning to live with a flinch, a faceless insurance bureaucrat, and a shootout over a dead woman and a seedy plastic surgeon. Now, when I returned after the week-end, I would face increased demand for my services and have a secretary—like most other self-respecting private eyes. And I certainly did not lack for self-respect.

What the hell did I get myself into?

END of Novel #10

C.T. FERGUSON WILL RETURN LATER in 2021. If this is your first foray into the series, you can start from the beginning with *The Reluctant Detective*. It's available by itself or as part of a three-novel box set. Enjoy!

THE END

Do you like free books? You can get the prequel novella to the C.T. Ferguson mystery series for free. *Hong Kong Dangerous* is unavailable for sale and is exclusive to my readers. Visit https://www.subscribepage.com/hkd2020 to get your book!

If you enjoyed this novel, I hope you'll leave a review. Even a short writeup makes a difference. Reviews help independent authors get their books discovered by more readers and qualify for promotions. To leave a review, go to the book's sales page, select a star rating, and enter your comments. If you read this book on a tablet or phone, your reading app will likely prompt you to leave a review at the end.

The C.T. Ferguson Crime Novels:

1. The Reluctant Detective
2. The Unknown Devil
3. The Workers of Iniquity
4. Already Guilty
5. Daughters and Sons
6. A March from Innocence

7. Inside Cut
8. The Next Girl
9. In the Blood
10. Right as Rain

The John Tyler Action Thrillers

1. The Mechanic
2. White Lines (summer 2021)

While these are the suggested reading sequences, each novel is a standalone mystery or thriller, and the books can be enjoyed in whatever order you happen upon them.

Connect with me:

For the many ways of finding and reaching me online, please visit https://tomfowlerwrites.com/contact. I'm always happy to talk to readers.

This is a work of fiction. Characters and places are either fictitious or used in a fictitious manner.

"Self-publishing" is something of a misnomer. This book would not have been possible without the contributions of many people.

- The great cover design team at 100 Covers.
- My editor extraordinaire, Chase Nottingham.
- My wonderful advance reader team, the Fell Street Irregulars.

Made in the USA
Las Vegas, NV
18 July 2021

26672464R00152